Into

the

Deep

ANITA K. GREENE

INTO THE DEEP
An Original work by Anita K. Greene

Published by Cedar Lake Studio
Copyright © 2014 by Anita K. Greene

ISBN 978-0-9886709-3-8

This novel is a work of fiction. Names, characters, places and incidents are either products of the author's imagination or used fictitiously. All characters are fictional, and any similarity to people living or dead is purely coincidental.

Cover Design by Wicked Smart Designs
Interior Formatting by Author E.M.S.

Published in the United States of America.

To my husband, Ed, and my son, Kent.
Thank you for putting up with overcooked meals as
'just one more sentence' becomes a scene.
Without your encouragement and understanding,
I would have given up on this journey.
Love you both!

To this nation's Wounded Warriors,
Thank you for your service.
I pray our country never forgets your sacrifice.

Acknowledgement

To Brian Gavitt, MD, MPH
Major, USAF, MC

Thank you, Brian, for brainstorming injuries with me and answering all my questions concerning trauma and medicine. You were a great help in making Jack's story 'real'.

Note: Any error (or creative license taken) is mine alone and in no way reflects on the professionalism of my nephew and go-to-guy for all things medical.

Into The Deep

SeaMount Series Book Two

SeaMount agent, Jack 'Preach' Conroy's assignment is to bring Lucinda Lavalle home to her worried grandmother. The island country teeters at the edge of civil war. A former Army Ranger, Jack has the skills to do the job. What he isn't prepared for is Lucinda's resolve to stay on the island or his growing attraction toward her. Sassy and irreverent, she challenges his faith at a time he's fighting his own losing battle with God.

Lucinda Lavalle can't go home. Her grandmother's safety depends on her staying away, but there is no reasoning with the determined agent, or her traitorous, unlucky-at-love heart that wants to trust him. Committed to protecting her at any cost, Jack dares her to stop running from God and him, and believe she is worthy of their love.

A Note from Anita

Each story I write strengthens my conviction that I do not write alone. After pouring hours of prayer into a story, asking that it not be mine, but His, why am I still surprised when it unfolds in an unexpected way? As I write and plan future stories, I'm discovering that like real life, each man of SeaMount has his own unique faith walk. My prayer is that God will use Jack and Lucinda's story to encourage you to go deeper with your faith. Don't be afraid to step 'into the deep'. It is there that you will find your greatest blessings.

Thank you for being the most amazing readers! I love hearing from you. I'm only a tweet, email, or Facebook message away.

God bless you on your journey,

Anita

Glossary

Command Bird – A helicopter that circles overhead and directs the action on the ground.

FRAGO – A Fragmentary Order is an abbreviated form of an operations order, usually issued on a day-to-day basis, eliminating the need for restating information contained in the operations order.

OPORD – An Operations Order is an executable plan for a specific military operation.

PFD – A Personal Flotation Device more commonly called a life vest.

PZ – A Pickup Zone is a geographic area used to pick up troops or equipment. (In the Army this is done by helicopter.)

Technical – An improvised fighting vehicle.

He stilled the storm to a whisper;
the waves of the sea were hushed.
They were glad when it grew calm,
and he guided them to their desired haven.

Psalms 107:29-30

Into

the

Deep

Chapter 1

Jackson "Preach" Conroy leaned an elbow on the sticky tabletop, fighting to douse the flare of anger embedded in every cell of his body. He searched each face wreathed in the acrid fog of cigarette smoke. The place was the devil's den. How many wives were home weeping? How many kids were going hungry?

Stop it, Conroy. Don't go there. He scrubbed a hand across his mouth and blew out a breath.

He'd fought to get out of this mission, knowing too many ghosts would rear their spectral heads. But the director of the SeaMount Agency had refused to listen to any argument, and within twenty-four hours he had been on a flight headed for St. Beatrice, this troubled island country.

A cacophony of hoots and whistles swelled like a living thing in the dimly lit room. Whatever the sassy waitress said appealed to the club's rough crowd. Teetering on ridiculously high heels, she tossed her bottle-blonde hair over one shoulder and sauntered to a nearby table, the short hem of her floral dress swishing with each step.

Jack couldn't take his eyes off her.

Lucinda Lavalle.

His one and only reason for being in this bar.

He detested her line of work. That alone should put him off, but she intrigued him. He hadn't expected that.

A small woman—just under five feet compared to his six-foot-three frame—she was a bit of a klutz. He hoped she didn't have a strong attachment to the shoes. They'd have to go. Right after he pitched the shirt and sandals he wore. On this mission, dressing in costume meant looking like a stinking idiot.

She wobbled up to his table, her eyes on his tropical green mug still as full as when she'd set it down fifteen minutes ago. Drinking the contents would be a breach of his ironclad code. He was *not* his father.

"You're not drinking." Lucinda lifted a sweating pitcher in his direction.

The parrot-shaped handle of his mug pressed against his palm. "Taking my time."

"Hot day." She fanned her face and fluffed her hair giving Jack a glimpse of a heart-shaped mole on her temple. The distant pop of gunfire swung her gaze toward an open window. "That's not good." Her hazel eyes, tipped up over high cheekbones, came back to study him. "You on vacation?"

"Something like that."

She frowned and shrugged. "The fighting will blow over. Always does."

Wasn't gonna happen. He'd stepped off the plane and had boots on the ground before he had all the intel he needed, but what little he knew indicated the political unrest had reached a boiling point and was about to blow with volcanic proportions. The impending civil war advanced the timeline of his mission, the focus of which stood before him preening with the hope of earning a good-sized tip.

The entrance door squeaked and an older gentleman

walked in followed by a hulking brute who appeared to be his muscle.

"Esteban!" Lucinda's lush lips widened in a welcoming smile. She teetered away.

Alarm slithered down Jack's spine. He dumped his drink in the soil of a half-dead potted plant. The assurance that he knew all the players in the scenario he was orchestrating had taken a direct hit and gone down in flames. The man dressed in the tropical-weight white suit was a surprise.

Jack didn't like surprises.

Chapter 2

Lucinda hurried as fast as her heels allowed. She hadn't seen Esteban in over a week. He was her one bright spot in this miserable job. She kissed his whiskery cheek, ignoring Rico, Esteban's bodyguard, hovering in the background. Rico petrified her.

Esteban accepted her kiss as his due and took her hand in his. "Lucinda." Censure shone in his pale gray eyes. "Manuel tells me you've been riding again."

She glanced at the club's owner, Manuel Mingau, as he approached to greet Esteban. *Tattletale.* "I have to run the bike every now and then." Much older than her, Esteban expected her to act like a lady. In his world, ladies didn't ride motorcycles.

"If it must be ridden, let Manuel ride it."

She ground her teeth together. Manuel had a shed filled with bikes. He didn't need hers, the *toad.* She wanted to swat the gloating grin off his wide mouth. She'd spent a pretty penny on her used bike. Finding one to fit her small frame hadn't been easy. Hiding her free hand in the folds of her dress, she crossed her fingers and forced a smile. "Okay."

He patted her shoulder and turned to Manuel. "There's a shipment arriving this week."

Lu stepped away from the table. They never wanted her

around when they discussed business. *I should stay just to annoy them.* Stepping up to the bar, she handed her pitcher to Tito. "Slow afternoon."

He nodded and smiled, his gold tooth glinting in the low light. "Everyone's on the beach."

Two months ago she would have been on the beach, too. Lifting the now full pitcher, she glanced toward the corner of the room. The tourist's intense blue gaze caught and held her attention. A shiver raced along her spine.

Today marked his fourth visit to the club. His short black hair and ocean blue eyes were a mesmerizing combination. Dressed in a tropical print shirt, his watchfulness set him apart from the crowd. He wasn't here to party with the locals or forget his real life by drowning in the island rum.

His mug was empty.

She rarely read a customer wrong, but this man baffled her. *You're here to push the booze, Lu. Do your job.* She moved between the mostly empty tables. They wouldn't deposit a single cent in her pocket. Unfortunately, neither would some of the occupied tables where the money was poured into a glass.

"I'll take more of that." A meaty hand latched onto her wrist.

This Neanderthal was the worst of the regulars. "Hands off, Roberto." Before he could tighten his grip, she yanked her arm away. Her foot twisted. The exhilaration of success got lost in a fight to regain her balance.

Beer sloshed over the rim of the pitcher. She dropped it and grabbed the closest chair. The pitcher landed on its side atop the tourist's table, spilling a tsunami of cold beer straight into his lap. He shot up from his seat, a wet patch spreading across his shirt and dark khaki cargo pants.

Sprawled across a captain's chair, Lu ignored the catcalls

and unhelpful suggestions from the rowdies. The chair's arm dug into her ribs. She tried to rise with grace—impossible to do in platform heels.

The tourist reached for her.

"I'm so sorry." Her breath rasped loud in short gasps. Expecting his touch to be rough with anger, the hand gripping her elbow was surprisingly gentle. For a long moment she stared into his eyes, drowning in unfathomable depths as blue as the deepest water off the island coast.

He set her on her feet, holding her as though she were fragile. "You okay?"

His question reminded her to breathe. Sucking in air, a sharp twinge shot through her side. She nodded. "I'm sorry."

His gaze shifted and sharpened. "Boss is coming this way."

The sour taste of dread coated her tongue. This wasn't her first spill. But it was the first one of such magnitude.

"Lucinda!" Manuel's voice speared through her. "Clumsy *vaca*!"

She tried to shake off the tourist's hand, but his grip tightened.

Manuel's hand fell heavy on her shoulder. "You are bad for business but Esteban, he likes you. Go clean yourself."

Biting her lip to hold back an angry retort, she glanced at the tourist in apology.

He wasn't looking at her. The concerned gaze of only a moment ago had cooled dangerously and was trained on Manuel. "No woman deserves to be called a cow."

"Ah, *amigo*. This is not the first *acidente*."

The tourist's blue eyes iced glacial.

Lu shivered. His interference would make the situation worse. "Sometimes I *am* less than graceful."

He released her arm, never taking his eyes off Manuel.

She hobbled to the kitchen and tossed the cheap plastic pitcher into the sink. One shoe felt spongy. The heel had loosened when she twisted her foot. She braced her hand against the wall and pressed her fingers against the throbbing ankle. It didn't hurt as bad as a sprain, but she'd strained it for sure. Her ribs were tender and her dress needed to be laundered. She had a spare outfit in her tote bag. Several accidents taught her the wisdom of having an extra on hand.

Lu straightened her shoulders, ignoring her co-workers' baleful glances. Native to the island, not one of them offered her a word of solace. Her earlier attempts to make friends had been rejected, so she'd given up. She needed the job, not friends.

Leaving the kitchen, she limped along the hall and ducked into a room off to the right. A rabbit warren of narrow passages wound between cases of liquor stacked so high they'd crush a person if they toppled.

She shut the door and made a beeline for a small neon-pink carrier where two coal black eyes peered out in happy adoration. "Finny." Unzipping it, she pulled out a pure white Maltese puppy.

Released from her prison and reunited with her mistress, the pup whined and writhed in ecstasy.

Cuddling the soft little scamp, Lu dodged the moist tongue darting out to give kisses. A gift from Esteban, Finula had wrapped her tiny self around Lu's heart. She adjusted the pink collar set with clear sparkly gems.

"I need to change, sweetie." Taking her purple tote off the wall hook, she slipped it onto her shoulder. "Then I'll take you out back for a quick potty."

"No you won't."

Lu spun around.

In the darkest corner, the tourist leaned against a stack of boxes.

A frisson of fear prickled across her shoulders. "What are you doing back here?"

"Looking for you."

Her breath caught and she hugged Finny close. "I'm sorry I spilled beer on you." She stepped back, unsteady on her broken shoe. He wasn't wearing his bright shirt and appeared to merge with his surroundings. "I'll pay to have your clothes cleaned."

"You're coming with me."

"Yeah, *right*." She backed another step toward the closed door. *Keep him talking, Lu.* "I suppose you think you're God's gift to women."

His smile tipped up on one side. "I'm God's gift to *you*."

Another step back. "I don't need God giving me gifts. But thanks, anyway."

He shifted, no longer leaning against the boxes. "Everybody needs God's gifts. Your gift is getting out of this vile place. You don't belong here."

"You sound like Deacon Beam. He likes to remind me I'm on the fast track to hell." *You're babbling, Lu. Shut up.* But she couldn't stop talking any more than she could stop the tremors rippling through her body. "Well, *duh!* Like God would want *me* in heaven."

"Your grandmother sent me."

She froze in place. "Gran?"

A sharp knock shook the flimsy door. "Lucinda, hurry."

Manuel! She dove for the door. A warm hand clamped over the bottom half of her face and stopped the scream filling her chest. Pulled back against a solid wall of muscle, she vibrated with shock.

Manuel hammered on the door. "Esteban is waiting."

"Say, 'give me another minute' and nothing else or the dog dies." His words whispered hot across her temple.

She whimpered beneath the strength of the hand controlling her.

"Lucinda?" The doorknob rattled. "Open up!"

Her gaze flew to his eyes, then down to his boot jammed against the bottom of the door. She inhaled through her nose. His hand smelled of soap and warm male. He must have sensed her acquiescence because his hand loosened.

"G-give me another minute." She tried to keep the fear from her voice. If Manuel suspected something was amiss, he'd insist on investigating and Finny would die. "I-I'm changing." She held her breath.

"Esteban is impatient." Manuel pounded his fist against the door once more for good measure and left.

"Give me the dog."

Hot tears spilled down Lu's cheeks. "You said—"

"Now." His hand went to his belt.

The pit of her stomach knotted rock hard. She should have seen *this* coming.

He yanked his dark T-shirt from his waistband and held out his hand. "Give it over."

"Wha…what are you doing?"

Finny disappeared beneath his shirt before he tucked it back into his waistband.

"You're *stealing* my dog?" Eyes on the wiggling bump beneath his shirt, she didn't see the hand come up to cover her mouth. The weight of it dropped but sticky tape remained, sealing her lips.

Her hands went to her face only to be caught in his iron grip. In one swift motion he fastened a white plastic strip around her wrists. Her stomach rolled, and the bitter taste of bile burned the back of her throat. The man wasn't taking only Finny. He was taking her, too.

She shook her head. "Don't do this." But the words, smothered by the tape, were nothing more than a tormented moan. *Think, Lu!* Large hands gripped her waist. She rocked on her broken shoe and then was airborne, landing upside down over his shoulder. Her nose bumped against his back. *God, help.* Like that would happen.

She beat at her assailant's back and bottom with her bound hands. A strong arm clamped hard behind her knees. Her feet harmlessly paddled the air. He swung around fast. She grabbed his belt as an anchor, her tote bag dangling between her bound wrists. Desperate, Lu jammed her elbows into his back.

Chapter 3

Jack jogged down the dingy hall, filled with the stink of booze and greasy food, toward the rear service exit. The firebrand draped over his shoulder growled and pummeled his back while inside his shirt a cold nose skated across his ribs. He bit back a smile. Weirdest job he'd ever been on.

He hadn't wanted to frighten her, but with the escalation of street fighting and the entrance of the older man, he didn't have time to talk some sense into her. He had to go with Plan B. Snatch and grab.

Beyond a rack of cleaning supplies, a thin slice of light outlined the backdoor. Tightening his grip on her, he opened it a crack and listened before easing through the door and into the alley. He had studied the back of the club as closely as he'd scrutinized the front. Behind him a shout rang through the thin walls of the building.

The owner of the club was on the hunt for his barmaid.

Jack's gaze lingered on the three-sided shed filled with a fleet of motorcycles. Tempted by speed, the noise and flash would make him an easy target.

Hotfooting it along the alley, his burden bounced on his shoulder. Just short of the main street, he ducked into the recessed back entry of an aging hotel and slipped her from his shoulder. The hem of her dress hiked up her thigh. His pulse tripped over the expanse of pale skin webbed with delicate blue veins. He yanked the hem of the dress into place causing her to wobble on her heels.

He pushed her up against the brick wall. "Here's what you're gonna do. You will walk when I walk. You will run when I run. You will not fight me. You will not say a word. Am I clear?" Fear shadowed her eyes, and shame washed through him. Right now, he needed her cooperation at any cost.

Her eyes swooped to the bulge in his shirt that shifted from his right to his left and continued to move around his side. The tears leaking from her gold-flecked hazel eyes didn't dampen the sparks of anger shooting his direction. She nodded.

A truck rumbled past, shaking the ground beneath their feet. The hum of traffic was punctured by the *tat-tat* of a firefight. Much as it would make taking her simpler, he couldn't waltz down Main Street with her gagged and bound. The natives overlooked many things on this island, but kidnapping wasn't one of them. He slipped his finger beneath the tape and peeled it off her trembling mouth.

She licked her lips, the chemical bite of the tape's residue causing her to grimace. "May I have Finny?"

"No. The rat is my insurance." He leaned down and pulled a knife from a boot sheath.

She went rigid, her unflinching gaze on the fixed blade. "Finny isn't a rat."

"Hold out your hands."

She clamped them tight against her stomach. Her breath hissed between her teeth when the flat side of the blade grazed her skin.

With a flick of his wrist, Jack cut the flex cuff then sheathed his knife. Keeping one small hand in his, he checked his six then turned back. "I'm—" *Crack!* His head snapped to the side and pain exploded on his cheek. The copper taste of blood coated his tongue where his tooth had sliced the inside of his cheek.

Calling himself every kind of fool, he snagged her clawing fingers before they took out his eye. He wrestled her around and pushed his forearm against the back of her neck, nailing her cheek to the wall. Using his body mass against such a tiny opponent was almost criminal. Her breath whistled in short distressed pants. Taking care not to squish the bundle of fur tickling his ribs and yapping, he leaned against her back. "We don't have time for this. Your grandmother wants you out of here."

Her gaze swung back over her shoulder trying to find him. He accommodated her by leaning around to look her in the eyes. "She's worried about you."

"Leave my grandmother out of this."

"I can't. She's why I'm here."

Beneath his arm, the muscles in her shoulders softened. She was listening. "We can do this the easy way or the hard way, but you're coming with me. It's up to you whether your dog lives or dies." He knew he was being a real piece of work, but she'd awakened something deep inside him. He didn't like the feeling, whatever it was.

He swung her around to face him, prepared to counter another attack. Pulling on his shirt, the puppy fell into his hand with a startled yip. He tossed aside the clothing in her tote and tucked the pup inside before slinging the long handles over his shoulder. *A man purse.* Determined to make the sacrifice and wear the thing, he clamped his elbow against the restless pup.

Her bottom lip trembled. Anger sizzled in the honey gold depths of her eyes, but she didn't fight him when he pulled her from the entryway and headed toward the main road. He propelled her around the corner of the building and into the stream of pedestrians.

A shout echoed in the alley behind them between the buildings. Jack caught a glimpse of Esteban's muscleman.

"How do you know my Gran?"

He ignored the question, concentrating instead on maneuvering her through the flow of foot traffic. She limped from her fall off those blasted high heels. Why she chose today to wear them was Murphy's Law in play. The honk of a horn echoed between the stucco buildings. They dodged a bicycle weaving through the crowd.

"I asked, how do you know my grandmother?"

Keeping her hand wrapped in his, he pulled her close. "She called us."

"Us?" She glanced at him. "Who *are* you?"

"Jack Conroy. Your grandmother contacted the agency."

"What agency?"

"SeaMount Agency. We rescue little girls like you."

The tension in her escalated. He draped an arm over her shoulder and, under the guise of an infatuated lover, steered her into the cool shade of the storefront awnings. The tantalizing scent of strawberry shampoo had him leaning closer. Funny, he hadn't taken her for the strawberry type. "Your grandmother wants you back in Ingersoll, Kansas."

She jerked at the mention of her hometown.

Behind them a commotion broke out. Rebel soldiers jumped out of a pickup truck, tricked out with a machine gun mounted in the bed, and forced the occupants of a civilian transport into the street. The M-15s the rebels waved around looked new, as did the technical they drove. The door displayed a blue square bisected by a green line, the insignia of the Island Voice of Reform Party.

"Hustle it, Lulabelle." The street crowd had thinned. The short hairs on the back of Jack's neck jumped to attention. The locals were ducking for cover. The worst was coming on fast. Snugged close to his side, she struggled to keep up. The heels had to go. He guided her into a protected alcove. "Give me your foot."

Bracing her hand against a window showcasing gaudy sequined shirts, she touched her tongue to dry lips. "Why?"

He reached down and pulled her shoe off. With one quick snap of his wrist, the heel broke off.

"You broke my shoe." She spoke as though she didn't quite believe what she'd witnessed.

"You can't walk in these shoes, much less run." He held up what was left of the shoe and frowned. A steel shank ran through the sole, shaping the arch. Held horizontal, the toe pointed up as though it belonged to an elf.

She stared at the mutilated footwear and repeated herself. "You broke my shoe."

"The heel was already loose. I finished the job." He glanced at her other foot. If he made a matched pair, she still wouldn't be able to walk in the things.

Close by a ruckus flared in the street and gunfire rattled.

He dropped the shoe. "Get out of the other one. You're going to have to hoof it barefoot."

Her nose wrinkled in disgust. "The street is hot and dirty."

"I can carry you."

The threat had her shucking her other shoe, mutiny in each jerky move.

He pulled her from the alcove. She tried to shrug his arm from her shoulders, but he tugged her closer. "Don't fight me, Lulabelle." She stumbled. He tightened his hold to keep her upright, surprised how right she felt snugged up close beneath his shoulder. He'd been unaware of the empty spot she filled.

"The bottoms of my feet are blistering." She hopped and skipped a step.

Up ahead a shop owner hurried to pull his wares off the sidewalk.

Jack steered her toward a tub piled high with sandals. "Find what you need. Be quick about it."

A burst of gunfire, closer than before, echoed down the alley across the street. The shopkeeper's frightened eyes appeared to take up half of his dark face. He hesitated, wanting to refuse them service. Jack pulled out a bill and forced it into his hand.

Glancing at the money, he stuffed it into his pocket and began pulling sandals from the heap and dropping them on the pavement.

She slipped her foot into one and wiggled her toes.

"Take that one." Pulling out another sandal that looked the same size, Jack dropped it beside her other foot. "Hurry."

"They don't match!"

The V of fabric across the top of her right foot was a riot of yellow flowers. Solid red fabric cut across the top of the left.

"They'll do." Thanking the man, he tugged her to his side and took off, forcing her to run to keep up with his long stride.

An ominous whistling streaked overhead.

Jack slammed her against the wall, shielding her with his body. An explosion split the air. The ground shook beneath his boots.

"Wh-what was that?" Her heart played a rapid tattoo against his chest. Her hair tickled his neck.

"The beginning of civil war." Between them, in the tote, the puppy squirmed and whined.

"Finny?" She pushed at his chest. "You're squishing her."

He sucked in his breath and shifted, pressing against her as another grenade came smoking in, closer this time. She braced against him for the pounding explosion that choked the air with thick dust. Dirt and tiny bits of debris peppered his neck and back. He pulled her away from the wall. Across the street, a pink two-story building had a smoking hole in the second floor. "Run."

The wide street they followed sloped to the waterfront of a large bay, stretching turquoise blue to the horizon. Multi-million dollar yachts bobbed at anchor in the gently rolling water. Where land ended, the street morphed into a wide pier reaching out into the bay.

Jack tightened his grip on her hand and plunged into the panicked crowd leaving the pier and the entertainment they'd been enjoying. *Nothing like a few grenades raining down to break up a party.*

"Ow!" Lu raised her arm to ward off the stampede. "We're going the wrong direction." She yelled to be heard above the din.

Dreadlocked musicians scrambled to pack their steel drums. Food vendors dropped the awnings on their shacks and dashed for cover. Ocean breezes whipped through abandoned racks of T-shirts and sundresses. Transports and party boats moored along the edge of the pier were alive with frantic sailors untying vessels, desperate to get underway.

"Keep moving." Shielding her and the pup, Jack fought against the crowd. The *tat-tat* of gunfire sent another wave of terror through the throng. He clutched her to his side, afraid she'd be separated from him. "Move faster, Lulabelle." He pushed her toward the end of the pier and the transport waiting there.

"Why are they bombing us?"

Not bombs, but now wasn't the time to explain the finer points of munitions. "Nothing personal. Just war." He veered to the edge of the wooden pier where the crowd grew thinner, but more obstacles were underfoot. Boat motors revved to life and men shouted to be heard.

Lu tripped on a coil of rope.

Hooking an arm around her waist, he hauled her upright then swept her into his arms. She squeaked in surprise but didn't fight him. Instead she wrapped her arms around his neck and hung on. The tote rested on her tummy, and he could feel the pup scrambling to right itself.

He dodged a stack of crates and a small ice chest. *Another hundred feet.* Whit waited with a modified service boat that looked like all the others traveling between the pier and the yachts.

Overhead two high-pitched whistles, one right after the other, sliced through the air.

Jack dove to the side, landing against a bright yellow shack advertising fishing excursions.

An ear-shattering *BOOM* followed a blinding flash. With a screeching roar, the pier exploded around them. Wood disintegrated beneath his boots and he was falling. The ringing in his ears muffled Lucinda's scream. Holding her tight, he prayed this wasn't their last minute on earth.

Chapter 4

His back slammed against a slick object. Cold water closed over him. The puppy's tiny feet patted at his chest, and Lucinda's blonde hair swept across his face in a tickling wave. Whatever he'd landed on bobbed to the water's surface.

Jack lay on his back, dazed and coughing up seawater. Waves lapped across his legs. His bottom slipped on the smooth surface. Lucinda lay beside him. Rising on one elbow, the tote holding the puppy slid off him to rest on Lucinda's chest.

The blast had capsized a small runabout, and they were draped across the hull. He took a quick inventory of his injuries. The adrenaline pumping through his veins masked the pain of cuts and bruises.

His attention cut to Lu. Unsure of the stability of their perch, he pulled her close. Her eyes were closed, and she lay quiet as death. Running shaking fingers up her neck, he checked her pulse. She was alive. A graze across her brow beaded with blood. He ran his hand over her shoulders and down her arms checking for broken bones. His exploring fingers swept from her ankle to her knee before her hand flailed and landed with a splash in the water. She sucked in a breath and moaned.

Around them the water churned with people crying out in fear and pain as they thrashed about, grasping at anything that floated. The macabre call of seagulls added to the clamor of the tragedy. Fuel tanks caught fire, blanketing the bay with black sooty smoke.

"Snap out of it, woman." She responded to his harsh words with a flutter of eyelashes. "Come on, Lulabelle. We're sitting ducks. Another grenade could drop."

The muscles of her throat contracted. She pursed her lips and wrinkled her nose. "Smoke." A sharp bark came from the tote on her chest. Her eyelids opened wide, then closed and opened again. "Finny." She moved to sit up.

Jack captured her jaw in his hand and leaned over her. "Be still. We're afloat but not secure." Turning the tote upside down, the wet puppy spilled out. It staggered to a stand on her stomach and gave a half-hearted shake. Oblivious to their surroundings, it wagged its tail. He placed the soggy ball of fur in her searching hands. "Keeping it alive is up to you." The pint-sized puppy should have drowned. He hoped giving her the responsibility of her precious pup would push her to fight through what was to come.

Fire crackled and the smoke grew thick, billowing on the prevailing ocean breeze, making it difficult to breathe. Overhead feet thudded across the remains of the pier. In the distance, sirens screamed.

Eyes glazed, Lu shuddered. "Don't like fire." She fumbled with the tote, tucking Finny inside.

To their left, amidst the debris, bobbed a body. Shielding her from the sight, Jack pulled their float closer to a steel piling. Beneath the surface of the water, colorful sea sponges clung to the metal post. Overhead jagged boards poked in all directions. Heat from the burning fishing shack scorched his skin.

20

The end of the pier was gone. Whit would have been there, grinning and ready to rock and roll. The man had been the brother Jack never had. A painful hole gaped open in his chest, followed by a wave of molten fury. He struggled to tamp out the fire and focus on his job. He had to get Lucinda to the alternate pickup zone.

The telltale smoke trail of another grenade wobbled across the sky, and a million dollar yacht blew out of the water in a ball of fire. Waves from the explosion rocked their perch.

Lu whimpered as one leg slid into the water.

"Don't move!" He slipped into the water and hooked his arm across their fiberglass island.

She twisted toward him, her face ashen. Lunging, she wrapped her arms around his neck.

He went under and surfaced spitting saltwater. *Should've seen that coming.* Nose to nose with her, he tread water. "You're gonna drown us."

She tightened her grip.

The tote rested on his shoulder, and the puppy squirmed against his ear. Underwater, her legs tangled with his, giving his heart a workout for all the wrong reasons. He ran his hand across her back, helpless to fight the response rocketing through him.

"I hate fire." She trembled and he pulled her closer. The gold flecks in her eyes sparked bright. Hair slicked back from her face exposed the heart-shaped beauty mark. "Get me out of here."

Her hoarse whisper fanned his face with warmth, making his nerves jump to attention. The hyper-awareness that had served him well as a former Army Ranger was destroying him when it came to this woman. "Can you swim?"

She shot him a hesitant look then shook her head to the negative.

Figures. Nothing was going to be easy on this op. He gripped her arm and squeezed the locked muscles. "You have to trust me."

His whispered words drew a look of resignation. Beneath his hand she quivered.

"Relax." He murmured close to her ear noting its delicate topography. *Get your head back in the game, Conroy.* Holding her with one arm he swam and clawed his way to a bench seat cushion bobbing in the carnage. "Get on." He helped her stretch out on her belly with the pup nestled beneath her chin. "Keep your head down."

She did as told without argument.

Grasping the strap handle at one end, he sidestroked with caution through the water, chunky with debris. Instinct kept him beneath the remaining fragments of the pier. From the narrow gap between the water's surface and the boards, he watched a small boat filled with armed men push through the wreckage to the closest yacht. Yelling ensued, followed by the pop of gunfire. They were taking no prisoners.

He looked over his shoulder. Lucinda had her head buried in her crossed arms, the pup peeking out from under her chin.

The cushion snagged on something and tugged at his hand. Giving it a yank, he got it moving forward, though slower this time. He'd picked up wreckage floating beneath the surface. Letting the steady lap of the waves carry them toward shore, he guided the cushion between jagged rocks.

"Doing okay, Lulabelle?" Her hair hung in rattails, she had rips in her dress, and she'd lost the mismatched sandals he'd paid dearly for.

"No." The word was a muffled snarl.

He welcomed her anger. It would keep her in the fight. The cushion pulled again. He glanced back. From between her naked heels, peered a pair of chocolate eyes. His heart bumped against his ribs. He pulled on the cushion, and it sailed past his position. He lunged.

The eyes grew wide before the person ducked underwater.

Jack followed and grabbed a skinny ankle. The water erupted in a churning frenzy. Digging his boots into the pebbly bottom of the bay, he pushed to a stand hauling his catch to the surface.

A kid! Not more than nine years old.

"Aagh." The boy struck out.

Jack wrestled him into submission, covering his mouth. "You're lucky to be alive."

He didn't look at Jack, instead rolling his eyes in Lucinda's direction.

The threat neutralized, Jack removed his hand and gave the boy a helpful push toward shore.

Too small to touch bottom, he tread water. "She's going."

Jack glanced in the direction the boy was looking.

Lu's cushion had floated out of reach. She had one hand in the water paddling hard.

Dodging wreckage, Jack went after her. Coming alongside, he grabbed the strap handle.

Beneath the black streaks of eye makeup, her pale cheeks flamed pink. She looked daggers at him and batted at his hand. "Let go."

"No."

"You're gonna get me killed."

"That's not my intention."

"Could've fooled me. Let go."

Ignoring her angry yammer, he hauled her ashore then

helped her off the cushion. He led her across the beach to a sun-warmed rock. Her knees gave out and she sat with a bump. Shivering, she hunched her back and held the puppy close.

Survivors of the blast were swimming ashore, stumbling out of the surf dazed and bloody.

"She okay?" The boy peered at Lu, hitching up his dripping shorts every few seconds. His pockets bulged, heavy with stuff pulling the pants off his nonexistent rump.

Not wanting an audience, Jack waved toward the growing crowd. "Go find your mother."

"No *mama*."

"Then go find whoever you were with. They'll be worried about you." Jack turned his attention to Lu. The scrape on her head had stopped bleeding, but she'd been left with a goose egg. Her skin was cool as satin to his touch. He gave into the urge to rub his finger across the small heart-shaped beauty mark. "You'll have a headache."

"I had one before I got blown into the water."

The episode hadn't stilled her tart tongue. All things considered that was something to be thankful for.

"We have to get out of here." He helped her stand and led her along the shore, putting distance between them and the rebels looting the pier and boarding the boats floating in the bay.

The boy followed, tugging on his pants every few steps.

Lu stumbled and Jack caught her. "Go easy, Lulabelle."

She snorted and whacked his hand away.

He needed her to ditch the short dress that flipped up at the most inconvenient times. *A pair of pants and footwear— again.*

Gently lapping waves washed the first surge of rubble ashore. On this end of the beach, opportunists were already combing the sand for anything that could be used or sold.

"This place, *hefe*."

"I'm not your boss."

The kid ignored him and ran to the bank of riprap. He climbed the uneven tumble of rocks with practiced ease. Reaching the top, he spun and flashed Jack two thumbs up. "Easy."

Jack studied the route the boy had taken, noting the natural handholds and steps. In another half mile the embankment butted up against a sheer rock cliff. This appeared to be the easiest way off this end of the beach.

Lu swayed. Exhaustion lined her face. "I can't climb that."

"You don't have a choice. Hand over Fifi."

She frowned. "Finny."

"It's not a fish."

Her eyes sparked, and she stiffened as he'd hoped she would. "Finula is her full name."

Jack pushed her toward the base of the rocks. "Dogs should have names like Brownie or Scruffy."

"Finula is neither brown nor scruffy." She swept her hand over the puppy's head poking out of the tote and adjusted the sparkly collar. "Her name means white shoulders."

"Fancy name for such a small dog." He held his hand out. "I'll take her so you can climb."

She looked up at the uneven pile of rocks and the dark holes gaping between them. "You might drop her. On purpose."

That hurt. Though he *had* threatened to kill the pup. Her dubious expression meant he'd done his job well. Regret threaded through him. "I promise to be careful." He tried to tone down the impatience lacing each word as he pried the tote from her resisting hands. They were losing valuable time.

He patted his pants pocket and the SAT phone safe in its waterproof pouch. Once they were in a secure place, he'd contact Sam. If the boss didn't hear from him, a recovery operation would be set in motion. He'd never hear the end of it. Not after insisting he could do this simple extraction alone.

He glanced toward the pier. His chest squeezed tight, making it hard to breathe. Were the others aware that Whit had been lost in the explosion? Once again, slinging the tote filled with puppy onto his shoulder, he encircled Lu's waist with his hands and lifted her onto a rock. "Climb."

Chapter 5

Lu gripped the rock's rough edge. From the bump on her head to her scraped toes, every inch of her body hurt. She bent her knee, searching for a spot to place her bare foot. Jack's hand closed over her arch. She jumped, heart racing. Strong and sure, his hand guided her. "It's your fault we're in this mess." She pulled herself up, puffing and grunting with exertion.

"You're doing okay." His breath stirred the hair at her temple.

She reached up, each move taking concentration. His heat blanketed her back as he shadowed her, guiding her feet and hands to the next step and handhold. One slip and she'd disappear into the dark crevices. Halfway up, her muscles trembled from the effort. "I'm tired."

He placed his hand at the small of her back. "Take a minute to catch your breath."

She clung to the stone, studying the hand covering hers. Large with long fingers and short nails, his hand pressed her palm against the rock, assuring she would not fall. Stiffening her legs, she reassured herself that his closeness had nothing to do with her wobbly knees.

"I'm ready." She bent her knee, scraping it on the stone's

face. She sucked in her breath and tightened every muscle, afraid she'd plunge to her death.

"That hurt?"

"A little. I don't want to fall," she whispered, not daring to check if she'd drawn blood.

"I won't let you fall. Try again."

Surprise jolted through her when his hand grasped the back of her knee. Moving carefully, she soon reached eye level with the top of the embankment. She paused to gather her strength for the last push. A firm hand cupped her bottom, sending shockwaves through her. An unexpected boost sent her sailing over the edge to land on the flat top of the rock. On hands and knees, she crawled to sandy soil carpeted with rough grass. Muscles quivering, she collapsed and rolled to her back and looked up at the smoke-filled sky. She'd done it. Not gracefully, but she'd made it to the top in one piece.

A dark face dipped over her. The boy's round-eyed gaze traveled the length of her. "You look bad."

"No kidding. I could be worse." She struggled to sit up, arms and legs shaking. "I could be dead."

Finny landed in her lap. Halfway out of the tote, the pup stretched to give her mistress a kiss before being tucked back inside.

The sandy strip butted up against a street. On the opposite side, shops and restaurants faced the water. Along this busy thoroughfare, some folk rushed toward the pier while others ran away.

"Let's go." Jack extended his hand to help her up.

Ignoring it, she rolled to her knees and stood. She planted her feet wide, hoping she wouldn't embarrass herself by falling. He steered her across the street to the sidewalk.

"We have to find you sandals—again."

"You need *sapatos*?" Shadowing them, the kid dug into a deep pocket on the leg of his shorts and pulled out a pair of sandals. A thin leather wallet dropped to the ground. He bent to scoop it up but Jack beat him to it, holding the wallet overhead out of the boy's reach.

"*Meu!*" The kid spoke in rapid-fire creole that Lu couldn't follow. He dropped the sandals and tried to climb Jack to reach the wallet.

Holding him off with one hand, Jack flipped it open with the other. "Your name Sven Olsen?" Blue eyes frosty, he looked down at the boy. "What else do you have in those pockets?"

The kid danced backward, eyes darting between the wallet and a way of escape.

Jack advanced on him like a tiger stalking its next meal.

"Don't hurt him." Lu drew back, closer to the building. "He's just a little boy."

"He's a pickpocket."

The boy dodged left, then right. Jack mirrored each move.

A lack of gunfire emboldened curious spectators. Heart in her throat, Lu stepped into the crush of people. Keeping a large woman in a jungle print dress between her and Jack, she strode several steps before daring to peek around her living shield. Jack's piercing blue gaze cut through her. Heart tripping, she ducked into an alley and ran. Bare feet slapping the rough concrete, she dodged bits of windblown trash. Behind her, rapid footsteps beat against the pavement.

A few yards from her goal, the dark silhouette of a man stepped into the sunlit entrance blocking her escape. Fueled by desperation, she didn't slow her headlong rush. Too late she realized her error.

Rico! Esteban's man.

His thick arms closed around her. Nose jammed against his chest, she choked on his sour odor. His arms tightened and he thrust her away. She fell against the building. Her head snapped back and cracked against the stucco wall. The world reeled. Stars danced in front of her eyes. The sickening pound of fists against flesh slashed through the ringing in her ears. In the shadows, two dark forms wrestled.

Rico and Jack.

Lu slid down the wall and sat in the dirt and leaf litter caught at the base. *Get away.* Crawling with one hand, she clutched Finny wrapped in her tote, in the other. Her breath scraped harsh in her throat.

A hand closed on her shoulder. Rising up on her knees, she lashed out. Her hand was caught and held in a vise-like grip.

"Lulabelle, stop."

She stiffened. Jack towered above her. A thin thread of relief swirled through the fear and anger roiling inside her.

"Hand over the dog."

She clutched the puppy to her chest, her body wracked with tremors.

"Give her to me and slip these on." He held up the sandals the boy had pulled from his pocket.

She released her grip on the puppy. Knees scraped and burning, she bumped to her bottom on the pavement. Beyond Jack's legs, Rico lay on the ground unmoving. Bile seared the back of her throat. "Y-You killed him." Her stiff lips could barely form the words. Hands shaking, she attempted to slip the sandal thong between her toes.

Jack knelt before her, blocking her view. "I didn't kill him." Taking the sandals from her, he gently slipped them on her feet. "Though I probably should have." A look of confusion rippled across his handsome face. Helping her up, he kept her hand in his and led her out the far end of the alley into the late afternoon sunshine.

Here, away from the waterfront, the cobblestone street was quiet. The buildings were older homes where sweet scented bougainvillea cascaded in pink and white waves over walls and wrought iron fences. A small flock of bananaquits flashed yellow feathers and sipped nectar while scolding each other in wheezy squeaks. A fountain splashed in a nearby courtyard. From atop a gently waving palm drifted the mournful coo of a dove.

Lu took a deep breath wanting to inhale the peacefulness. How had her normal routine day turned so harrowing in the space of minutes? The man beside her was responsible for the upheaval, and yet she had this crazy desire to trust him.

"You okay?"

"I didn't die. Why didn't I die?" She didn't have an ounce of bravado left to hide behind.

"God has plans for you here on earth." He slipped her hand into the crook of his elbow.

She kept it there, the warm strength grounding her careening emotions. "If it's more of the same, I don't want Him fiddling with my life."

"The choice isn't ours to make, Lulabelle."

"Why do you call me that?"

A hint of a smile slipped across his solemn face. "Because no one else does."

Too unsettled to figure out the meaning behind that comment, she focused on keeping up with his long stride, taking two limping steps to his one. None the worst for wear, Finny peeked out of the tote hanging from his shoulder.

The tinkling of shattered glass broke the tranquility. His gaze searched the street behind them. From the direction of the waterfront, a truck loaded with rebels rumbled up the street.

"Go down the next side passage." The words were no sooner out of Jack's mouth than government security forces blocked the other end of the street.

He scooped her up. Her arm caught between her ribcage and Jack, she grabbed his T-shirt with her free hand. He lurched sideways diving for cover as the two opposing forces opened fire. The roar of weapons solidified into a wall of sound buffeting her ears and lungs. Eyes scrunched shut, she burrowed her face into his chest. His boots drummed a steady rhythm on the pavement.

Hugging the shadows of a pink stucco residence, he slowed and stopped. He set her on her feet and shoved her behind him. "Stay with me."

She'd be a fool to do otherwise. Tangling her fingers in the fabric of his shirt, she resisted the urge to plaster herself against his back.

Keeping to the shadows, he led her to the back of the house and the unpaved access alley running behind the homes on this street. Deeply rutted and edged with a rough weedy fringe, the laneway functioned as a collective service yard. Bicycles, washtubs, and rusted pieces of cars competed for space with small fire pits ringed with chairs in every state of disrepair.

Her hand in his, Lu stumbled after him. A flock of chickens squawked and scattered. A goat, its udder heavy with milk, watched them pass. The area was devoid of people.

She tripped and fell to her knees. Biting her lip, she kept from crying out. Pieces of gravel dug into her skin. Helping her up, he led her to the end of the alley and behind a thick annatto bush growing at the base of a high wall.

Lu sagged against the mossy bricks. She rubbed her palms against her dress, dislodging dirt. Over Jack's hip,

Finny peeked from the tote, wiggling and hoping for attention. Unable to resist, Lu scratched behind her small companion's ear.

"Listen." Jack tilted his head.

She strained to hear over the bang of her heart and the breath pumping in and out of her aching lungs. Nearby, a withering barrage of gunfire blended with the crackle of shattered glass.

"Come on."

Muscles protesting, she followed him along the wall to an arched iron gate. She peered between the bars and a cold chill ran up her spine. Ledger stones and sarcophagi stained and crumbling with age, filled the cemetery of an old church.

Jack unlatched the gate, pulled her inside, and hustled her to the foundation of the church.

"What are you doing?" The old burial ground amplified her whispered words.

"Finding a place to hole up." He stopped at a low door made of wide boards set deep in the rock and mortar. An ancient padlock hung from iron hardware.

"I'm not going in there with you." She stepped back.

"You haven't a choice."

"There are always choices." She hiked her chin a notch and clamped her lips together to stop their trembling.

His gaze strayed to her mouth, and a lopsided grin flashed and faded so fast Lu blinked. "The best choice you can make right now is to stick with me."

He released her hand and she felt lost. Her instincts told her to run. Instead she pressed close, held in place by indecision.

Slipping a small tool from his pocket, he worked on the lock.

"You're breaking into a church!" Even *she* knew that was a bad move. "God's not going to like that."

This time his grin reached his eyes causing warmth to unfurl in her chest.

"It's okay. Bible says God is my refuge."

"You're crazy."

"Yeah, that too." The heavy lock rattled as he pulled the latch from the staple and flipped the hasp. The door swung open and a whiff of dank air, redolent with an earthy scent, stuck in Lu's nostrils. He curled his arm around her waist and nudged her toward the dark entrance.

"People die in places like this." She tried to turn away, but his arm tightened, drawing her to his side.

"You better not die." He cleared his throat. "Your grandmother would be upset."

Her attempt to dig her heels into the rock step failed. He propelled her forward. Another burst of gunfire flared close. Startled, she stumbled down the short flight of steps where darkness engulfed her. His arm slipped from her waist leaving her adrift in a sea of black. She blinked to adjust her vision.

A silhouette passed before a small square of light.

Relief trickled through her. The darkness wasn't absolute. Every few yards, a terracotta grate covered with wire mesh allowed the weak, early-evening sunlight to filter into the underworld of the building. She placed her hand against the rough wall. The foundation sat half above and half below ground, a shallow hole hacked from volcanic rock.

His hand clamped around her arm, startling her. It slid down to take her hand.

"We're out of the way here."

A red beam flickered across her face. She flinched away.

He lowered his flashlight. "Relax and don't do anything foolish."

"What exactly constitutes foolish? I'm in the basement of a church with...with *you*." Her voice faltered as she swallowed back the terror trying to overtake her.

"Foolish would be trying to escape. I'll find you. Save yourself the trouble and me the time." His shoulders were hunched to prevent his head from knocking against the low beams.

Outside their hideaway, boots crunched on gravel. The thin beam of light disappeared. His hand rested on her shoulder then skimmed up her neck, raising goose bumps. His fingers trailed across her jaw to cover her mouth. He stood unmoving, waiting.

Gunfire and shouts filtered into their dark hiding place followed by a heavy silence.

His hand fell away. She stepped closer to him wanting to feel the heat of his body. The dim evening light caught in his eyes, making them shimmer like the path of the moon on water.

"May I have Finny?"

He considered her request before slipping the tote from his shoulder and pulling out the puppy. His fingers were wrapped around her as though she were nothing more than a small stuffed toy. "This is not a dog." His thumb ran along the stones set in the collar. "No self-respecting dog wears jewelry." His glance flicked between her and the puppy licking his fingers. "Important to you, isn't it."

"Esteban gave her to me."

"Did he now?"

His serious consideration of her answer encouraged her. "She was a gift."

"Esteban have a last name?"

"Duro."

"Promise not to run?"

She nodded, crossing her fingers behind her back, fully intending to break the promise.

His observant gaze made her uncomfortable, and for a moment she wondered if he'd read her thoughts. "You know my Gran?"

"Not personally. I'm the lackey charged with the job of bringing you home."

"I can take care of myself."

"Your grandmother's worried about you."

Lu held her trembling hand out to Finny. The dog's tiny pink tongue tickled her fingertips. "I don't want to go home. Things happened that Gran doesn't know about."

"What things?"

"That's none of your business." Her brave words contradicted the quaking in her stomach.

"Everything about you is my business. Your grandmother made it my business when she contacted SeaMount." He stroked behind Finny's ear. The puppy leaned her head into the scratching finger, eyelids at half-mast with contentment.

Little traitor. "How can I be sure you aren't kidnapping me and holding me for ransom?"

In the shaft of light, his eyes gleamed an unnatural blue. "You're grandmother doesn't have the resources to pay a ransom."

"Oh, *that* puts my mind at ease."

His hand shot out and closed around her wrist. Without a word he pulled her farther into the basement to a hall framed with ancient planks of wood.

She walked through a spider web, making her skin crawl. She scratched the phantom itches in her hair, on her arm, behind her knee, and back to her hair.

"What are you doing?" His question hissed in her ear.

"Spiders."

He pushed her into a small room and leaned close, his face inches from hers. "You aren't covered with spiders."

"You don't know that." She dug at her neck and her scalp. "They're everywhere in dark damp places."

His gaze drifted from her tangled hair to her tattered dress. "I'll be back."

Hot fear sizzled through her. "Where are you going?" She wanted to bite her tongue for sounding needy and frightened. She couldn't depend on a man who had kidnapped her.

His eyes glimmered blue. "To take a look around." He stepped closer. "I will not abandon you."

Her heart panged as though wounded. She crossed her arms. "I-I didn't think you would."

He brushed her hair back from her temple. "Didn't you?"

She stared at him, unable to answer. He handed her the puppy. Snuggling Finny close, tears blurred her vision. The puppy whined and wriggled with joy. Barely hearing a soft squeak and snick, she glanced up.

He'd left her.

She pulled on the handle. It didn't budge. A shard of fear cut through her. "Hey."

"Quiet." The muffled command filtered through the door. "The men in the street will hear you."

"Good!" Panic overrode caution. "They can rescue me."

"Don't count on a happy ending with that, Lulabelle. They're out for blood, emotions at fever pitch. You don't know that they'll hold themselves to a code of honor."

A tremor ran through her. If his purpose was to scare her, he'd succeeded. He was her lifeline. He was crazy and had pulled her into more trouble than she'd ever dug up—and that was saying a lot—but because of him she'd survived. "Don't leave me here." She hated the desperation edging her plea.

"Rest." His disembodied voice remained calm. "I'll be gone only a short time and I'll be back. I promise."

Chapter 6

Jack listened, his hand on the iron latch bar. He waited for her to take her wrath out on the door. Her silence surprised him and didn't bode well. Had he underestimated her? He admired her spunk. She was a fighter. Now if she'd only realize he wasn't the enemy and quit fighting *him*. He should have kept the dog. The minute he had the thought, he dismissed it. The puppy was hot, its tongue hanging out. He needed to rustle up potable water. Having to provide basic necessities created another kink in his plan. The escalation of the fighting would make moving to the secondary PZ tougher.

Praying for divine guidance, he walked the few yards left of the narrow hall and stepped into a large open room. Odd bits of discarded furniture lined one wall. A bent candle stand stood sentry duty at the base of a set of steps carved into the rock wall. He climbed them to the closed door at the top. Hoping he wasn't about to frighten a priest going about his evening duties, he lifted the latch. The door swung open on oiled hinges, and he stepped through into a small alcove tucked into the north transept of the church.

The scent of incense and beeswax swirled around him, transporting him back to the church of his childhood. He rubbed his face. In a church much like this one he'd been introduced to God the Father, and his Son, Jesus Christ. His breath hitched in the back of his throat. He should have never stepped foot inside this church. Memories nipped at his heels as he hugged the wall, moving beneath the stained glass windows rising high between the vaults and glowing in the evening sun.

Focus, Conroy.

Entering the vestry, he passed the cabinets and drawers storing vestments and linens and entered a smaller room used by the young servers. He found a cupboard filled with the paraphernalia that accumulates in an area frequently used. One shelf held a cache of bottled water. Scooping up several bottles, he dumped them in an empty linen sack. He found a first aid kit in the tiny bathroom. To assuage his conscience, he tucked several paper bills of island money into the top drawer of the linen cabinet.

Using the pillars running the length of the nave for cover, he worked his way to the back of the church. In the narthex, to the side of the entrance, sat a large woven basket filled with clothing donations for the needy. *That's me, Lord.* He desperately needed Lucinda out of her dress and into something less revealing.

He dug through and found a pair of lightweight pants and a top that looked her size. He added a beach towel emblazoned with the name of a five-star hotel. Stuffing the clothing and towel in the sack atop the water, he crossed the narthex to a door set back in the dark wood paneling. The church bell tower would be an excellent observation post.

He went to work on the lock with his multi-tool. Within seconds he opened the door gaining access to the steep stairs. At the top he pushed through the trapdoor and, on all fours, crawled beneath the huge bronze bell to the small balcony jutting from the side of the tower. Sheltered by a solid half-wall, he rose up on his knees to spy over the lip.

All that remained of the sun was a mauve streak on the horizon, casting an ominous glow on the buildings below. To the north, the pop of gunfire followed flashes of light. The chaos at the waterfront had eased. First responders had the area lit with spotlights, risking their lives to continue rescue efforts.

Jack sank down and turned to sit with his back against the wall. Exhaustion washed over him. He needed to call in a situation report. The boss wouldn't like this SITREP. Pulling out his SAT phone, he punched in the numbers that would connect him to the agency director, Sam Traven.

"You're alive." The director's rough voice had an edge to it.

"Ran into trouble." Jack shifted, folded his knees up, and braced an elbow on them. "They blew off the end of the pier." He cleared his throat. "Hear from Whit?"

"No contact yet."

Jack's gut took a nosedive leaving him nauseous.

"Do you have her?"

Jack pulled his focus back to his mission. "Got her locked up." He didn't try to keep the bite out of his voice. "Need you to check out an Esteban Duro." Jack filled him in with a brief summary of events. "We're in a hot zone."

"I'm sending in the team."

"Don't." Having accepted this mission as his job, he would do it his way. "We'll get to the alternate pickup zone."

"ETA?"

Jack jammed the phone between his shoulder and ear. *Think.* He cracked a knuckle, searching for the best possible answer. "Two days." *And then I'm coming back to find Whit.*

Signing off, he sat with his arms crossed on his knees. Two days may or may not give him the time he needed. On his own, he could hoof it out by morning. With a civilian in tow, he'd have to secure transportation and hope they didn't get caught up in the fighting. He rubbed his face. For more years than he cared to count, he'd relished these challenges. He *liked* his job. So why did his heart want to sit this one out?

You know.

He dropped his head to his folded arms. "No." He denied the soul-deep whisper, knowing he could no longer ignore the battle being waged between his heart and his mind. *I'm not ready to give it up*.

Weary, he crawled back to the trap door and retraced his path through the church. Lucinda had been on her own too long. Had she believed him when he'd told her he wouldn't abandon her? Would she be angry and gunning for a fight or had she used up all her adrenaline and crashed? Truth was, he expected to go back and discover she'd found a way to escape.

The door remained secure. He sent a quick prayer of thanksgiving heavenward. Cautious he prepared to counter an attack.

He stepped inside and found her sitting sideways on a low bench, her legs stretched along the dinged surface, her back against the plank wall. The frou frou pup on her lap spotted him first. It stood and waggled all over in a happy greeting. The welcome didn't hold true for its mistress. The rest had revived her, and fire snapped in the golden flecks of her hazel eyes.

"Have a drink of water." He offered her a bottle from the bag.

Suspicion played across her face before she accepted it. A sip was followed by several moments of guzzling.

He fisted his hands at his sides, unable to take his eyes off the muscles working in her slim throat. Though he objected to her lifestyle, he didn't find *her* in the least offensive. In that small body, she had an inner strength of huge proportions. In the past, he'd seen men twice her size struggle through days like today. She was resilient and determined to meet the challenge. Didn't make things easy on him, but he'd rather deal with her stubborn streak than a sniveling wimp that fell apart on him at every turn.

She drank half the bottle of water then offered some to her dog. Tiny as it was, her cupped hand created the perfect bowl. Several times she refilled her hand. "How long do I have to stay locked in this room?"

"We'll be here most of the night." The optimal time to move was under the cover of dark. But he'd had to find provisions, and she needed first aid treatment and rest. Supplies in hand, he approached her. "Your knees are a mess."

Wary, she held out her hand. "I'll take care of them."

"Not on your life." *Given the circumstances, not the smartest thing to say, Conroy.* Setting the supplies on the far end of the bench, he uncapped a bottle of water and dumped it over her knees.

She shrieked and swiveled to get away. Legs akimbo, she toppled from her perch.

He caught her before she hit the ground. One arm around her back and a hand on her hip, he leaned over her small frame and drank in her sweet scent. Her lips were a breath away from his. A jolt of attraction arced through him. Every nerve sizzled and sang, jarring his self-control. The force of his response shook him to his core. In the low light, the whites of her eyes glistened. Her hand, small and warm, clung to him.

No. No, no, no. God Almighty. Not now. Not this place. Not THIS woman. The prayer banged around in his head, which at the moment was empty of all rational thought.

She glanced up at the grate, breaking the strong current connecting them. Her gaze snapped back in his direction, her words an indignant whisper. "You did that on purpose."

Well, yes, but not to get this *response.* She shoved at him, but he didn't—couldn't—let go. He righted her on the bench, catching the pup as it started to slide off her lap.

"I'm sitting in a puddle." Rearranging the hem of her dress, she scowled. "Why'd you do that?"

Jack eased back, blindly groping for gauze. "To clean your wound." *Payback for the feelings you stir up in me.*

"Give me that." She snatched the white square from him. "Do you have more water?"

He pulled another bottle from the sack and unscrewed the cap before handing it to her. Palming his flashlight, he flipped up the red lens. Shielding the white light with his hand, he directed it at her torn flesh. Legs stretched along the bench, she dabbed at her knees and picked gravel from the cuts. The curious pup stood on her lap, sniffing and trying to move closer. She pushed it back. "No, Finn."

In the backwash of light, he studied her. The strain of the day was evident on her face and in the set of her shoulders. A medicinal scent drifted through the heavy air as she patted ointment on her knees. He ripped pieces of white waterproof tape from the roll and secured the gauze in place.

"I want you to change out of that dress." He set the linen sack on the bench and dug out the clothing. "These should fit."

She studied the pants he held up. "Where did you get them?"

"Donation basket."

"When you leave, I'll change."

"I'm not leaving."

"Then I'm not changing." She held his gaze, her fear of abandonment seemingly overshadowed by the desire to have some control of her situation.

He'd lost too many skirmishes to an untrained opponent. Frustration tightened his chest. He dimmed the light with the red lens. "Who's Esteban?" The man's appearance had lobbed a frag grenade into his mission.

She looked at him from the corners of her eyes before turning her attention back to her knees. "A businessman."

"What's his business?"

Fiddling unnecessarily with her bandages, she didn't look at him. "He sells things. He and Manuel talk about getting deliveries."

"Deliveries of what? Groceries? Furniture?"

"I don't know." She flipped her hair off her shoulder and shot him a pointed look. "When he and Manuel discuss business I'm dismissed." She stroked the pup with the tips of her fingers. It had settled and lay snoozing on her lap.

"You let your lover dismiss you?" His gut lurched. *There, he'd said it.*

She looked away, rubbing her earlobe. "Esteban is old world."

He buffed a hand across the top of his head. Her body language confused him, giving him little to work with. "You aren't the timid type. Gold digger? Maybe. Shrinking violet? No way."

Her wounded expression wasn't what he'd expected. He'd hoped for an anger that matched his own. At the very least, he wanted a fit of pique so she would speak without thinking. But all he'd done was cause her to look as vulnerable as the tiny pup cradled in her lap.

"He gave me Finny." Her whispered words verged on tears.

"For that scrap of fur you stay in a relationship with a man who dictates what you can say and do?"

She jerked as though taking a direct hit. "That's none of your business."

"He doesn't let you ride your bike."

"You were listening."

"Yep." No woman deserved to be chained to an abusive relationship.

"Esteban is good to me."

How can she believe that? "Better than the son of the mayor of Ingersoll, Kansas? What's his name? Trip? Trot?"

"Trent." Shock then panic flashed across her tired features before fear settled over her. "How do you know about him?"

"Your grandmother was a fount of information. Big news when the crown prince of Ingersoll dumps his fiancée."

She looked down at the pup and fiddled with the silly pink collar. "What else did she tell you?"

"Two months ago when you landed on this island, you should have been a newlywed on your honeymoon. Instead, you came alone, the trip a consolation prize handed out by the ex-groom." Hair falling across her cheek, he couldn't see her expression, but the stiff line of her shoulders revealed her distress. He waited for her to lash out. Call him a few names and tell him to mind his own business.

She did none of that.

Careful to keep the pup balanced in the crease of her thighs, she pulled on the hem of her dress, folded her legs up and hugged her knees. Her unexpected silence fell between them like a coil of concertina razor wire.

He'd gone too far. She'd shut down. Anger with himself

burned hot in his chest. His attraction to her had muddled his thinking, and he'd messed up. He needed a breather from this tough little enigma wrapped in a strawberry scented package. He draped the pants and shirt across her feet and placed the flashlight on the bench. "Put these on. Please."

Chapter 7

Lu kept her head down. His footsteps crunched across the dirt floor, and the door latch clicked. Sniffing, she wiped her nose with the back of her hand. When he caught her mid-fall, she saw in his eyes he had wanted to kiss her. Why didn't he take what he wanted? She'd never met anyone like him—so in control of himself and everything he did.

Lifting Finny, warm and furry, she unbuckled the collar and pocketed it. "That more comfortable?" She held up the clothes. Given the situation, they'd be more practical. She stripped off her dress. Pulling on the dark brown pants, she took extra care lifting them over her bandaged knees. The cuffs hit her mid-calf and the seat clung tight across her bottom. The rust colored cotton top floated loose around her middle. She looked like a drab little house sparrow.

Picking up Finny, she stepped to the doorway to test it, unsure she'd have the strength to do anything if she found it unlocked. The wide boards squeaked, and the latch bar rattled but held.

"Don't bother." Jack was on the other side of the door. "You won't get far."

Lu pulled a face. She shuffled back as he opened the door and re-entered the room.

"You need to rest." Pulling a towel from the sack, he

spread it on the floor near an interior wall. "Lay on this."

Almost cross-eyed with fatigue and having a hard time thinking straight, she had no trouble figuring out that stretched prone on the floor, the spiders would have greater access to her. "You're kidding, right?"

"Nope." Arm hooked around her waist he escorted her to the towel. "It's clean."

"I'm not lying down." As last stands went, it was a feeble attempt. Clutching Finny and lacking all grace, she sat and leaned back against the plywood wall. Her eyelids drifted down on their own accord. "I'm not going to sleep." He brushed against her as he lowered his lean body onto the towel. He was positioned between her and the door. Warmth radiated from him and she leaned closer soaking it up. "I don't trust you."

"I've been truthful with you."

She had doubts about that, but for the life of her she couldn't remember what they were. She needed a quick rest and it would all come back to her.

Lu woke to a soft rustling. The soft surface pillowing her cheek bunched hard, the movement accompanied by a crinkly whisper. Her shuddering breath brought silence. Pressing her cheek against warmth, she struggled to wake up.

"Go back to sleep, Lulabelle."

Her eyelids popped open. The earthy scent and red glow snatched her from a sleepy stupor. Earlier events flooded back with vengeance, and she wished she could close her eyes and hide once more in the bliss of sleep. Her racing pulse made that impossible. "What time is it?" Lifting her head, she pushed away from his well-muscled arm.

"Too early to be awake."

"You're awake." She shoved her fingers into her tangled hair and trailed them across her cheek, creased from resting on folds in the sleeve of his T-shirt.

"I'm on watch."

She yawned. "What're you watching?"

He didn't answer, but his unwavering gaze spoke volumes she didn't want to hear. Time to change the subject. A book rested on his legs. "What're you reading?"

"A Bible I found on those shelves." He lifted his chin in the direction of the opposite wall.

Lu sat up straight. "Where's Finny?"

He pointed to the corner of the towel. Her pup lay sleeping in the middle of her bundled dress.

She leaned back against the wall and rubbed her eyes. "Has the fighting stopped?" As if on cue, a wave of gunfire crackled across the city. Her hands dropped. Her gaze flew to his face. He looked at her with a steady assurance that only made her more irritable. She glanced once again at the Bible in his hands. "Shouldn't you be doing something to get us out of here?"

"I am." He flipped a couple of pages, stirring up the scent of mold before running his finger down the right side of the page and stopping three quarters of the way down.

Lu leaned close to peek over his arm. "What does it say?"

His gaze drifted across her facial features before he turned back to the Bible, shining the red lens of his flashlight on the page. *Though I walk in the midst of trouble, thou wilt revive me: thou shalt stretch forth thine hand against the wrath of mine enemies, and thy right hand shall save me.*

She wrinkled her nose. "Sounds old and pompous."

"There are more modern translations available."

Lu mulled over the words he'd read. "Does that mean

God will save me from you?" His surprised expression made her heart bump with satisfaction.

"I'm not your enemy, Lulabelle."

She clutched her hands together. "So *you* say." How many times had she tried to figure out this very point? "See, that's the thing about people like you."

"People like me?" His eyebrows jumped toward his hairline.

"You read those words," she pointed at the book on his lap, "and apply them to the situation from *your* perspective."

"That's right."

"So where does that leave me?" She held her breath hoping this time she'd understand. "Does the Bible apply to you and not to me?"

He looked at the book on his lap and fingered the edge of the pages. His answer was slow in coming. "God in His sovereignty works out His will for each of us."

The same simple answer she'd heard before. It explained *nothing*. Why should she let a God she didn't understand dictate what happened in her life? She grasped for the conclusion she could live with at this moment. "Then there *is* a possibility I won't have to go with you."

In the red glow, his expression became dark and fierce. "*Not* an option."

Disappointment bubbled through her. "Well then, so much for *God's* sovereign will."

The Bible closed with a slap causing her to jump. Jack's lips were clamped in a tight unwavering slash.

"Don't be angry with me."

A muscle quivered in his jaw. "Why would I be angry with you?"

Lu scratched a bite on her arm. "I've been told I ask impertinent questions." She inspected the bump. "A spider bit me." She dared to look up at him. "I have to go to the bathroom."

The woman was driving him to insanity. Her eyes were heavy with sleep, and she sat so close her musky woman scent surrounded him. She asked questions debated by theologians while remaining oblivious of his fight to maintain a semblance of self-control. "You have to—"

"Go to the bathroom." She got to her knees and checked her puppy. "Two bottles of water does that to a person."

Jack cracked a knuckle then roughed a hand through his hair, her accusation "people like you" still circling in his head. She'd lumped him into a group that...that... He wasn't sure what group she'd dumped him in, but he was sure he didn't like it. "You can't wait?"

She looked over her shoulder at him. "For what? Doesn't this church have a restroom?"

He wanted her to go back to sleep. He wanted her out of his hair, which wouldn't happen until he delivered her to her grandmother. But mostly, he wanted to kiss her silly.

Setting aside the Bible, he snapped off his light and rose. "Let's get this over with." A dim glow from street lamps sifted in through the grates, giving him enough light to maneuver.

Picking up her puppy, she stood with a groan. "I hurt all over."

Palming her elbow, he opened the door to their hideaway. "Go right." He hustled her along the dark passage and into the room with the stone steps. "Careful, they're uneven."

She stumbled and muttered under her breath.

He hauled her up, pausing at the door to listen before

opening it and leading her through. Between her sore muscles and a whole lot of rubbernecking, she didn't move fast enough to suit him.

"This place is spooky." Her whisper echoed as white noise in the vaults.

Retracing his steps from earlier, he steered her past the end of the communion rail. "Surely you went to church with your grandmother."

In the ambient glow created by the moon and streetlights, she looked around. "Her church isn't fancy."

He tugged on her hand to hurry her along. "I grew up in a church like this."

She stopped. "You did?"

"Keep moving." He placed his hand in the small of her back and pushed her forward. "I grew up in an Irish Catholic family." Would she notice the absence of the word "good" that usually prefaced that descriptor? Being the son of Seamus Conroy had not been "good". "I learned all the rules as a kid then tried to break every single one as a teen."

She swiveled, looking up at him. A patch of light coming through the stained glass window haloed her hair in a soft yellow and pink aura. "But you read the Bible."

"Yeah." He pulled her out of the dancing colors before he did something crazy, like kiss her sassy mouth. "Eventually figured out knowing God isn't about rules."

"It's not?" She frowned.

"Nope. God wants relationships."

Under his hand, her shoulders fell a fraction. "Oh."

"God doesn't do relationships like mortal men, Lulabelle." He hustled her through the vestry to the tiny windowless lavatory. "In here." He snapped on the wall switch, took the pup from her and stepped out.

She entered.

An anguished howl filled the tiny room.

Diving back inside, he thrust her against the wall and crouched defensively hunting for what caused her outcry. Finding no immediate danger, he caught her gaze in the spotted mirror. "What is it?"

"I'm a mess. Why didn't you tell me?"

"Tell you what?"

"Look at me!"

He turned away from the mirror and stood his full height. She needed to be more specific. "What am I looking at?"

She huffed and shoved at him, but he refused to give ground.

Her hands touched her hair. "I look like a freak." Leaning to the side, she tried to peek in the mirror, but he sidestepped, blocking her view.

"You came," he hesitated, choosing his words with care, "close to losing your life." His heart skipped a beat.

"My hair is a rat's nest!" She jabbed her fingers into the wild mane. "And I have raccoon eyes."

He squinted at her and shrugged. "No different than camo face paint. On an op, we look ugly most all the time."

She squealed in outrage and tried to duck past him.

"What'd I say?" He hooked an arm around her to keep her from running into the wall.

"Get out." She whipped her hand up to point at the door and cracked it against the doorjamb. "Ow." Her face crumpled with pain. She shook her hand.

"Excuse me?"

"Leave. Please."

Evidently her sanity had returned. He stepped aside, and she dove for the thin bar of soap. Turning on the water, she scrunched her eyes shut and lathered her face, all the while doing a funny little dance with her feet, her original need overridden by the desire to look like herself again.

Heart heavy, Jack stepped out of the tiny room and closed the door, giving her privacy. He'd hauled her through a life-changing incident and it wasn't over yet. She could scrub away the exterior grime, but all the horror she'd witnessed had left its mark on her. That she couldn't wash away.

The doorknob rattled and she stepped out. Her skin glowed. She'd gathered her hair up in a rubber band exposing the intriguing little heart on her temple. Desire curled in his gut, and his breath hitched in his chest. Not trusting his voice, he gave her the pup. Taking hold of her hand, he pulled her back the way they'd come, past the rail to the side aisle.

"Jack."

Hearing his name on her lips for the first time spun him around. She slammed into him, rocking him back against a pillar.

"Did you see that?" She pointed across the empty pews, her words soft and breathy.

He dragged his eyes away from her and looked in the direction she indicated. "What?"

"Over there. A little girl." Her voice shook. "In a dress."

A child? Arm around her shoulders, he stood unmoving, trying to concentrate on quartering the nave with his gaze. He came up with nothing on the child and a whole lot of feelings for the woman at his side. "Let's go." Forcibly turning her around, he prodded her toward the basement door.

"Do you believe in ghosts?"

Would the woman never stop talking? His life was riddled with ghosts. "No."

He went ahead of her on the stairs to catch her when she

fell. Negotiating them took all her concentration and, wonder of wonders, she didn't trip once, much to his disappointment. Any reason to put his arms around her held a certain appeal.

Back in the basement, she walked to the towel and sat down without a word. At this distance, cloaked in the shadowy darkness, he couldn't get a fix on her state of mind. Only minutes ago he wanted her to button her lips. Now he wasn't so sure that was a good thing. "You okay?"

"What's next on the agenda?"

Jack leaned against the door and crossed his arms. "You should get more rest."

"What about you?"

I need to get away from you so I can think. "I'll be close by." Last evening, he'd hoped the rebels would lose steam and the government security forces would gain the upper hand. The fighting had quieted down during the night. He needed eyes on the situation to determine his next move. The dusky shadows of early morning would serve his purpose.

"Try and go back to sleep." Reluctance dogged him as he left the room and flipped the latch into place. In the space of a night, leaving her had become harder to do. Praying she'd be there when he returned, he exited the church through the door set in the foundation.

Chapter 8

Lucinda smoothed a hand down her ponytail. The man was driving her crazy. He'd kidnapped her and dragged her into the path of danger, then rescued her and protected her. His actions had her bouncing between being outraged by his heavy-handed control and wanting to curl up in his arms and hold on. *Forever.*

Memories of yesterday crowded her thoughts. Bodies tangled in debris. Rico, a motionless heap in the alley. Her stomach twisted. Jack had tried to shelter her from the worst, but for all his diligence, he'd been unable to hide the horror.

Looking for a distraction, she picked up the Bible he'd set aside and fingered the edge of the soft cover. The gold letters stamped into the old leather had lost their shine.

That someone as self-sufficient as Jack Conroy would depend on God surprised her. Her Gran loved God and depended on him, but Lu had never found God reliable. When her father walked out on her mother and her, she'd prayed and prayed to God to bring him home. But Daddy never came home, leaving Lu with a gaping hole in her little girl heart.

Growing up trailing after her mother from one small town to another, she tried to fill the emptiness, but no person or thing ever came close to easing the ache. Not the many "uncles" her mother brought home. Not boys or the party life.

If what Jack said was true and God wanted a relationship, He would skip right over her. She didn't do relationships very well. Only Gran understood Lu, taking her in when she needed a place to belong.

Lu tossed aside the Bible. The gray light of dawn brightened the square grates. Now may be her only opportunity to return to Esteban. She crossed to the rickety shelves where she found hymnals, prayer books, and old crockery coated with a layer of fine grit. Picking up a small bowl, she flipped it over noting the lack of chips or wear.

"Trent loves old stuff, Finn." She fingered the pottery mark in the base, waiting for a wave of loss. But only anger surged through her. Anger because he'd dumped her and wouldn't tell her why. Anger because she had to leave town when her Gran was in danger.

She set the bowl back on the shelf. It hit something with a *klink*. Brushing the tip of her fingers through the dust, she uncovered a thin rod. She held in her hand. The flat end was followed by a series of twists before lying flat again and ending with a small cup shape. A candlesnuffer.

She stepped over to the door. Holding her breath, she slipped the flat end of the handle through the crack between the door and the jamb. The decorative twist stopped the handle a fraction shy of the bar on the other side.

Exhaling to calm her pounding heart, she pulled the handle out before jabbing it in again and again. Yanking it out, she used the end to poke and chip tiny pieces of wood from the edge of the door. She needed another eighth of an inch to reach the latch.

A cold nose poked her ankle. "Finn, get back on the towel." Scooping up the puppy, she set her on the island of fabric. "Stay." She wasn't sure why she bothered with commands. Finny ignored any she deemed unnecessary, which was all of them.

Getting back to work, she gouged wood from the frame, taking care to avoid splinters when she picked away the small chunks. Inserting the rod handle, she worked it beneath the bar. Holding her breath, she lifted it off the hook.

"Freedom." Heart hammering, she opened the door and peeked into the gloomy hall. Seeing no one, she ducked back inside. Tossing aside the tote bag, she shook out her tattered dress with shaking hands. Tearing and knotting, she fashioned a sling that lay close to her body. She tucked Finny inside and slipped the candlesnuffer through the knot, hiding the handle in a fold of fabric. Looking for something else she could use as a weapon, she snatched up the Bible and slid it in next to Finny.

Drawing a deep calming breath, she stepped from the room. She'd heard Jack leave by way of the heavy door in the foundation. Turning in the opposite direction, she crept along the dim passage leading to the room with the stone steps. She climbed them, taking care not to fall. At the top she opened the door and stepped into the church.

She skirted the alcove and made a beeline for the closest pillar. The beauty of the church stole her breath away. Dark polished wood and intricately carved moulding framed stained glass windows that glowed vibrant with color and details in the early morning sun. The aroma of incense, lemon polish, and candle wax teased her nose.

Peeping into the sanctuary, she looked toward the spot where she'd seen the little girl pop out from between the pews before disappearing. Her heart jumped in a painful start. Halfway back, a floral hat bobbed above a pew. Determined to prove to herself the child hadn't been a trick of her imagination, she hurried down the side aisle. Disappointment squelched her hope. The hat sat atop the head of a small elderly woman dressed in khaki pants and matching jacket. Kneeling, she had her hands clasped close to her chest and her head bowed in prayer.

An explosion outside shook the sanctuary.

Lu's knees wobbled and she grasped the closest pew.

The elderly woman looked up, eyes wide with surprise.

Shaking, Lu slid onto the pew beside her. She wiped her damp palms along the sling holding Finny. "Hello. Have you been here all night?"

"Goodness, no!" The woman shook her head. The flowers on her hat swished to and fro. "I arrived a half hour ago."

"Did you see a little girl in here?"

From beyond the wall of the church a heavy piece of equipment rumbled by.

"No. No one except you, of course." She looked around as though trying to memorize every detail. "My late husband Reginald and I were married here."

A *BOOM* shook the floor beneath their feet.

"It must have been a beautiful wedding." Lu forced the words past the knot in her throat.

"Yes. My name is Ava."

"Lucinda."

"I'm an old fool reliving memories before I leave."

"Leave?"

"Yes. Word came over the radio a couple of hours ago. U.S. citizens are advised to leave the country."

The building quaked under the pounding of another explosion. A chunk of plaster fell from the ceiling and landed on the pew in front of them. Something thumped against the side door entrance. Engines whined and wood splintered.

An uproar from the outside poured in through the broken doors. Jack's words about a lack of honor echoed in Lu's mind. "We have to get out of here." Heart lodged in her throat, she set off down the side aisle toward the back of the church with Ava and her enormous purse in tow. Halfway back an empty candy wrapper and cookie crumbs littered the floor. Lu paused before the crack of wood breaking apart pushed her on.

Coarse shouts and the rattle of metal against metal echoed in the vaults. Lu ran to the large double doors in the narthex. Her hand gripped the curved iron handle. She hesitated as a large vehicle rumbled by outside. The rush of running feet on the wood floor made her heart roll then thunder in her ears. The rebels had broken into the church.

"This way." Ava tugged her toward an enclosed winding staircase.

The commotion at the front of the church covered the squeak of the stairs as they grasped the wrought iron railings and ascended. At the top, Ava got down on all fours. Lu followed her into the organ loft where massive brass pipes hung on either side.

Finny's sling shifted. A soft whine followed a sneeze. Lu pulled her out. Ava gasped in surprise.

Holding Finny close, Lu crawled past the organ's manuals and the narrow choir benches to the front of the loft. She rose on her knees and peeked over the low wall.

At the altar, silver flashed as candlesticks were passed among the men. To one side several yanked on the fringed hem of a tapestry. She was the least religious person she knew, but she wasn't stupid enough to believe actions like this would go unpunished by the God her grandmother and Jack whole-heartedly worshiped.

Chapter 9

Gone! Jack threw the tote bag to the floor and circled the crude little room. He'd been out longer than he'd planned, trying to discover why the men and equipment had converged on the city square half a block away.

BANG! The building shook on its foundation. A cloud of dust sifted down around him.

He fingered the splintered wood on the doorframe. She'd found something long enough to reach the bar latch. He'd have seen her if she'd left the church through the basement door. Which meant she was running loose indoors.

The building shuddered. Overhead, triumphant shouts swelled along with the tramp of booted feet. With his heart stuck in his throat, he ran for the carved stone steps and mounted them. He opened the door a crack to listen. The noisy rebels were at the front of the church. Slipping into the alcove, he hunched low staying close to the wall. At the corner where the alcove joined the side aisle, he took a knee and peeked around the wall. His blood run cold then rushed so hot it burned through him as he monitored the action behind the communion rail.

Silver clanked as chalice, candlesticks, and incense thurible were tossed in a heap. Off to one side a short rough-looking man hefted a weapon in one hand and a heavy bronze cross in the other, laughing and gesturing like the fool that he was. Wishing he could mete out punishment by his own hand, Jack prayed that God take the initiative—preferably this instant.

Lucinda wasn't in their midst. He drew back, flattening his spine against the carved moulding of the wall. With a practiced gaze, he quartered the nave searching for a sign of her. Movement in the organ loft caught his attention. Nothing looked out of the ordinary in the shadows. A pale pink flower floated above the half wall before disappearing. He held his position.

The flower rose into view again, this time followed by a colorful garden planted on the brim of the hat above a pair of eyes. A second female civilian.

He clenched his hands into fists. He wasn't responsible for everyone in the path of the rebels. Lucinda was his priority. Ready to turn away, another head popped up. The dark roots in the center part of blonde hair flagged her. *Lucinda.* Relief poured through him.

Shouts erupted at the altar, and both women ducked out of sight.

Leaning forward, he tracked the men as they disappeared through the door to the vestry. Staying low, he slipped from pillar to pillar toward the back. Entering the narthex he bore right and climbed the enclosed spiral staircase. At the top he dropped to the floor, his gaze hunting the loft's shadows. Lucinda crouched on the floor at the front. Beside her sat the elderly woman with the hat.

Low crawling, he was almost on them when Lu spotted him.

"Ja—"

He hushed her with a sharp shake of his head. Scooting closer, he placed a finger to her trembling lips. A maelstrom of emotion busted loose in his chest making it hard to breathe. *Idiot, Conroy.* He gestured for her to follow him. Now wasn't the time to remind her they wouldn't be in this predicament if she'd stayed where he'd put her.

He crawled between the low risers. Hat skewed over one eye, the elderly woman followed fearlessly behind him dragging a huge purse. Lucinda slipped Finny into a sling she wore bandolier style and brought up the rear.

At the back of the loft, he motioned for Lu to come up next to him. Only then did he notice the sling was crafted from her dress.

He leaned close to her ear. "We go out the front door. Stay low and be quiet." Every second counted. The men were occupied in the rooms behind the altar, but they wouldn't be for long. "When we get outside, break left and run. Don't look back. I'll be right behind you."

She hooked her arm around the woman's shoulders. "Ava, will you be able to do that?"

His innards sank with resignation. This op was circling the drain, ready to spill into the sewer of bad decisions. He could never leave an old woman to fend for herself. Dread seeped through him. He now had two of them to keep in line.

"I'll do it." Ava nodded causing her hat to slip another half inch.

Breathing a half formed prayer for protection and swift deliverance, Jack took the lead descending the stairs.

One of the women stumbled.

He glanced back. Lu's hands were braced on the both railings. Ava's hands dug into her shoulders, hat covering both eyes. He shook his head. If they made it out in one piece, he'd be a lucky man. He hit the bottom step.

The door swung open.

Jack's heart leaped.

The rebel soldier standing on the other side gaped in surprise. He raised his weapon.

Lucinda's scream echoed in the stairwell as Jack stepped forward and pushed the long barrel aside with his hand. In a matter of seconds he'd wrapped his other arm around the butt, drew it snug to his armpit, pulling the soldier toward him and at the same time letting fly a swift jab to the man's chin. Bones crunched and the man slumped in a heap blocking the door.

Shouts echoed at the front of the church followed by the thrum of boots.

Jack spun. He jerked his head to one side to avoid poking an eye out on the short rod Lu wielded like a saber. Snagging her around the waist, he swung her across the rebel's body. "Out the front. *Now.*" He turned back and Ava threw herself into his arms, rocking him back on his heels. She was only a bit taller than Lu, so he scooped her up, stepped across the soldier and ran for the front doors. He lunged after Lu, heart hammering his ribs. Behind him, a chaotic babble erupted as the men discovered their comrade.

Lu ran around the corner of the church and stayed close to a high, untidy hedge of hot pink ixora. He followed her using his body to shield her from the bullets snapping past. Leathery leaves and flower clusters whipped his face. The sharp burn of a bullet creased the side of his neck. A cold sweat drenched him. With each step he pounded out, Ava squeaked. Catching up to Lu, he pressed in on her, steering her down a side street and through several back alleys before he eased the pace.

Panting, she slowed to a limping walk.

"Put me down, you poor boy." Ava released her hold on his neck as he lowered her to the ground. "My car is back there." She pointed in the direction they'd just come from.

She can't be serious. "Keep moving." Between two tall buildings, he pushed them to walk faster through the urban canyon. The slap of bare feet on cobblestone swung him around.

The boy from the pier. Beside him ran a tiny girl dressed in a pale pink dress. A cloud of soft curls framed her face.

Lu gasped. "That's her. The little girl in the church."

"*Hefe*, this way." The kid ducked into a nondescript doorway past men in threadbare clothes loafing on the stoop. A spicy aroma wafted from the open door.

A technical rattled past the end of the street and halted, tail lights visible. The pickup's backup lights flashed on. Gears ground. Praying he wasn't making a mistake, he hauled Ava and Lucinda past the men in the doorway.

Two bare light bulbs hung by wires from the ceiling, lighting a room crowded with small tables and mismatched chairs. In the back, a tall rawboned man stood before an ancient black stove stirring a pot of savory red beans and rice. His gaze skipped over the women and landed on the boy. He raised an eyebrow. "Simao. What mischief have you gotten into this time?"

Jack didn't wait for the boy to answer. The back of his neck prickled with apprehension. "Do you have a back way out of here?"

The man turned off the flame, set down the oversized spoon and wiped his hands on a towel threaded through a bit of rope he used as a belt. He held out his hand. "Timothy Pyle."

The knock of the pickup's engine grew louder. Jack was barely civil with introductions.

Feet shuffling in place, Simao rattled off a spat of Papiamentu. Timothy's sharp gaze darted to the door where the pickup came to a clattering halt. "Follow me."

Their host stepped through a curtained doorway. Lucinda and Ava were right behind him. Jack brought up the rear guard. He stepped behind the curtain as several armed rebels approached the loafing men who instantly became nosy, bumbling citizens. Why they chose to help him was as mysterious as Simao's coming and going. The boy had already disappeared taking the little girl with him.

The corridor made a sharp turn. The occasional closed door didn't give any clues about the place. The back of Jack's neck tightened. He was ready to call a halt for fear of a trap when the man leading them stopped and pressed a hand to the wall. A section of the wall slid to one side. With one step he disappeared from sight.

Pushing Ava aside, Jack scrambled to keep Lu from following, but he was too late.

She walked through, clutching her metal rod.

He dove after her, ready for a fight, but stopped short.

Books. Everywhere. Expensive leather bound books lined all four walls. Gilt lettering glimmered in light cast by a lamp in the center of a round polished table. A worn burgundy leather chair sat in a pool of light in one corner. A quiet snick spun Jack around. The door they'd walked through had disappeared into the wall of books.

Lucinda helped Ava to the chair before removing her sling and taking out a whining Finny.

Timothy went to a small cabinet and pulled out a white box with a red cross on the lid. He nodded at Jack. "You should dress that wound."

Jack wiped the stinging spot on his neck. Blood smeared his fingers. He'd nearly bought the farm. "Branches of a hedge got me."

Timothy shook his head. "No branch did that." His sharp eyes met Jack's. "And you know it."

Uneasy, Jack didn't move. "Who are you?"

Timothy glanced at Ava before setting the first-aid kit on the table. "I'm chief cook and bottle washer for the poor."

"Why are you helping us?"

"Simao can be persuasive. He says you rescued him after the explosion at the pier." Timothy handed him a small packet of sterile gauze.

Jack tore it open and doused the pad in alcohol. "The boy's a thief." He slapped the pad against his neck and gritted his teeth, waiting for the sting to subside.

"Light-fingered and a reliable source of information. Most adults pay little attention to a small boy hanging around listening." Timothy walked over to the chair where Ava sat holding Finny. "Ava Endicott Smythe Fairfax. You don't remember me do you?"

From beneath the bent brim of her hat, Ava studied him. "No. Should I?"

His smile added crinkle lines at the corners of his eyes. "I knew your second husband, Ellison Fairfax."

"Were you in banking with my Ellison?"

"Investment banking. After the economic downturn I was without a job. Your husband encouraged me to do something more with my life. Here I am."

"Ellison had a way about him." Ava's gaze drifted dreamily for a moment before turning back to Timothy and patting his hand. "I married again after Ellison's death. Reginald Meriwether."

"The oil man?" Timothy's surprise brought a smile to Ava's face.

"Yes. He was a rock after my Ellison passed. And one thing led to another."

Impatience tumbled through Jack. The stroll down

memory lane, informational as it was, would have to wait. "What else did Simao tell you?"

"You have an enemy." Timothy glanced a Lucinda. "Esteban Duro."

Chapter 10

Lucinda approached Jack. The sight of his blood did crazy things to her insides. She picked up a clean gauze pad and upended the bottle of alcohol. "Let me help you." Confronting his fierce gaze head on, she applied pressure to the wound. "Another half inch to the right and you'd be dead."

Something flickered in the blue depths of his eyes. "Don't sound so disappointed."

She flinched and pressed harder. His breath whistled between his teeth. "That's a mean thing to say." She thought for a moment. "I was in that church filled with soldiers because you kidnapped me and took me there," she shifted her gaze to his neck, not wanting him to see the lie in her eyes, "maybe I have every right to wish you dead."

A surprised chirp came from behind her. She looked over her shoulder at Ava. "Well, it's true. I was perfectly happy minding my own business when he tossed me over his shoulder and carried me off. He says my Gran sent him."

Jack clenched his jaw.

Fascinated by the play of muscles beneath her fingertips, Lucinda couldn't pull her gaze away from his finely sculpted features. "I have my doubts." Her gaze drifted along his hairline. His military cut needed a trim. "Of course Esteban is your enemy. You took me." The declaration didn't bring the satisfaction she hoped to feel. She looked away from his turbulent eyes before they ripped a current straight to her soul. Let him believe what he wanted. She was on St. Beatrice for one reason—to protect her grandmother.

Timothy eased onto the overstuffed arm of Ava's chair. "Duro is a bit of a mystery man. Been on the island almost a year. If you've made an enemy of him, be careful."

Lu threw the used gauze into a small wastebasket. What if Timothy was correct and Esteban, *her* Esteban, was dangerous? Had she left the situation at home only to walk into another set of bad circumstances beyond her control?

Jack applied ointment to the wound on his neck. "I told Simao to go home."

"You weren't that nice about it." She crossed her arms. "'Beat it, kid', I believe were your words."

A smile played across Timothy's lips. "Simao rarely does what he's told." He stepped over to the hidden doorway. "I'll have transportation for you by nightfall."

Lucinda flicked hair back from her face. "Someone will take me back to the club?"

Jack's hand closed around her forearm. Tension radiated from him. "Get me a vehicle. I'll do the rest."

"The rebel forces may set up roadblocks." Timothy pressed his hand to the bookshelf. The wall slid open. "You'll need someone who knows the island to drive you." He stepped beyond the wall and disappeared.

Lu pulled away from Jack. She swept her hands over her hair and fell back against shelves. "Let me return to the club, and you won't have Esteban after you."

"That will not happen."

Confused by the trickle of relief running through her, she

glared at him. He stood directly in front of her, staring over her shoulder at books. She wanted to grab his T-shirt and shake him. *And hang on—forever.* He lifted his hand and her tummy jumped.

Pulling a book from the stack, he let loose a low whistle. "Amazing." The soft wonder in his voice melted a layer of the protective shell around Lu's heart.

Worn around the edges, the book looked fragile in his hands. Intrigued by his awe, she stretched up on tiptoe to peek at the yellowed pages he reverently leafed through. He stopped at a drawing of Christ on the cross. The words weren't in English.

She glanced up, straight into his intent blue gaze. Her pulse slammed hard. Embarrassment surged hot across her cheek. She stepped back.

Returning the book to the shelf, he continued to read the spines of the others.

Thinking she'd bust wide open if he didn't say something, she blurted, "What are we going to do?"

Preoccupied, he murmured, "About what?"

Holding her temper, she tapped her foot against the wooden floor. "Tonight. We have no idea what type of transportation Timothy is providing. For all we know he could be on the side of the rebels. If he hears about the church and the soldier you killed—"

He grabbed both her shoulders and pulled her close. His nose a scant breath from hers, she blinked to focus.

"We're in the middle of a war zone. My mission is to bring you home, and I will use every skill I have." His gaze drifted from her eyes to her lips and back. "Be it by force or by guile, I will get you home alive."

The air between them quivered with the heat of his declaration. Unable to drag her gaze from his, he held her in place by his fierce certainty that nothing would stand in his way. After a moment, he returned to the books.

Dragging in a deep breath, she walked wobbly-legged to the chair where Ava sat holding Finny. Dropping to the floor, she leaned against Ava's legs. Face to face with her puppy, she stroked from ears to tail. "Men make me crazy."

Ava chuckled. "That happens only when you care about them, dear."

Lu huffed and glanced at Jack. His back was to them as he methodically looked through the wall of books.

Ava patted her shoulder. "Men can be a maddening bunch, but I wouldn't trade the time I had with each of my husbands for anything in this world. With Reginald, love sprang up new all over again."

Lu sighed. "I thought I'd found that kind of love."

Ava rested a hand on Lu's shoulder. "What happened?"

"The mayor's son, the most eligible bachelor in town, fell crazy in love with *me*, Maudie Lavalle's granddaughter. But one day, Trent got all weird." She shook her head. "On top of that, I received threatening phone calls."

A soft thump from Jack's direction startled her. She glanced at him, but he continued to study the books, his back to her and Ava.

"How awful, dear. Did the police help you?"

Lu shook her head. "They said the calls were pranks and told me to change my phone number. Ingersoll, Kansas isn't exactly a hot bed of criminal activity. Trent didn't want to hear about the calls. He was more interested in dumping me." She sighed. Trent was old news. "How do you know when it's really love?"

Ava thought for a moment. "When you would give up anything, including your life, for that person."

That sounded drastic to Lu, but who was she to argue.

Lifting Finny from Ava's lap, she shifted to find a comfortable spot for her shoulders then leaned her cheek against Ava's thigh. "Think I'll rest a few minutes."

～&

Her shoulder was pinned. She couldn't break free no matter how hard she struggled.

"Wake up, Lulabelle."

Jack! Did he see her arm caught between the boards of the pier?

"Come on. You need to eat."

The horror faded. She blinked orienting to waking in the room filled with books. The strength of Jack's hand on her shoulder soothed her now that she was fully awake. A tantalizing aroma filled the room. Her stomach growled. She clutched her tummy and glanced at him from beneath her lashes.

His lips tipped up on one side. "Come eat something." Finny looked down at her from the crook of his arm.

She rubbed the sleep from her eyes. "Finny needs potty time."

"She's all set." He reached out and helped her stand. "Timothy showed me the side door. I fed her, too."

She glanced around the room. Two small condiment bowls sat side by side on the floor. One held water the other contained a remnant of...*oh puh-leese!* "You fed her *cat* food?" Whisking Finny from Jack's hold, she held the pup close. "What did these mean men feed you?"

"The best we could do in the circumstances."

Huffing, she turned away and approached the table at the center of the room where their host had laid out a small feast of red beans and rice, steamed callaloo, and fried breadfruit. Mouth watering, she set Finny down and filled a plate.

Rather than disturb Ava napping in the chair, she sat on the floor, her back against shelved books. Finny trotted over to sit beside her. Using her fingers, Lu popped a slice of breadfruit into her mouth, closed her eyes and chewed. Jack dropped to her other side, his plate heaped high. "Let's say grace."

Lu paused mid-chew, looked at him then at her plate. *Gran would approve of this man.*

His voice lowered to a more intimate tone as he talked to God as though He were a close friend.

From the corner of her eyes, she watched him, hearing little of what he said until the "amen". He dove into his food, focused on the meal with the same single-minded purpose he'd displayed when it came to protecting her. Whatever the man did, he was all in.

Flustered by her train of thought, she scooped up a forkful of the beans and rice and jammed it in her mouth. Heat blossomed, scorching her tongue with a nuclear blast. She grabbed her napkin and spit. Eyes watering and nose dripping, she gasped for breath. She dabbed at her eyes with the corner of her napkin. "How can you eat this?" Her voice rasped.

Jack took another forkful of the fiery entrée and chewed as he considered her question.

She uncapped her bottle of water.

"That will only help for a minute. What you need is milk. It binds to the capsaicin."

"Thank you, *Einstein*." In the absence of dairy products, Lu chugged the water to get a small measure of relief. She wiped her mouth and took a bite of breadfruit hoping it would help relieve the burning sensation.

"You should've grown accustomed to hot and spicy by now."

"I tried. All I ever got for the effort was a stomach ache." She poked at the steamed, spinach-like callalloo with her fork. "Are the greens spicy?"

"Nope."

She twirled a tiny bit on the end of her fork and taste-tested to be certain. "Tell me again who you work for?"

"SeaMount Agency."

"And they are who exactly?" He didn't seem inclined to answer so she jumped into the silence. "If I have no choice about the company I'm to keep, I want to know who I'm with."

He set his fork on the rim of his plate. "SeaMount stands for Strategic Emergency And Mobile Operations UNiT."

"I'm an emergency?" She stared at him, her meal forgotten.

"To your grandmother, yes. We've brought missionaries out of hotspots. Helped in disaster stricken areas. Wherever there's a need."

"Do you work for the government?"

He stabbed a piece of breadfruit. Sure he would try to dodge the question, she leaned closer, ready to pounce, but his fork paused mid air. "That is never acknowledged."

That wasn't encouraging. "If the rebels catch you, the U.S. won't help?"

He didn't answer, which spoke volumes. Appetite gone, she set aside her food. The risks he faced on her behalf were greater than she'd realized. "Like a seamount in the ocean, you operate under the radar. Why do you do it?"

He poked at his dinner plate. "The Bible says we are to do good, seek justice, rescue the oppressed."

"So, you jump right in. Both feet." She didn't understand people like him.

An explosion shook the building. Several books toppled to the floor.

Holding his gaze, fear prickled up her arms. When nothing further blew up, she pushed a curious Finny away from her plate and rose. "I want another bottle of water."

The next few hours were spent in a fitful attempt to pass the time. Occasionally a staccato outburst of gunfire penetrated their small haven. Timothy insisted they leave after dark. Jack kept his own counsel on the matter.

"What are you reading?"

With her nose buried in an old black and white picture book showing the island before it became a tourist mecca, she hadn't seen Jack approach. She held the book up.

"If this civil war continues, the island will regress to its former state." For a moment his expression became grave with unspoken thoughts. "Come on. It's time to go." He held up the sling she'd fashioned earlier, amusement softening his features. "A Bible and a candlesnuffer?"

"I needed a way to defend myself." She lifted her chin daring him to laugh.

The muscles in his cheeks twitched. "Debating theology or in hand-to-hand combat?"

Lu eyed the floral fabric holding her primitive weapons. "Would thumping you over the head with the Bible be considered a theological debate?" She had no idea what his strangled grunt meant so she ignored it. "Are you taking them away from me?"

He shook his head. "I wouldn't dare disarm you." His

throat worked on a noisy gulp. "Put the sling on and keep your hands free."

That didn't sound promising. "Why?"

"Just do it." He glanced at Timothy and Ava speaking in low tones near the exit.

Complying with his order, Lu slipped the sling over her head. She placed Finny inside next to the Bible.

Jack leaned in close on the pretense of adjusting her getup. "Remember what I said earlier—by force or by guile."

Lu sucked in a breath, her gaze colliding with his in one heart-stopping crash. "I can't take much more excitement." Her whispered words brought a fleeting smile to his lips before he snared her hand. Giving it a reassuring squeeze, he led her to where Timothy and Ava stood.

"We're ready."

She wanted to argue that statement. *He* may be ready, but she wasn't. Not at all.

Chapter 11

In the dark hall, Jack crowded Lu against the wall, positioning his body between her and the exterior door. Night had fallen. At his insistence, the indoor lights had been turned off so his eyes could adjust before leaving the safety of the building. Ava stood in front of him smiling up at Timothy, nodding at something the man said. She wasn't much of a shield but Jack would take what he could get. A fact he wasn't proud of but collateral damage happened. A rivulet of perspiration ran from his temple. When had these choices become so difficult?

Timothy turned to Jack. "The man I've hired knows the island. I told him where you want to go. He'll get you there."

No he won't. To keep the location secure, he'd given Timothy a point well short of the PZ.

Timothy opened the door. In the uneven shadows cloaking the alley a small hatchback of questionable vintage idled.

Lu slid across the backseat to sit behind the driver. Ava climbed in after her. Jack slammed the door then faced Timothy, the tension palpable between them. "Why are you helping us?"

"Call it a favor repaid. Ellison Fairfax would have expected me to help his widow. I don't like it that she's mixed up in your plans, but you're her best bet for getting off the island."

Jack raised his head like a dog catching a scent. "Why?"

"The rumor is the rebels have taken control of the airfield. No planes are coming in or going out."

"She's not my responsibility."

"Not officially. But I'm a good judge of character, and you'll do your best to ensure she makes it off the island."

The man knew nothing about him. Only a few minutes ago he'd been willing to forfeit Ava's life in order to save Lucinda. Without a word, he folded his length into the small car.

"Pedro will drive you good." The man with a wiry build and a cap of tight gray curls floored the gas pedal.

The women gasped, their hands slapped to the seat to hold on.

Pedro kept talking. "Roadblocks won't stop Pedro. You'll see. Yes?"

Jack's skin crawled as Pedro negotiated cart paths and narrow alleys. The car bumped off the gravel and careened over patches of grass before racing through a yard where a nanny goat jumped out of the way.

The winding route wasn't taking them to the outskirts of the city as per Jack's instructions. Every red flag he'd developed over the years prickled and jumped beneath his skin. "Pull over."

Pedro grinned big. "Soon. Soon. Mr. Timothy said to deliver you straight away. You'll see." He wheeled onto a cobblestone walkway between two buildings.

Jack broke out in a sweat as the door handles on both sides of the car scraped the cement buildings and threw sparks. Free of the alley, they bumped off the edge of the sidewalk.

"Stop the car." Jack reached for the wheel.

Pedro pushed him away and gunned the engine. The car sailed across the road and onto the median strip where high grass and low scrub slowed them. Tossed from side to side, the women squealed.

Grabbing the wheel, Jack dodged Pedro's elbow and struck a double blow to the side of his neck. Pedro's eyes rolled back, and he slumped sideways. The car swerved into a thick stand of ginger thomas. Leveraging up, Jack leaned across him and thrust open the car door. Yellow trumpet-shaped flowers rained down. He pushed Pedro out.

Ignoring Lucinda's frightened shriek, Jack maneuvered around the shift and beneath the steering wheel. He yanked the door shut and rammed the car into reverse. Gravel pelted the undercarriage and the tires caught. The hatchback hit the pavement, and he jammed the shift into drive.

The blunt muzzle of a weapon dug into the base of his skull.

His blood crystalized. Cold shards ran painfully through his veins. He looked in the cracked rearview mirror.

Ava's hands were wrapped around the grip of a snub nose revolver.

Eyes wide with fear, Lu pressed against her door.

"Don't think about it, Jack dear." Ava's hands, with their parchment thin skin and age spots, held her weapon steady.

Feigning calm, he kept his hands on the wheel. "Don't think about what, Ava?"

"About taking this gun away from me."

"Where'd you *get* the gun?"

"Timothy." She didn't take her eyes off the back of his head.

"Why did he give it to you?"

"For protection."

"From me?"

A tiny smile tweaked her pale lips. "Timothy wasn't specific about that, but Reginald always said I needed to be able to take care of myself." Determination radiated from her. "Turn here."

He'd let his guard down and the old woman had gone rogue. Furious with himself, he swung onto the wide boulevard, into the wealthier section of the island.

"Go left at the royal palm." Ava pressed the muzzle into his scalp.

Tamping down anger over his slip-up, Jack followed her directions. "Where was Pedro taking us?"

"I don't know."

Lucinda shifted, her gaze intent on Ava.

Foreboding crackled down Jack's spine. She was planning something foolish. Like rescuing *him*! Hadn't he told her to keep her hands free? He'd implied she might need to use them. He'd been thinking a leap from a moving car or running for her life. *Not* disarming a gun-wielding granny.

"How're you doing back there, Lulabelle?"

Her gaze flew to the rearview mirror. He winked and some of the tension left her face and shoulders.

"Ava," Lucinda's voice trembled, "put the gun down."

Never taking her eyes off the back of Jack's head, Ava smiled. "You wait. You'll thank me." Her head bobbed and the flowers on her much abused hat flopped pitifully. "Take a right up here at the corner. Lucinda, open your window."

Lu lowered the window as they drove up to a gatehouse complete with a red and white striped security arm. A man in uniform stepped from the small booth.

"Alfred!" Keeping the weapon steady at the back of Jack's ear, Ava leaned across Lucinda.

"Mrs. Meriwether?" He peered inside the shadowy interior of the car. "You're out late tonight."

"Yes, and I'm tired. Do be a dear and let us through."

The man hustled to do Ava's bidding. The arm lifted, and she prodded the back of Jack's head with her weapon.

The poking ticked him off. Having an old woman get the drop on him made the incident that much worse.

The neighborhood they cruised through reeked of money. Behind high walls and iron gates, he caught glimpses of two-story stucco mansions laced with white gingerbread and grillwork covering windows. An abundance of foliage and flowers fringed the wide street.

Following Ava's directions, he pulled into the driveway of one of the larger homes. Exterior lights blinked on, illuminating the front walk and doorstep.

"Who lives here?" The trepidation in Lucinda's voice ripped a hole in Jack's heart.

"I do." Ava's hands remained steady.

He put the car in park and turned the key to the off position. "Now what?"

Indecision flitted across her lined face. Out of the car he'd have room to maneuver, and she'd be no match for him. "We go in and clean up and rest. I'll collect a few things I want to take with me." She poked him with the revolver at Jack. "Get out."

She'd hijacked the car to collect a few possessions? He started to shake his head in disbelief then thought better of it. He did as she ordered pocketing the car keys. "You'll have to put your weapon down sometime."

Behind him, Lucinda opened her door and climbed out. Pale and drawn, she stepped up beside him—right into the line of fire.

He pushed her aside. "Get away from me."

She stumbled sideways, her expression confused and hurt.

"Don't want you shot." Why he felt the need to explain was beyond him. Relieved to see her expression clear with understanding, he was annoyed that it mattered to him.

"Move." Ava punched the air with her weapon.

Jack set off up the paved walk toward the front door with Ava on his heels. Behind them, loud pounding broke the night silence. He wheeled around at the same time Ava looked over her shoulder. Seizing the opportunity he lifted her arms into the air and disarmed her.

She squealed in outrage.

The weapon in his control, he checked the cylinder. God help him, she had a live round chambered. One good bump in the road and she could have blown his brains out. Feeling lucky to be alive, he approached the rocking car where yelling now accompanied the banging.

Revolver trained on the car, he keyed the lock. The hatch sprang open.

Simao lay on his back, feet in the air.

"*Hefe!*" Seeing the gun, his smile wavered.

"Don't kill him." Lucinda's tearful cry flipped Jack's stomach.

Oh for Pete's sake. Jack glanced toward heaven then reached in and pulled the boy out setting him on his feet. He leaned down, hand braced on his knee to go face to face with Simao. "What are you doing here?"

"Watching your back, *Hefe*." He glanced at Ava and Lucinda. "Where's Pedro?"

Could things get any more complicated? "Where's your sister?"

Hands behind his back, Simao rocked on his sandaled feet. "Safe."

Jack didn't ask any questions for fear he'd feel compelled to go rescue the boy's sibling. "Do you know where we are?"

The boy looked at the palatial home then out through the open gate and nodded his head.

"If I told you to go home, would you?"

Jabbing the ground with the toe of his sandal, he shook his head.

Jack looked down in defeat before standing straight and pushing Simao toward the wide-eyed women. "Everybody inside." He closed the gate at the end of the drive and caught up with them on the walkway.

Ava withdrew a beaded key fob from her oversized purse and unlocked the door. She flipped a wall switch, and light flooded the foyer illuminating the marble floor and sweeping staircase. A massive orange ball of fur with a fluffy tail bound into the room, yowling and weaving through her ankles.

With a protective hand on Finny's sling, Lu stared at the beast.

"This is Pumpkin." Ava reached down and scratched the animal under its hairy chin. "A big baby, aren't you, pet?"

A sinking feeling burned hot in the pit of Jack's stomach. He was certain Ava would insist on taking the cat with her. He loomed over her. "Explain yourself."

Ava eyed the gun he held at his side. "Timothy said you're my only chance of getting off the island."

Lucinda's eyes pooled dark with concern. "Jack, is that true?"

"Unconfirmed." His biting reply didn't stop Simao from butting in.

"It's true." He fingered an antique silver bowl resting on a small piecrust table.

"I-I'm sorry." Ava's shoulders slumped. Beneath her much-abused hat, her parchment-thin skin was nearly transparent. "I couldn't leave without my Pumpkin or the ruby bracelet Reginald gave me on our anniversary."

Her apology appeared real, but Jack wasn't ready to let her off the hook. "If I hadn't eliminated Pedro, would you have pulled the same stunt on him?"

She looked away.

His blood ran cold. That was all the answer he needed. "Don't pull another trick like that. Understood?"

She nodded. A flower fell from her hat and drifted to the floor.

Jack looked at the weary women and then his watch. It was past midnight, and they had a long way to go. A trained team would be making a sprint for the PZ. He rubbed his hand down his face. The women were running on empty. This would be the safest, most comfortable place for them to regroup before pushing through. "A quick meal then a short rest. We leave in three hours."

Ava climbed the stairs with her mammoth cat on her heels.

He let her go. Wilted, like her poor abused hat, she appeared to be no danger at the moment. His hand at the small of Lucinda's back, he pressed her along the hall. Simao followed in their wake, handling everything he passed.

Guiding her to the breakfast nook, he pulled out a chair. She dropped into it and swept a trembling hand over her hair. The flecks of gold in her hazel eyes had lost their sparkle. She drew in a shaky breath. "I was afraid she'd kill you."

Simao set about opening drawers and cupboards, exploring the contents of the kitchen.

Swinging the cylinder of the revolver open, Jack removed the cartridges. He tucked the weapon in the back of his waistband before grasping the knot of fabric on Lucinda's shoulder and lifting the sling off over her head. Digging the puppy from its folds, he handed her to Lu. "You were ready to try and rescue me." Absurd as the idea sounded. "Thought you wanted me dead?"

She shivered and looked away. "I don't want you dead. Just, just..." She waved her hand in the air.

"Gone?"

She nodded, but uncertainty shadowed her eyes. "Did you kill that nice man, Pedro?"

He barely caught her whispered words. How do you explain to a civilian the instincts that have kept you alive in places dangerous beyond their imagination? He squatted next to her, pushing a strand of hair behind her ear, exposing the intriguing heart-shaped fleck on her temple. Her pallor worried him. "We were headed for trouble."

Her almond eyes pooled liquid, searching his face.

His heart dropped. *She thinks I'm a cold-blooded killer.* He went to the refrigerator. Pulling out a carton of orange juice, he poured a glassful and he set it on the table in front of her. "Drink all of it."

Her hands shook as she tried not to spill the contents on herself and her little dog.

The desire to take her in his arms and soothe away her fear overwhelmed him. *Fool!* She wouldn't welcome any comfort from him. Stuffing his hands in his pockets, he backed away and leaned against the counter.

The story he'd overheard her tell Ava hadn't been part of his briefing. Her grandmother had said nothing about threatening phone calls. Had she kept that information from her grandmother? Sam needed to know. He rubbed a hand down his face, weary of the twists and turns cropping up on this mission.

Ava entered the kitchen and went to the refrigerator. Simao had all but crawled in while exploring the abundance of food. Stepping out of her way, he held a bottle of milk in one hand, a brick of cheese in the other, and a sesame bagel clamped between his teeth.

Opening the cupboard at his back, Jack found a plate and set it on the table. "Sit here, Simao."

The boy unloaded his bounty and sat.

Handing him a table knife, Jack turned back to Lu. He had to hear the rest of her story. To prove she wasn't right for him? To convince him she had good reason to leave Kansas and her grandmother? He had no idea what he was searching for, except maybe peace of mind.

Chapter 12

"Why did you leave Kansas? The truth, Lulabelle."

Lucinda set her glass down with a thump. Orange juice sloshed onto the back of her hand. She wiped it off. The sweet acidic juice had revived her flagging energy. His gaze was heavy-lidded and intent causing her tummy to tingle.

"Why do you want to know?" *Good one, Lu. Answer a question with a question.* It wouldn't distract him for long, if at all.

"You're grandmother said you had trouble with a man." He tried to look all casual standing with his hands in his pockets, but he hummed with tension.

Some perverse part of her wanted to shock him. "Gran thought I was pregnant."

"Were you?"

"No!" She'd expected self-righteous distaste not the concern roughing the edges of his voice. She leaped out of her chair. With Finny on her arm, she paced to the hall doorway and back. "I don't know why everything fell apart between us."

"The mayor's son."

She nodded. He'd heard her conversation with Ava. Her tired brain scrambled to find a way to redirect the conversation, but she came up with zip.

"Excuse me." Ava bustled past carrying the fixings for roast beef sandwiches. She clattered about pulling out a cutting board and knife.

Jack eyed the knife and side stepped, putting distance between him and the little white-haired woman.

Lu couldn't hold back a smirk and became the target of his narrow-eyed gaze. She looked away pretending interest in Simao as he attacked the brick of cheddar with the knife Jack had given him. Sneaking a piece, she nibbled a corner.

She had no "other woman" to blame. No heated argument or harsh words. She didn't want to tell him any part of the sorry story but knew he wouldn't be put off. "Trent used all the excuses. 'We aren't right for each other.' 'This isn't working.' Which wasn't true. We had a great relationship until..." She stopped and glanced at him from beneath her lashes. He'd think she was nuts.

"Until what?" The gentleness in his voice, so at odds with his tough exterior, melted all resistance to him and his many questions. She sat with a bump. Unable to look at him, she finger-combed Finny's coat and traced the pup's tiny ears. "Until Billy Wilson got involved."

Jack shifted his weight against the counter and crossed his arms. "What did Billy Wilson do?"

"He was angry with me and said things to Trent."

"Angry about what?"

"I don't *know*!" Exhausted and miserable, she lifted Finny to her cheek, closed her eyes, and whispered, "I don't know." She couldn't hold the tears back. They dripped off her jaw. Finny's coat absorbed the moisture. "This...this is the part where I feel stupid because I don't have the answers. I can't find the answers because I don't know what the questions are."

Cloth rustled. "Then let me help." Jack's voice, soft and rough with emotion, was close to her.

She opened her eyes. He had squatted beside her, one arm on the table, the other on the back of her chair. Her brain couldn't wrap around the concept of this Jack. Gentle and caring. Was it a ruse to get her to talk?

"You're not stupid, Lulabelle." His smoky blue gaze touched on each feature of her face.

She couldn't look away. She wanted desperately to believe him.

"What were you doing when Billy got mad?"

"I drove my car to the garage." The words hovered on a whisper. She cleared her throat and forced herself to talk louder, stronger. "Gran needed new shoes, and my car was making an odd noise so I wasn't sure it would go the distance to the city. I stopped at the garage early in the morning." She ran out of air and stopped to breathe. She'd never told anyone about that morning.

Across the table, Simao continued to stuff his face with the bagel and cheese. He'd be bound up for a week.

She jumped, surprised by Jack's fingertips resting between her shoulder blades. He began massaging small circles. She relaxed against his hand. If this was a new interrogation method, it worked.

"Then what?"

"I arrived a few minutes before business hours. The light was on and the door open, so I walked in. I didn't find him in the office so I stuck my head into the garage." She gulped to get rid of the lump in her throat. "He was there. He blew up at me for coming in early."

"Why?"

"I guess he wasn't ready. His tool bench had guns on it."

"Is he a sportsman?"

Lu nodded. "We take firearms in all the time at the shop." She frowned. "But these weren't for prairie chickens or deer hunting. They looked more like the guns the soldiers at the church carried."

Jack's fingers stopped then slowly started again. "Then what happened?"

"He told me to get in my car and he'd open the big overhead door for me."

"Did he?"

"He took his time." She glanced sideways at him. "When I drove in, the tool bench was clear." She shrugged and looked down at her hands.

"That's it?"

Lu sniffed and let loose a sharp self-deprecating laugh. "Yes. Sounds silly, right? But that evening…" She stopped, considering her words. That evening, she'd felt like a princess soon to be crowned queen. Trent had wanted his fiancée with him in front of the important people in town.

"That evening we attended a fundraiser at the VFW hall for a local charity. Trent had asked me weeks before to attend with him." She played with Finny's tiny paw. "I'd found a special dress and did my hair." She looked into his warm gaze. His fingers continued to caress small loops on her back. "Anyway, B-Billy was there. He spoke to Trent in private. After that everything changed between us. He even avoided me at work."

"The pawnshop his father, the mayor, owns."

She cast a sharp glance his way. "It was a good job in a small town." He made it sound so cheesy. "We carried some high-end items like antiques and expensive jewelry."

Ava set a platter of sandwiches on the table along with plates. "Jack, be a dear and get water from the refrigerator."

Squeezing Lu's shoulder, he rose leaving her bereft

without his comforting touch. She reminded herself to breathe. *Get a grip, Lucinda.*

The cat jumped into the chair beside Lu and stared at Finny with unblinking eyes. Finny stood on Lu's lap and sniffed. Her warning bark was met with a raised tail and angry hiss. Lu scooped the pup into the protection of her arms.

"Dear me. Pumpkin, be nice," Ava scolded.

The cat crouched low, tail twitching.

"Get down. Jack needs to sit there." With a practiced push, Ava removed the protesting cat.

Simao stuffed the last bit of bagel in his mouth and reached for a sandwich. Ava tapped the back of his hand in disapproval. "Grace first, young man." Smiling, the boy laced his fingers together in front of his nose.

Jack leaned close to Lu and whispered, "What do you bet the sandwiches disappear while our eyes are closed."

She muffled a giggle behind her hand. "I'll keep watch. I don't pray."

Something stirred in his warm blue eyes. He didn't reply.

The others bowed their heads and true to her word, she kept her eyes on Simao. He peeked once, saw her watching, and ducked his head again.

Jack thanked God for the food before them and for safety in the coming hours. Then he said her name. "Help Lucinda understand You want what is best for her. Bless us and keep us. Amen."

She stared at the sandwiches, her hand pressed to her stomach, desperate to calm the honeybees spiraling there. Hearing him pray for her felt intimate. Like he truly cared about her. But how could that be? She was just a job to him.

The sandwiches disappeared from her line of vision. He poked her with his elbow. "Take one now before they go past Simao." She dared a look at him. His crooked smile made her heart flip-flop. Hungrier than she realized, she packed away the sandwich and accompanying chips.

Under the scrutiny of the bad-tempered cat, Jack ate a second sandwich while Ava encouraged Simao to use his table manners, which appeared to be nonexistent.

Eating her fill, Lu covered a yawn with her napkin.

"You need to rack out for a couple of hours."

"If that means go to sleep, then I couldn't agree with you more. Preferably in a bed this time."

Jack rose, taking his plate and glass to the sink. "Ava, do you have a room for Lucinda?"

Ava handed the last half of a sandwich to Simao. "The second room on the right. You can take—"

"I won't need one, but thanks." He pulled out Lu's chair. "Come on, Lulabelle."

She didn't want him to accompany her, but she didn't have enough fight left in her to argue. Her sandals could have been lead boots for all the effort it took to climb the stairs.

The upper floor of the house was as beautiful as the lower. At the appointed room, she stepped through the door. The bed, covered with a puffy floral spread and plump pillows, beckoned. She wanted to fall in and never climb out.

Jack squeezed past her and rifled through the dresser drawers.

"That's rude." He looked out of place in the feminine luxury of the room.

"Making sure she doesn't have weapons stashed." He moved on to the nightstand.

Lu collapsed onto a small dressing chair and kicked off her sandals. "Ava apologized. Besides, there's a whole kitchen full of knives and other tools that can be used as weapons."

He searched the nightstand before moving to the closet. *Didn't the man ever get tired?* Finding nothing of interest, he stepped into the adjoining bath. Bottles clattered, drawers opened, and contents shuffled. "All clear."

"Oh goody." Her sarcasm was showing, but she didn't care.

He cut her a sharp look before opening the window and checking the security bars. "Come here."

Following his order seemed easier than arguing. She wanted a shower and time in that lovely bed. "What?"

"Look down there. What do you see?"

Gripping the bars, Lu rested her forehead between two of them and peered down. She hoped he wasn't grading her on this quiz. "Bushes."

"What type bushes?"

"I don't know, Jack. What type bushes are those down there?"

He pulled her back and closed the window. "Yellow allamanda. The sap causes an itchy rash."

"And you're telling me this why?" She had an idea but she was done with the guessing game.

"Don't even think about trying to escape." His hands bracketed his narrow hips, biceps bulging.

"The only thing I'm thinking about is a hot shower and a soft bed."

He eased Finny from her grasp. "Then go on. Get started."

"What are you doing with Finny?"

"Guard dog that she is, I'm taking her with me while I go through the rest of the house. I'll take her out for her bedtime run and then bring her back." He lifted an eyebrow daring her to argue with him.

"Don't let Pumpkin get her."

"She'll be safe from that devil-cat. Go on, Lulabelle. Get your shower. You're falling asleep on your feet."

There was that gentle Jack again. The one that made her want to take Finny's place and curl up in the crook of his arm. *Stop it, Lucinda.* She stumbled to the bath, closed the door, and listened for him to leave. Several minutes ticked by before the bedroom door closed. She studied her reflection in the mirror. She looked like she'd been dragged through Hades and back.

By all accounts, she had.

Chapter 13

Jack closed the door to Lucinda's bedroom and leaned against it. A whirlwind of emotions whipped through him. Leaving her alone in that room made him ache with the desire to hold her close. Courageous as she was, he wanted to stay at her side and protect her. He wanted to be the one who swept the shadows from her eyes. Trent Ingersoll was a fool. A fact that worked in Jack's favor.

A tiny tongue licked his arm. He held the puppy high in one hand. "Your mistress is a distraction. She's driving me bonkers."

The puppy smiled.

He shook his head. His mission was to bring one petite woman home, and here he was tangled up with a frou frou puppy, an old woman, an ornery cat, and a boy who would give Oliver Twist a run for his wallet—or whatever else his sticky fingers came in contact with.

He was long overdue contacting Sam. The director would be planning a recovery operation for Whit. Jack swallowed hard around the lump in his throat and pushed the grief away. He had a job to finish.

Hearing Ava in the kitchen talking to her cat and tidying up, he began a detailed recon of the second floor. In each room he checked drawers, closets, and all the places folk liked to believe no one else would look when hiding their secrets. In the small study off the master bedroom, he hit pay dirt. Reginald Meriwether, oil tycoon, had a penchant for antique weaponry.

A Sharps rifle was mounted on the wall behind the desk. From the bottom desk drawer, he confiscated the modern day black powder cartridges for the American Civil War era rifle.

On the cherry credenza, a WWII fighting knife with worn leather holster was showcased under glass. Over a small settee hung a WW1 Naval officer's dress sword. Leaving the sword where it hung, he took the fighting knife as backup.

Finished clearing the second floor, Jack headed for the stairs. He paused in passing Lucinda's room and listened for the soft splash of running water before going down and out the front door. He set Finny on a tiny patch of green lawn.

Keeping an eye on her, he stood in the deep night shadow of an African tulip tree. The damp breeze carried the tang of salt and the distant sound of sporadic fighting. Had Ava's neighbors escaped off the island? The rebels wouldn't be long in coming to this area to go through the empty houses looking for valuables. The dutiful gatekeeper, Alfred, wouldn't be able to keep them out. Jack hoped the man was safely away before that happened.

Finny finished her business and he picked her up. The tiny scrap of fur was growing on him. Staying close to the wall enclosing the property, he walked the perimeter. At the back of the house, light from the sliding glass door filtered across a patio created with stone slabs and ringed with flowering bushes and low palms. In a corner, water cascaded from a dolphin fountain.

The bright kitchen light silhouetted Simao standing in the door.

The hair on Jack's arms prickled. Simao's knack for collecting information was a valuable asset. A boy with no family could support himself—and his sister—bartering and selling information for basic necessities. Behind Simao, Ava shook out a canvas grocery tote.

Timothy had Jack pegged. He would not leave an elderly widow, no matter how feisty, no matter how many pistols or ancient weapons she had, to fend for herself.

Widows and orphans.

He went rigid, the words echoing through his mind. He rubbed a hand across his chest. *I have a mission to complete. Can't deal with this now.* Pushing aside the prodding of the Holy Spirit, he hurried through the rest of his recon. He moved Pedro's car to the side yard out of sight of the street. In the garden shed, he found a full gas can. He poured the fuel into the car before returning to the house through the front door.

Simao waited for him.

"Miss Ava go up." He pointed to the stairs before hitching up his shorts.

Jack stepped into the formal living room. Simao followed. Switching on the light, Jack placed Finny on the sofa and set about checking windows, pulling drapes, and searching the room. "Did Pedro know you were in the trunk of the car?"

Simao shrugged. His sharp brown eyes followed Jack as he checked the tops of bookshelves, behind pictures and under the low settee.

The rooms on the first floor of Ava's home surrounded a central hall and stairway. Jack entered the small family room with Finny and Simao on his heels. He followed the same routine as before, but this time Simao mimicked him, looking where he looked, touching what Jack touched.

Going into the formal dining room, he searched the china cabinet.

Simao crowded close. "You look for something?"

He'd wondered how long it would take Simao to ask. "Yes. I'm looking for something." Jack closed the cabinet and moved on to the sideboard. A polished tea service held center stage. He considered the wisdom of opening the silverware drawers but figured the boy couldn't fit much more in his already full pockets.

Jack opened the two doors and Simao poked his nose in.

"You can't find it?"

"Not yet."

"Maybe Simao can help." He stood before Jack, looking hopeful.

Jack rubbed his chin feigning thoughtfulness as though the idea could have merit. "I'm not sure about that."

The boy didn't give up easily. He spread his hands wide. "Tell me what." At his feet, Finny barked as though echoing the question.

Jack smiled, ready to negotiate a deal. "First you tell me what."

Simao nodded his head.

"What do you do with your loot?"

Confusion clouded his chocolate eyes. "My *loooot*?"

Jack pointed at the bulging cargo pockets that had long ago lost their buttons. "Those things."

Simao backed away.

Jack grabbed him and swung him beneath his arm. Clamping Simao tight to his side, he used his other hand to defend his manly man parts from the boy's flying fists. A torrent of Papiamentu and barking rang in Jack's ears as he stepped into the kitchen. He flipped Simao upside down and gripped his skinny legs.

The boy screeched. His hands slapped down on the tile floor, and his legs stretched toward the ceiling in an assisted handstand. His shirt fell, revealing an expanse of dark skin covering a washboard of ribs.

Presented with a face to kiss, Finny didn't hesitate. She dove in and brought the screeches to a sputtering halt.

Jack shook him. A fork clattered to the floor. A silver saltshaker and bag of almonds followed. A spoon and three pens slipped from his pockets narrowly missing Finny as she worked on an ear. The boy's squeals ended in a sharp cry when a pair of scissors clipped him on the chin. Fearing a knife would fall out and slit Simao's throat or stab Finny, Jack set him on his feet.

Simao stood amid the items, yanking at his shirttail and shorts, pockets still holding a few items.

Jack pointed at the floor. "Loot, *amigo*."

The wheels were turning behind those big brown eyes.

"No story. I want the truth." Jack crossed his arms. "Do you work for someone?"

Simao shook his head. A smile broke across his face, and he poked a finger in his own scrawny chest. "Businessman."

The titter of laughter alerted Jack to the audience standing in the hall listening to him interrogate a nine-year-old. "You sell these things?"

Simao nodded.

"What do you do with you money?"

Another swift smile. "Feed my sister, Angelina."

The poverty on the island was as extreme as the wealth. That division led to the rebellion now playing out in the streets. How could he fault a boy for trying to provide for his sister?

"Everything out of your pockets." Jack stood back and

waited while Simao removed a pepper shaker, silver sugar tongs, and a wallet that looked famil—"

"Hey," Jack snatched it from his hands, "that's *mine*!" He glared at the women dressed in robes and giggling like schoolgirls.

Looking at Lu was his undoing. Her hair was hidden beneath a twisted towel emphasizing her tipped-up eyes and high cheekbones. Fresh from the shower, she looked soft and feminine in a short pink robe. The sight of her hit him low in the gut.

Ava, dressed in a floor length purple robe, held her hand out to Simao. "Come with me, dearest. I'm sure I have something nicer than a pair of old salt and pepper shakers for your sister."

Simao, knowing a good thing when it presented itself, took her hand. Looking back, he smiled and gave Jack thumbs up.

Unable to hold back a grin, Lucinda watched Ava lead Simao away.

After the two days they'd had, he welcomed her smile even if it was at his expense, however he still wanted to grumble. "Ava doesn't take his stealing seriously."

She tipped her head to one side. "You can't change a lifetime of conditioning in a day."

No, he couldn't, but he could point out the error of the kid's ways. "I can't condone his behavior." For his sanity he needed her to hightail it up the stairs to bed. He checked his watch. "Soon it'll be time to leave. You should sleep. No telling what the day will bring."

She stifled a yawn and stepped into the kitchen. The fresh scent of soap teased him as she padded past on bare feet and picked up Finny, busily snuffling the items littering the floor.

He'd forgotten all about her frou frou puppy.

"Hi sweetikins."

The sugary greeting should have made him nauseous. Instead, it curled his toes in his boots.

The puppy whined and waggled all over.

"I know. It's been a long day." She snuggled it close scratching beneath its chin with one finger. She padded by him once more giving him a weary smile before leaving the room.

Ten minutes passed before he moved. Half the time he'd prayed—for Simao and his sister, for Lucinda's struggle to know God, for deliverance from whatever had him wrapped up in her. The rest of the time he worried, which revealed a serious lack of faith on his part.

He walked around the first floor turning off the lights. Stepping outdoors, he looked toward the east. No flashes of light highlighted the skyline. The rebels had chosen to call it a night. He pulled out his SAT phone. The director answered on the first tone.

"Expected to hear from you before this."

Jack ran a hand along his chin, scratching a two-day beard. "Ran into trouble." He briefed the director on the most recent developments including the phone calls Lucinda had received in Kansas. If any of this pertained to his mission, Sam would connect the dots. Unsure how to explain Ava, he only said they had stopped for a short rest. He signed off without asking about Whit. Foolishly, he wanted to hold on to hope.

Taking up position on the stairs, Jack sat with his back to the wall. If anyone came down, they'd have to step over him or leap the railing. He crossed his arms and leaned his head back. "Father God, show me what I'm to do with this bunch."

Chapter 14

Lucinda sat at the top of the stairs watching Jack. His head and shoulders rested against the wall. His knees leaned against the railing. Eyes closed and lips parted, his black hair stood on end. Her palms itched to smooth the wayward spikes into place. Instead, she curled her fingers into the hem of her borrowed nightshirt and buried them between her knees.

She'd slept only a short time before a dream had jarred her awake and left her with a sick stomach. She'd lived through the events of the past two days. She didn't want to reenact them in her dreams. Shivering, she glanced at the Bible on the stair beside her, unsure why she had grabbed it when she dashed from her room holding Finny.

Resting an elbow on her knee, she cupped her chin in her hand. Jack was convinced he knew what was best for her in this situation. Could he be right? Would Esteban agree to let her leave the country until the fighting quieted down?

Her stomach clenched rock hard. Going home meant facing Trent. Had the danger passed? If Gran were still receiving threatening phone calls, she wouldn't tell anyone. She would simply take matters—and her ancient shotgun—into her own hands.

Jack shifted, opened his eyes, and pinned her in place

with his electrifying blue gaze. The connection arcing between them left her breathless.

He climbed the stairs to sit next to her. Swiping a hand through his hair, he mussed it even more. "Why are you up?'

His beard was dark and well defined, and she wanted to run her fingertips across his jaw. Would it feel bristly or velvety soft? "Finny needs to go out. I didn't want to wake you."

"I wasn't asleep." He held out his hand.

She handed Finny to him. "Your eyes were closed."

A secretive smile tipped his lips.

The honeybees went airborne in a tummy-tickling swarm.

He held Finny up in front of his face. "Tell me again why Duro gave her to you?" The puppy squirmed, stretching to lick the tip of his nose.

"She was a gift."

He turned his clear gaze on her. "But *why*?"

The two words hung between them. Her heart slogged heavy in her chest. She crossed her arms on her stomach and gripped her elbows. He wanted a specific answer she didn't have. "What do you want me to say?" She hated that her voice broke.

His heated gaze raked over her face. "The simplest answer: 'Because he loves me'."

The words thrust deep and painful, splitting her open. A million little pieces of her heart tinkled against each other as they fell to the pit of her stomach. Wounded, she hunched her shoulders. Neither indignation nor sarcasm came to her rescue.

Rising, Jack thumped down the stairs.

Lu stared at her toes, relieved he had nothing more to say. Love was the obvious answer, but not the answer she could give. She didn't know. Esteban had never said. He was a gentleman. Other than the occasional kiss on the cheek, there was nothing physical between them.

Drawing in a trembling breath, she wiped a wayward tear from her cheek. Within a space of thirty-six hours her life had turned upside down, and the man disappearing into the kitchen was the catalyst. If she believed him, he was also her salvation. Refusing to sit in a puddle of self-pity, she dashed down the stairs and through the kitchen to stand at the open slider. In the early morning gloom, she watched Jack cross the stone patio and set the puppy on a grassy spot.

Simao walked over to stand beside her, a dusting of powdered sugar outlining his lips. He wiped his forearm across his mouth. "Today we leave?"

Jack came indoors and handed Finny to Lu. "Today you go home, Simao, and we go to our homes stateside."

"We stay with Miss Ava."

"No. We can't stay with Miss Ava because she's leaving, too." Jack pulled out a can of coffee and the electric percolator. The quantity of grounds he scooped into the basket made Lu's tongue curl.

Simao was in the fridge again, the food still a fascination. "We can stay."

Pumpkin stalked into the room, tail twitching with disdain for the strangers that had invaded his house. He joined the boy at the fridge, hoping food would fall to the floor.

Jack filled the pot with water and plugged it in. Pulling Simao out of the fridge, he led the boy to the kitchen table and pointed to a chair. "Sit."

Lu smiled, well acquainted with this Jack.

He squatted on his heels beside Simao's chair. "Miss Ava, Miss Lucinda, and I can not stay because of the fighting."

"No planes flying."

"I have friends who will come for us."

Lu wondered how Jack could be so sure his team could help? Hadn't one of them been at the end of the pier when it blew up?

The boy frowned. "Where are the friends?"

Jack hesitated before he answered. "On another part of the island."

"Simao take you there."

"You must go home."

Simao shook his head emphatically. "Bad men out there. I show you the way."

Jack scrubbed the heel of his hand across his mouth. "The rebel forces are holding the city. They may not be in the remote areas yet."

"Not them. Rico from Paradise and others."

Esteban's man? Lightheaded, Lu sank onto a stool by the counter. She must have made a noise because Jack looked her way before turning back to Simao.

"Why is Rico bad, Simao?"

He stopped to think then simply said, "He has guns."

Unable to breathe, Lu waited as Jack considered what Simao had said. Of course, Rico had a gun. Lu had seen it.

The coffee pot hissed. Jack stood and poured a cup, the nutty aroma circling the kitchen. He took a sip, grimaced, and drank some more.

Ava came downstairs, dressed for the day. "I smell coffee. Let me make some toast before we leave." Pumpkin greeted his mistress. She scratched beneath his chin.

The only one still in nightclothes, Lu hurried up the stairs to her room. A pair of cinnamon-colored capris and a coral T-shirt lay on the bed. The clothes Jack had found for her in the church donation basket were nowhere in sight. She needed to find them. Finny's collar was in the pants pocket.

Giving the pup the run of the room, she used the small trial-size tubes and packets of make-up she'd discovered in the bathroom the night before. She tied her hair up with a circle of stretchy gold fabric.

"Come on, Finn." Opening the door, she stepped back. Jack stood in the hall, leaning against a wall, sipping coffee.

His gaze traveled the length of her.

"Don't be rude." Too short to look down her nose at him, she settled for a pointed glare.

"Deciding which outfit I like better. This one or the one you wore yesterday."

She tugged at her clothes. Whereas yesterday's pants hugged her bottom, the capris bagged on her thighs and in the seat. In place of yesterday's full tunic, the knit tee hugged her curves. She huffed and spun toward the stairs. Jack's hand closed around her arm, arresting her forward momentum.

"Not so fast, Lulabelle."

She swung around, at the last minute remembering to look annoyed. Cocking her head to one side, she lifted her chin. "I need to find my pants from yesterday. Finny's collar is in the pocket."

"I'll take care of it." He pushed away from the wall. "Tell me what you know about Rico."

"He works for Esteban."

"In what capacity?"

"Bodyguard." She thought for a moment. "On occasion he leaves the club when Esteban is with Manuel."

"Now why would a bodyguard leave the man he's hired to protect?"

"To run an errand?" She held her hands up. "I don't know. I've never had a bodyguard."

Jack's eyes glinted as a half-smile tipped his lips. "You have me."

"Oh that's right. God's gift to women."

"No." He pushed away from the wall. "God's gift to *you*. It's not the same."

She couldn't hold back a snort so unladylike Jack's eyebrows lifted in surprise. "Number one, God has no reason to give me a gift. Number two, even if He did, of *all* the gifts He could give me, why you?"

"You're wrong, Lulabelle. God has a good reason to give you a gift. It's called unconditional love. He loves you."

She tsk tsked.

"Even if you don't love him back." He paused, choosing his words. "He knows all about you, Lulabelle."

Anxiety raced up her spine. "Scary thought."

"Nothing surprises Him."

Change the subject. "But why you?"

Jack stared at her, the light in his eyes shimmering warm and unsettling.

Intrigued by his loss for words, she waited.

The comforting scent of warm toast wafted up from the kitchen. "Eat something and then it's time to go." He ran down the stairs.

Her heart contracted with disappointment. She wanted an answer this time, unlike the day he'd whisked her out of the club and she'd assumed he was a religious kook and serial killer all wrapped up in one gorgeous package. Needing time to rein in her thoughts, she dawdled down the stairs.

Finny's collar was on the breakfast table, sparkling in a shaft of sunlight. She sat down at the table and buckled it on the puppy before taking a slice of toast and buttering it. Lu savored the simple fare. In the middle of all that had happened, warm buttered toast felt normal. Right now, she needed normal.

Ava brought another plate with more hot slices and a small jar of peach jam. Her mouth was set and her eyes glistened, but no tears fell. Snatching the empty plate from the table, she hurried to the sink.

Lu wanted to cry for her.

Jack took a seat across from her. "She'll be okay, Lulabelle. She has other homes." His words were whisper-soft meant only for Lu.

"I know. But sometimes when you have to give up what you have right now, it's hard to see the other good things waiting for you."

"Is that why you insist on staying with Duro? You can't see the other good things waiting for you?"

Ouch. "Low blow, Jack Conroy."

"Your grandmother loves you, Lulabelle."

"And I love her."

Jack seized her hand. His thumb bumped across her knuckles. "So stop fighting me and accept that it's time to go home."

She snatched her hand away. "I'm not sure I can."

"Why?"

"Because sometimes loving a person means you have to do something you don't want to do so they will—" Her throat closed up.

"So they will what?" His voice was a soft caress reaching across the dirty dishes and jam jar.

She couldn't get the words past the lump in her throat so she whispered, "Be safe." A tear fell to the linen tablecloth followed by another. On the other side of the table, Jack's face wavered in her watery vision. "So she'll be safe."

With jerky movements, Lu stacked the dirty plates.

Jack rose and turned on the radio. He stood before it, coffee mug in hand, listening to the English-speaking channel. He looked up, alarm in his eyes.

Heart in her throat, Lu joined him.

Suppressed panic threaded through the announcer's voice. Distressed, his island accent became more pronounced, and she had to concentrate on every word to understand him. "Government buildings are now in control of the Island Voice of Reform Party. We have unconfirmed reports some members of parliament are dead."

Lu's hand covered her mouth.

Jack tipped his head, listening. The station went silent. He tried to fine-tune the scale and reception, but received nothing until an odd vocal note blurted from the radio followed by the trembling voice of the announcer.

"I've been given a paper to read." He cleared his throat. "The Island Voice of Reform Party has declared victory and is now the new government on our beloved island, St. Beatrice. The seaport, the airport, and all communication systems," the announcer's voice faltered, "including this radio station, are now under the jurisdiction of the Island Voice of Reform Party."

Jack turned off the radio.

Lu stared at it, not wanting to believe what she'd heard. Beside her, Ava breathed as if she'd run a great distance. Lu helped her to a kitchen chair. Thoughts in a spin, she poured a glass of cold water from the fridge and offered it to Ava.

In a matter of hours the government had fallen, giving way to a new regime. Odd how quickly a person's perspective can change with words of such magnitude. The problems at home seemed small in comparison. Today, Kansas felt like a safer place. But was it? If she left the island, would she risk her grandmother's life to save her own?

Chapter 15

Jack hustled Simao down the hall to the formal living room. Like it or not the kid was his best bet for immediate information. "Sit."

Simao scooted back on the settee, drew his knees up, and rested his bare feet on the cushion. His dark eyes followed Jack as he crossed the room to the bookshelf he'd searched last night. He pulled out a stack of pamphlets and maps. They were the type available to tourists visiting the island paradise.

On his flight to St. Beatrice, Jack had memorized the general layout of the island, including the city and all major roads. To stay away from the more populated coast and the fighting, he now needed specifics of the island interior and the many secondary roads that traced through the mountains. He unfolded the largest, most-detailed map on the low coffee table and pointed to their current location. "We're here."

Simao nodded. "Yes, *hefe*."

Uncertain who Simao may talk to, Jack indicated the general area of the secondary pick-up zone. "I want to go here." The beach wasn't much more than a dent in the coastline on the rugged more remote side of the island.

"I go with you?"

Jack's gut tightened. What would happen to this boy? "Your sister needs you."

Troubled, Simao looked down at the map. His brown finger traced a narrow line through the mountainous heart of the island. "Follow this."

Jack cracked a knuckle and studied the road that wound through the volcanic peaks of the interior. Could he trust Pedro's car to go the distance? Vehicle maintenance wasn't a high priority for most islanders. Under his breath, he offered up a quick prayer. *Lead me, Father. Not my way but yours.* "Where is your sister, Simao?"

He pointed to a tight grid of streets near the mission where they'd hidden. As the bird flies, it was only a few miles from their current position.

"She needs you, Simao. You must go. Now." He was sending the boy back to the streets. He rubbed a hand across his chest, unable to calm the disquiet simmering there. "Angelina needs her big brother." Folding the map, he tucked it into his pocket. Was he condoning the kid's stealing in order to take care of his sister? He reached into his front pocket where he'd begun to keep his wallet with the hope of keeping it out of Simao's reach. He pulled out all the island currency he had. The money would do him no good in the States. "Here. Take this."

Simao's eyes grew wide. Taking the money, he stuffed it into a pocket. "Thank you, *hefe*."

"As your *hefe*, I have your word that you'll return to your sister?"

The boy nodded.

Jack held out his hand to shake on it.

Simao, eyes so big it was a wonder they didn't fall out of his head, placed his hand in Jack's.

Jack started for the front foyer but the boy hung back.

"We have a deal, Simao."

"Yes, *hefe*." He ran to the kitchen where Lu and Ava sat hand in hand. They looked up when he barreled into the room. Hands tucked behind his back, he looked at each one in turn. "Miss Ava. Missy Lu. Thank you." He ran out the slider and crossed the stone patio to the corner where the burbling dolphin fountain splashed water. Using the fountain as a stepstool, he climbed up and over the wall.

Jack stood at the sliding door. "Godspeed, Simao." The horizon glowed softly with the first light of day.

Lu came to stand beside him. "Where is he going?"

"I've sent him back to his sister." He continued to stare out into the yard not wanting her to look too closely at him. He'd made these kinds of choices before and never struggled like this. What had changed?

You know.

He spun away from the door, pushing the small voice aside, unwilling to listen. "We have to go. People will be fleeing the city."

"Refugees?" She whispered the word.

Jack nodded, thankful for her understanding. "Not that they'll get far on an island."

"W-we'll be refugees, too."

He couldn't offer her any reassurances. He could have thwarted Timothy's involvement and Ava's manipulation. Instead, he'd wrestled with his attraction to her and allowed his concerns for the two women and one little orphan to cloud his thinking. In the end, he wasn't able to save the boy. Simao was street smart. He'd find a way to survive. *Yeah, keep telling yourself that, Conroy.*

He looked over his shoulder at Ava, pale with shock. "Have her collect her papers and small valuables that can be easily carried in her purse." Not waiting for Lu to answer, he left the house. With one last glance at the corner where Simao disappeared, he went to take a closer look at Pedro's car.

The exterior had damage in several places where either Pedro or another driver had chosen not to give the right of way. The interior was as he remembered. Worn seats, missing radio knob, and the reek of fish. Jack lifted the hood, thankful to see a few parts were cleaner than others. Some care had been taken to ensure the car ran well.

Opening the hatchback, he pulled out a pair of rundown sneakers and empty soft drink cans. Pulling out a ratty blanket, something fell to the ground. His heart stopped, then thudded heavy as he stared at the shirt and the familiar white patch with a blue square bisected by a green line sewn onto the sleeve. He'd made the correct decision concerning Pedro. Dumping everything in Ava's trash bin, he took out his SAT phone.

The director answered on the first tone. "Where are you?"

"Still in the city." The heavy silence that followed was worse than the blistering reprimand he'd expected and deserved. "About ready to leave. Do you have any information on Esteban Duro?"

"We're tracing a connection to Ingersoll, Kansas."

Jack leaned against the car, his mind scrambling to remember all that Lu shared with him. "How does the woman tie in?" *The woman, Conroy?* He raked a hand through his hair.

"Don't know yet."

Jack focused on the next one word question. "Whit?"

"Nothing. I'm mobilizing the second team."

Jack blew out a breath. He knew Sam had been working on pulling together a second team. He regretted that their first op was to be the search and recovery of one of the men on his team.

Head back in the game, Conroy. Was Lucinda playing him for a fool or was she unaware of Duro's connection to her hometown? He shoved the phone into his pocket and entered the kitchen through the sliders.

Ava raced toward him leaning low with arms outstretched.

His heart ramped into overdrive. Something struck his legs, and pinpricks of pain pierced his skin. He looked down. A ball of orange fur clung to his leg.

Ava grabbed for the cat and missed.

Pumpkin changed course, jumped onto the kitchen chair then to the counter top only to come face to yawning door with the despised travel kennel. He let out an anguished cry, jumped to the floor, and dashed into the hall.

The pair headed into the dining room with Finny on their heels, adding her shrill bark to the chaos.

Lucinda flashed past the doorway. The pup squeaked with surprise and went silent.

Jack rubbed the back of his neck. How was he to get this circus out of the city? He went to the fridge to collect bottles of water.

Lu stepped into the kitchen, wrestling the excited pup. The dress-turned-dog-carrier draped over her shoulder had been cleaned and modified for less bulk. Tendrils of hair had slipped from the fabric loop that held it and brushed her pink cheeks. His fingers itched to caress the wayward strands of gold.

Ava's quick trotting steps followed the thump of Pumpkin running back into the kitchen.

Jack was ready this time. When the big cat galloped past, he tossed a dishtowel over its head. It paused just long enough for him to grab handfuls of orange fur and wrestle it into the kennel.

"Oh my." Ava fanned her face and plopped into the nearest chair, her hand on her chest. "I'm too old to run like that."

Ya think? Jack washed his scratched hands and forearms with antibacterial soap at the kitchen sink. This was the thanks he got for saving the ungrateful animal's hide. "It's time to go."

He carried Pumpkin's kennel out to the car and set it on the backseat. Lu slipped in beside it and lifted Finny out of the sling.

Ava locked the front door of her home. Wiping tears from her cheeks, she climbed into the front passenger seat.

Backing the car onto the street, Jack got out to close and lock the privacy gate. It would keep out curious passersby but was no match for the rebel forces. Putting the car in gear, he pulled away from the curb. Soft sniffles came from the seat next to him.

They were one hundred feet from the gatehouse when a white full-sized luxury SUV pulled in from the highway. Alfred stepped out of the guardhouse, smiling and waving.

"That's Esteban!" Lu's incredulous whisper sent chills racing up the back of Jack's neck. How had Duro found them?

A hand extended from the driver's window wielding a pistol. A shot split the air and the hand recoiled. Alfred dove back inside the guardhouse as a window shattered. The SUV crashed through the security arm. Splintered pieces of wood flew in all directions.

"Lucinda, get down." Jack's grip on the steering wheel tightened. Fear that she'd jump from the car and join Duro crawled through his gut. To his relief she obeyed his order and slipped off the seat to lay across the back floor, tummy over the drive shaft hump.

Grabbing Pedro's sunglasses from the console, he shoved them on his face. "Stay down." Her quiet sob twisted his jumpy insides. He fought the urge to speed up. The hatchback should not draw Duro's attention. The neighborhood housekeepers and gardeners drove cars the equivalent of the little hatchback.

Passing the gatehouse, Jack glanced in the rearview mirror.

The SUV wheeled around to follow.

Alarm careened through Jack. He pressed the gas pedal to the floor, recalling the details of the map he'd studied with Simao. At the next intersection he cut to the right, sideswiping the street sign. "Hang on." The car bounced over the curb. Lu groaned. He cut down a cobblestone walkway.

The SUV drove past, too wide to follow.

The walkway opened onto the main promenade of an outdoor mall. Weaving between park benches and around a marble fountain, he breathed a prayer of thanksgiving that it was too early in the day for the exclusive shops to be open. He pulled into the next wide alley between buildings wishing, for the first time in years, for a command bird circling overhead feeding him information so he wasn't blind to Duro's position.

Hurtling out the other end, he pushed the car for more speed, crossing the parking lot and leaving the mall behind. He ran the service road to the main road, shooting across it to another side road, hoping to avoid both of the warring factions. Had Simao reported their location and model of car to Duro? Jack's blood raced cold.

A quiet sniff drifted up from the floor behind him.

Sending the boy packing had been another error in judgment. He gritted his teeth till his jaw ached. This time, Lucinda was in the crosshairs with him.

Chapter 16

The vibration of the moving car hummed through Lucinda. Nose buried in the sandy carpet, her stomach roiled from the stink of dead fish and the wild motion of the car. The puppy lying beneath her chin tickled her neck. Bile burned the back of her throat. Cold seeped into her pores, and she couldn't stop shivering. She didn't bother to wipe away her tears.

Esteban had found her. Was Rico driving? Why had they threatened Alfred with the gun? Why breach the security gate as they did? Fear rolled through her. What did she know of Esteban? Her thoughts jumped from one memory to another, jumbled and stacked up like random freeze frames.

"You can sit up."

She wanted to ignore Jack's quiet words and keep her head buried in her crossed arms. *Coward.* Getting to her knees, she climbed onto the seat and settled Finny on her lap.

Ava peeked between the seats offering her a facial tissue.

Mumbling her thanks, Lu blew her nose. In the rearview mirror, she caught a glimpse of Jack wearing sunglasses, his mouth set in a straight uncompromising line.

They traveled rough back roads and alleys. She swayed and bounced so much, she felt sure her bones would shake loose from each other. Jack cut through places that were not part of the island's public road system until he reached a narrow secondary road. An unbroken line of traffic wound along the ribbon of pavement ascending into the mountains.

Traffic crawled for miles along the steep road. Even with the windows down, the interior of the car heated up as the sun rose high in the sky. In some places vehicles traveled two abreast, blocking the passage of anyone foolish enough to be bound for the city. Jack kept consulting his tactical watch and glancing at the sun in the sky, getting antsier with each passing hour.

Along the roadsides, people walked or rode bicycles. Others pulled small carts filled with items they deemed worthy of the effort. Outside Lu's window, a woman labored beneath a sheet filled to bursting. Two crying toddlers followed in her footsteps. A young man carried a small boy with arm and legs swaddled in white gauze bandages.

Lu wiped her wet cheeks. She looked at her bottle of water and half-eaten granola bar. Anger surged through her in a red haze. "It's unfair."

"Yes it is." Jack's voice was low, as though the sight moved him, too. Or maybe he was just angry because they were moving so slowly.

The traffic came to a halt. Up ahead, steam billowed from beneath the hood of an ancient automobile. With much gesturing and discussion, a communal effort was launched to push it off the road.

Lu sat forward gripping the back of the Jack's seat. "People want to live their lives the best way they know how. But along come these...these *men* who believe they have a better idea, so they blow up buildings and mess with the lives of the people they say they want to help."

Jack nodded. "That about sums it up."

She fell back against her seat, hands clenched into fists. "Why does God let this happen?"

Jack shook his head, a small tic in the muscle of his jaw. "God doesn't like this any more than you do. His heartache is greater than anything you feel."

Lu pushed forward again, shaking his seat in fury. "So why does He allow it? Why doesn't He stop the wars and all the suffering?" The words ground her throat raw. "I don't understand God." She sat back, arms crossed. "I don't understand Him at *all*."

"Welcome to the human race, Lulabelle." In the mirror she saw one corner of his mouth tip up.

"Not funny, Jack Conroy. How do *you* explain all..." she gestured toward the window, "*this?*"

Against the backdrop of a lush spill of rosy coralita, an elderly man leaned on his cane taking slow shuffling steps as others streamed past him.

"Free will. Each one of us has free will to do as we wish." He glanced up to see if she was listening.

"Well, some people don't deserve to have free will. All they do is hurt people."

"Are you saying God should have different rules for different people? Dole out freewill only to those worthy of His trust?"

Was that what she was saying? "Well, why not?"

"The 'unchosen' would be robots, doing only what their Creator deemed best." He looked at her in the mirror. "Talk about the haves and have-nots."

Lu wrinkled her nose. "Well, He could stop the really bad people."

Eyes on the road, Jack shifted into gear. The traffic was moving again. "God looks at all sin as bad. That's why Christ died on the cross, Lulabelle."

"You sound like Gran. I know all about Christ dying on the cross for my sins. And you don't have to tell me I'm a sinner. Deacon Beam reminds me every time I step into Gran's church."

He was quiet for so long, she thought she'd offended him. Finally, he spoke.

"If God did it your way, and revoked freewill for some sins and not others, where would He draw the line? Who would lose their freedom?"

Who indeed? The answer should have been easy but she hesitated, reluctant to make even a hypothetical choice.

A young mother had stopped to rest in the shade of a rain tree. Lu couldn't take her eyes off the baby in her arms. What kind of life would that baby have? "People should stop hurting others." That was simple enough. Surely God could do something with that.

"There are different kinds of hurts, Lulabelle. The pain of war is extreme and visual with enemies we can easily dislike, but what about the unseen less dramatic hurts. Like when a loved one chooses to leave home? Should God have denied freewill to the one who left so another person's heart isn't broken?"

The blow wasn't physical, but Lu ached from it. She'd known her Gran would be hurt when she left, but she'd gone anyway. She had no choice. "I had a good reason." A weak defense but the only one she had.

"Rationalization. The rebels have their good reasons, too." Jack slammed on the brake as a donkey stepped in front of the car. A young boy pulled on the rope wrapped around the animal's neck, but it refused to budge.

Rustling in the grocery tote, Lu pulled out the bag of carrots. She yanked on the door handle.

"Stay put, Lucinda."

She ignored Jack's sharp command. If God couldn't be bothered to help these people, she would do what she could.

At her approach, panic crossed the boy's face. Frantic, he shouted and pulled on his donkey. The animal simply leaned back, unwilling to give an inch.

She touched the boy's thin shoulder. He jumped, shot away from her and fell back, brought up short by the animal tethered to the other end of the rope. She smiled hoping to ease his fear. Opening the bag of carrots, she held one out to the donkey. Its ears swiveled forward, nostrils flared. Laying a carrot in the flat of her hand, she offered it up to the uncooperative animal.

He shifted his weight, curious but not ready to give up the ground he'd claimed. Had the animal ever tasted a carrot? It was, after all, people food. He stretched his neck, tempted but not ready to trust. His velvet-soft nose tickled Lu's palm, his breath warm and moist as he snuffled the treat. Cautiously, he lipped it from her hand.

Lu rustled the bag and pulled out another carrot. The donkey eagerly took it. When she turned to the boy, the animal stepped toward her and bumped her with its shaggy head. She held the bag out to the boy.

Eyes wide, he clutched it close to his body. The treats now in the possession of his master, the donkey nosed the boy's thin shoulder and followed him to the side of the road.

Thankful Finny had stayed in the car. Lu pushed her aside, climbed in, and slammed the door.

"Don't do that again."

Jack's angry growl couldn't spoil the moment. "I can't help all these people, but I could help him. And, frankly, that's more than I've seen God do in this situation." She waved to the boy and sat back.

The statement earned her a sharp glance. He'd removed

the sunglasses. She hadn't realized how late in the day it was. "We're the lucky ones. We have a way off the island."

Jack's attention snapped back to the mirror, the stinging slap of his gaze cracking her protective shell. She looked away stunned by her own words. When had she come to that conclusion?

Why this place? Why these people? I have too many questions, God. She straightened up, jerking her attention from the window to her hands clasped tight together. She was praying! Lucinda had spoken directly to God and a thunderbolt hadn't struck her down. Maybe God hadn't heard. He'd never expect her to pray so most likely He wasn't listening. She heaved a sigh of relief.

Chapter 17

Jack steered around a man riding a rusty bicycle. A metal coffeepot hung from the frame, clanking with each turn of the pedals. He glanced in the rearview mirror. Lu had settled down for a nap. He understood the anger and the helplessness she felt. He'd witnessed this same scene in every war zone. In a power grab like the one that had taken place on the island, the regular folk made the age-old choice: fight or flight. The same groups of people made the same decisions. The elderly, women, and children were the first to flee. The men stayed behind to protect what they owned before they either fled or stayed and fought with the side that had their allegiance.

A small moped wove between stopped cars and the shoulder of the road trying to make time in the traffic jam. Jack ground his teeth together. He'd tried to anticipate the traffic by taking a mountain road that originated in the interior, farther away from the city. His window for meeting the team within the specified time was slipping away. He would have a lot of explaining to do once this op was completed.

A child darted in front of the car.

Jack wiped a hand across his tired eyes. Where was Simao? If he had betrayed Jack, he'd done it to survive.

Would he join the flight or hunker down and do his best to support himself and his little sister? He prayed for Simao and then, for the umpteenth time, asked for an extra dose of patience as the traffic continued to creep through the throngs of people.

On the road's edge, the orange pom-pom flowers of lion's tail waved in the breeze. To the west, glimpses of the turquoise ocean flashed between the scrub trees. The day was waning, and hamlets created from tarps and bed linens began to pop up beneath the naseberry and mahogany trees. Automobile and foot traffic thinned to nothing the higher they traveled into the mountains. Here rugged bulwarks of volcanic rock towered high above the road.

Coming around a hairpin curve, the glare of the low sun momentarily blinded Jack. The bright light silhouetted a lone man on the side of the road. Beneath one arm, a crude crutch supported his weight. The wind tugged at his loose clothes.

Blinking to clear his watery vision, Jack steered the car wide around him. Why hadn't the guy stopped for the night along with everyone else? Jack studied him in the rearview mirror.

The evening sun washed the walker in a golden light. Loose-hipped, he swung on the crutch, a bush hat casting a shadow across his face. From beneath the brim, light hair skimmed his collar and shoulders reminding Jack of—*Whit.*

He ran the car off the road, leveling grass and flowers, and lunged from the car, chest so tight he couldn't breathe.

"Whit?"

The man stopped.

Jack didn't.

Free hand shading his eyes from the sun's glare, the man shifted his stance, bracing for the fool racing toward him.

"McCord!" The closer Jack got the more sure he was.

126

"Preach?" The cocky smile was unmistakable.

Skidding to a stop, Jack grabbed his friend, crutch and all. A bark of laughter and a hard thump on the back opened up Jack'chest. He dragged in air like a drowning man.

"Thought we'd lost you at the pier."

"Glad to see *you*."

They talked over each other grinning like fools until Whit nodded in the direction of the car. "Assuming they're yours?"

Jack swiveled.

Lucinda and Ava stood at the back of the car, watching the reunion.

"Yeah."

"Thought you were bringing out one." Whit headed toward the women.

"It's complicated."

Whit snorted. "With women, it generally is."

In his peripheral vision, Jack scrutinized his friend's condition. The wind-pressed fabric clung to his torso revealing the bulge of a wound dressing on his side.

"Quit lookin' at me." Whit swung on the tree branch he'd fashioned into a crutch.

Jack didn't bother denying the accusation. "What're your wounds?"

"Gash along the ribs. Not bad. And my leg. Tell me about the women."

"Tell *me* about the leg."

Muttering something uncomplimentary beneath his breath, Whit kept up his halting pace. "Fly thirty feet in the air and come down on wood and steel, you get banged up."

"Used your trauma kit?"

Whit cast a disgusted look his way. "I took care of it."

He'd have to take his teammate at his word. "Sam

mobilized the second team to search for you. We need to let him know you're alive." It felt good to say those words. *Thank you, God.*

"Lucinda doesn't want to leave." Jack ignored Whit's surprised look. "The rebels shut down the airport so I ended up with an extra."

"Howdy, ladies." Whit tugged the brim of his faded hat and introduced himself, cowboy charisma on full throttle.

Ava hurried forward. "Oh, you dear man." She held Whit's arm to "help" him to the car. "Jack thought you were dead."

Whit flashed a cheeky grin. "Don't pay any attention to him, ma'am. I'm a hard one to kill."

Jack ducked into the back seat and shoved Pumpkin's kennel to the center. Straightening up, he bumped into Lu. He caught her shoulders as she stumbled back. She clutched his shirtsleeve. The demanding look in her eyes squelched the automatic apology on the tip of his tongue.

"You didn't know he'd show up here?" The golden sparks in her eyes glistened in the early evening light.

"Wha—? No." Even now he found it hard to say the words. "I figured him for dead."

"He knows about the place we're going to?" Her gaze burned into him.

Some puzzle was shuffling around in the brain behind that look. "Everyone on the team knows the contingency plan."

"He hitched a ride up the mountain and then kept walking." She looked over her shoulder at Whit and Ava. "He could have gone the coastal route or stopped for the night or…or…" She ran out of steam.

Jack leaned against the car. "What're you trying to say, Lulabelle?"

She blew out a breath, stirring the wayward hairs hanging over her brow. "This wasn't a coincidence, was it."

"Is that a question or a statement?" How far would she have the courage to go with this line of thinking?

"A statement...I think. We could have missed him." With the toe of her sandal, she drew an arch in the sand. "But we didn't. Like God arranged it."

He kept his mouth shut, giving her space to think. In her own stubborn way, she was seeking God. It was a halleluiah moment, but he'd keep that to himself, too.

She glanced up at him. "Aren't you going to say something?"

"Only that you're right." Her look of surprise dinged him in the region of his heart. Had he been so hard with her?

"I've heard Gran talk about seeing God work and assumed she was stretching the facts. Now I'm not so sure. Your religious stuff is wearing off on me." She frowned and poked at his chest. "Stop grinning."

He tried, but his lips wouldn't stay straight. Grasping her hand, he hung on and leaned close. He breathed in the warm scent of her. Desire punched him low in the gut. Red highlights glinted like embers in the dark roots at the part in her hair, and her sunburned nose was peeling. She was nothing like the woman he'd always dreamed would be his, but he couldn't deny the feelings rocking through him.

Close by, Whit cleared his throat.

Jack didn't let go of her hand though she tugged on it. Feeling in his pocket, he tossed the SAT phone to Whit. "Call Sam."

Catching it, Whit turned away.

Jack could have stood there longer drinking her in, but they had to get moving. The day was nearly gone and they still had a long way to go. "Into the car." He stepped out of her way.

Ava pushed past her. "My turn in the back." She ducked in and plopped down next to Pumpkin's kennel. Eyes sparkling, she looked up. "Lucinda, you sit up front with Jack." Face beaming, she ran heavily ringed fingers through her curls.

Jack shook his head. Ava had succumbed to McCord's easy charm. "Com'on, Lulabelle. Looks like you've been routed." He helped her into the front before climbing into the driver's seat.

Whit's graceless entrance into the back jostled Pumpkin's kennel. The cat hissed.

"What's in there?" He peered in the front of the carrier.

Pumpkin struck out, claws unsheathed.

"Hey!" Whit jerked back, the stainless steel door saving his face.

Ava squeaked, her hands fluttering. "Hush, Pumpkin."

"Pumpkin? Never heard a pumpkin make a racket like that." He winked at Ava and tossed the phone to Jack. "Got a message for you. Sam is keeping the other team on deck as a precaution."

The mission was a mess. Jack rubbed the back of his neck. There was nothing to be accomplished by worrying about it, but with all that had gone wrong, something had finally gone right. McCord was alive. Even injured, the man was the best of the best in their line of work.

"So, Lucinda, Preach says you don't want to leave the island."

"McCord, stuff a sock in it."

"But you said—"

Jack cut him with a sharp glance in the rearview mirror. "Let it go."

Whit leaned back. "What's your dog's name?"

"Finula, but I call her Finny."

A bemused expression traced across his friend's features, as though he didn't know what to think of the name any more than Jack had.

"What've you been up to for the last two months?"

Jack bit back a few choice words before intercepting Whit's narrow-eyed gaze in the mirror.

"Working at the Paradise Club." Lu twisted to look at the man seated behind her. "I served drinks before Jack *kidnapped* me."

"You—." Whit choked on his words, shock in the glance he exchanged with Jack. "A bar? Preach hauled you out of a *bar*?"

"Threw me over his shoulder."

The car's tires bumped off the uneven edge of the road.

"Keep it on the road, man." Whit sat forward and punched Jack's shoulder.

"Quit talking about me."

Lu looked between the seats at Whit. "Why do you call him 'Preach'?"

Jack cast a dark look at McCord but it didn't stop his friend's mouth from running.

"It's what we call him. Wish I'd been at the bar."

"Why?"

Lu's sharp question sliced through Jack. Was she asking why the name or why did McCord want to see him in a bar?

Whit's sharp gaze snagged his in the mirror. "He hates them."

"Keep your eyes on the road, dear." Ava held her monstrous purse tight against her chest.

Jack's ears burned. Lu had gone quiet, but he was certain if he looked over, he'd find her staring at him.

"But why?"

O Lord, help. Lu's question hung in the air, choking him

like the oily black smoke of a tire fire. His life wasn't any of her business.

"Jack, why do you hate bars?" She leaned closer. "Does going into them break a religious rule or something?"

He wanted to ring McCord's neck. He glanced in the mirror. The idiot was smiling! *Fine, then.* Lu wanted an answer, and McCord wanted him to sweat.

Jack stared straight ahead. "My father was an alcoholic." His eyes were on the road, but he didn't see it beyond the memory of a pub, hazy with cigarette smoke and smelling of booze and body odor.

"I was ten the first time I stepped inside a bar and hauled my old man out. Ma wanted him home with us to celebrate my sister's birthday. He was so stinking plowed it would've been better to leave him on the barstool." He tried to relax his death grip on the steering wheel. McCord had never heard this story. Jack had learned long ago not to sugarcoat the truth. Made a person sound pathetic. He didn't want pity. "As soon as I was old enough, I walked away from that third story walk-up and never looked back."

"What happened to you mother and sister?" Lu's voice was whisper-soft as though she was afraid to ask.

"Ma died trying to save him." The old anger sparked to life. "My sister went to live with relatives."

"Where is she now?"

Jack shrugged. The woman didn't know when to leave well enough alone. "Don't know." Guilt squelched the fury in his gut. Self-reproach tied a knot in the pit of his stomach. He should have stayed. Protected her and his mother from the old man. But he'd been headstrong and angry. He had made the choice that kept him from occupying a jail cell for the rest of his life.

The sun dipped beneath the horizon painting the sky a

gaudy pink and gold. He switched on the headlights. An awkward silence lay heavy in the car. He had nothing to say that would lighten the mood. His childhood was what it was.

In the beam of the headlights, the occasional entrance to a side road flashed by, none of which had shown up on the map he'd shared with Simao. Most of them were nothing more than rutted cart paths leading to someone's home. One appeared newer, a gaping hole in the brush and trees with a graded roadbed.

In the dusky light, the peak of the mountain looked like a moonscape. Knobs of rock bumped black against the sky. Stars winked overhead. Several glittered low, caught in the gossamer web of scrub brush.

Coming off the mountaintop, Jack shifted into low. No guardrails edged the road. Around each curve the headlights pierced empty gloom before coming back to the winding road. The pavement was rough beneath the tires, pockmarked by the sharp fragments of rock that fell from the mountain's side. A few miles down the other side, Jack nailed the brakes.

The road ran right up to a chunk of rock the size of an Abrams tank.

He climbed out and stood in the V of the open door. Leaning his arm on the roof, he looked up. The face of the ledge had sheared off.

From inside the car Whit breathed a low whistle. "That's one big hunk of rock. You doing some heavy-duty praying, Preach?"

His heart slumped heavy in his chest. "We'll have to try one of the side roads we passed earlier." He refused to think about the real possibility they'd have to walk out.

Whit looked back the way they'd come. "People on the road were sticking together. Thought I was *loco* for going on alone."

Jack stared at the dead end. He had two women and a wounded comrade to get off the island and nothing was going according to plan. Not the agency's plan, anyway. God had other ideas. He swiped a hand across his face. God's will. Never easy or comfortable but one way or another always accomplished. *Would be nice if you let me in on the plan, Lord.* He ducked back inside the car.

Ava's purse was snug against her ribs, arms crossed over it, and eyes filled with questions. "What now?"

"We pray."

Lu frowned. "You expect God to move the rock out of the way?"

Whoever said she asked impertinent questions was right. "The Bible says He can move mountains, but I'm not in favor of sitting here and putting Him to the test."

"Oh, ye of little faith."

Ignoring McCord's quiet comment, Jack bowed his head. Whether anyone else followed suit, he didn't much care. Right now he needed divine guidance. "Father, you led us here. Now lead us out. Amen."

"That's it?" Lu's incredulous stare glittered. "You prayed longer over our meal at Ava's." Lu shifted around in her seat and looked at Whit. "Shouldn't he pray some more?"

Whit leaned across Pumpkin's kennel creating a stir within. "Praying isn't a magical incantation. You say what's on your heart."

She huffed. "Well, I can think of a whole lot more to say."

The Spirit didn't have to nudge Jack twice. "Then do it."

"What?" Lu looked from him to Whit and back to him.

"Say what's on your mind, Lulabelle. God already knows but wants to hear it from you."

"I don't *think* so." She clamped her lips shut and looked out her window.

Well, it had been worth a try. The darkness prevented her from seeing anything outside her window, so whatever she was looking at was all in her head. *Help her to know you, Lord.*

The flood of refugees made returning the way they'd come next to impossible. "We passed a side road that looked new. We'll try it."

Putting the hatchback in reverse, Jack twisted in his seat to look out the rear window. With no place wide enough to swing the car around, he went in reverse up the mountain with only the backup lights to show him the way. Foot on the gas pedal, he began the ascent.

Whit turned to watch, as well. Shrinking into her seat, Lu's eyes were scrunched shut. Ava appeared to be in suspended animation and turning blue.

"It's okay to breathe, ladies."

Lu's eyes popped open. Her lips barely moved as she whispered, "I don't want to distract you."

"Passing out would distract me."

She didn't smile, but she was breathing again.

At the top, a pull-off gave him room to turn the car around. A heavy sense of foreboding settled over him. Unease rippled up his spine. He glanced over his shoulder at Whit.

Eyes hidden in the shadow of his hat brim, Whit sat stiff, his lips a tight line.

Unable to shake the feeling, Jack considered his choices, but there were none. He was literally between a rock and a hard place. Jamming the car in gear, he drove back the way they'd come, on the lookout for another escape route.

Leaving the bald rock face and scrub trees on the top of

the mountain, the headlights skated along the monochromatic edge of the forest. A raw slash in the vegetation revealed the graded road they'd passed earlier. He slowed and took the turn, praying he wasn't headed for another dead end.

Following the path of least resistance, the road wound down the side of the mountain past rough shoulders of rock. Created using low-tech engineering and built for light traffic, it bore the markings of a hastily completed project. They descended into a valley surrounded on all sides by jagged mountain peaks and cliffs. In the distance a light pricked the darkness.

Jack's internal warning systems screamed on full alert. He pulled the car off the road onto a patch of dirt butting up against the base of a low rocky ridge. He switched off the headlights.

Whit thrummed his fingers on the top of Pumpkin's kennel. The annoyed cat spit and moaned.

"Why'd we stop?" Lucinda looked through the windshield at the light. "Maybe someone down there can give us directions."

He caught Whit's glance in the mirror and opened his car door. "I'll check it out."

Lucinda reached for the door handle. "I'll come with you."

"No!"

His verbal blast was met with surprised silence.

"I could use a restroom, Jack."

He felt like a brute having to deny her a most basic necessity. He looked at Ava, who simply smiled and nodded. The two of them stared at him as though he were being unreasonable.

"Lights don't necessarily mean safety or help." He

needed to look around before driving in and asking for directions and a restroom. Considering all the squirming in the seat next to him, that appeared to be an immediate need.

He stepped away from the car. Whit followed, tension rolling off him in waves.

"There's a flashlight in the tote. What do you have for weapons?" Jack hadn't seen a one, but he had no doubt McCord carried something on him, even if he'd had to make it.

"A couple of blades. The rest is on the bottom of the bay."

"Know how to shoot black powder?"

Alert with interest, Whit adjusted his weight on his crutch. "Grew up shooting my great granddaddy's rifle."

"There's an old Sharps in the trunk. Powder and mini balls are new." Jack faced his friend. "It could blow up in your face."

"I'll have a look."

Jack tossed him the keys to the car. "Got a WWII knife if you want it."

A cocky smile flashed beneath the hat brim. "You take it to balance the pea shooter you're packing."

Whit had done his own covert inspection and wasn't impressed with Ava's revolver. Jack looked back at the car.

Whit thumbed his hat. "I'll take care of them."

Those few words encompassed more than the women's immediate predicament. If he ran into trouble, Whit would do everything in his power to get them safely off the island.

Jack bumped a fist to McCord's bicep, swung around, and ran smack into Lu. He grabbed her shoulders. The car's interior light shone out the open door setting her hair aglow. He smoothed the fine flyaway strands floating in the light breeze. Tension radiated from her.

"Maybe you shouldn't go alone." She clasped her hands tight at her waist.

Her worried frown sent warmth fizzing through his chest. She needn't be concerned about him. He grasped her hands in his. "I work better alone."

"But..." She glanced toward the light. "You'll be okay and come back?"

"This is what I'm trained to do, Lulabelle." He tugged on her hands, pulling her to him. He surprised himself and her by leaning down and pressed his lips to the heart-shaped beauty mark on her temple. The scent of strawberries still clung to her.

"I'm sorry I made you talk about your father." He felt a tremor go through her. "When I was little, my dad left my mom and me stranded in a small town in Indiana. I don't like to talk about him, so I had no right pushing you."

He hugged her close, his heart swelling. This explained so much of who she was. "It's okay. You had no way of knowing." He had to get going. "Be good for Whit while I'm gone." He let go and turned his back on her while he still had the ability to walk away. Willing himself not to look back, he let the night close around him.

Drawing near to the light, the constant drone of a generator filled the night. Here in the bowl of the valley, the dense forest had been cleared away. Jack went down on his stomach, nerves pinging an alert. Pebbles and sawtooth-edged grass scratched his arms. He studied the set-up before him.

Two floodlights high on poles lit the clearing. In the center stood a building constructed of pre-fabricated metal.

Several vehicles were parked at the door, each bearing a crude rendition of the Island Voice of Reform Party insignia.

Off to one side stood a smaller outbuilding constructed of wood. Beyond that, hacked from the vegetation, another crude road bled into the darkness leading in the direction Jack needed to travel to reach the PZ. No way could he bring the women through here. He'd have to find another way. He pulled back, brush closing around him. The hairs on the back of his neck prickled.

A heavy boot jammed against his spine. His heart tripped once before pain exploded in his head and the world went black.

Chapter 18

Lucinda dug out the flashlight. "Ava, do you want to go first?"

"No, you go, dear."

Whit tugged on his hat. "Stay close."

Whit made her uneasy. His friendship with Jack didn't translate into unquestioning trust on her part. Walking back the way they'd come, she found a spot where tree ferns and small bushes grew thick beneath the trees.

The weak beam of her light didn't penetrate the shadowy layers beneath the forest canopy. The quiet rustle of leaves and occasional scratch of a skittering critter raised goose bumps on her arms, making her wish for Jack's protective presence. Her pulse tripped remembering the feel of his lips on her temple, his breath ruffling her hair.

She removed Finny from the sling and hurried the pup through its business before taking care of her own needs. An animal squealed in the trees overhead. Her heart leapt with fright, and she ran back to the car, stumbling over roots and rocks, her harsh breath knifing pain through her chest.

The car's hatch was raised, and Whit stood in the circle of light, cradling a rifle in the crook of his arm. Light splashed across the dark steel and gleaming wood. Ava stood beside him.

"That's my Reginald's gun."

"He kept it in good condition."

"It has been in his family since the Civil War." She touched the brass buttplate, earning a frown from Whit.

"Did he ever fire it?"

"In his younger days before we met." Her voice drifted off dreamily for a moment before pulling out of her reflection. "Reginald's family had men in every war this country fought."

"Your turn, Ava." Out of breath, Lu handed over the flashlight.

Ava trucked off up the road to find a private spot.

"Why do you call Jack, 'Preach'?" Lu had mulled over the question only half a million times.

Whit set the rifle down, leaned against the fender and pushed his hat back. "On occasion he preaches from the pulpit back home."

"Is he a real minister, with the collar and everything?" If he was an honest-to-goodness reverend, she was in *so* much trouble.

"No collar. He's an agent." Curiosity lit his green gaze. "Why fight Jack when he's here to help you?"

A warning, puzzling in its intensity, buzzed through Lu. "I told you why."

"Aw, come on." A lopsided grin eased across his good-looking face. "He rescued you." He cupped her elbow in his warm hand. "Knight in shining armor. Damsel in distress."

She yanked her arm from his grasp and jammed her fist into his sternum. "Keep your hands to yourself. And so you know, I wasn't in any distress."

He raised an eyebrow. "There's the war."

"Not when he grabbed me. Well, the fighting had only begun." She shoved him.

Lightning fast, his hand circled her wrist. "What game are you playing?" The easy-going cowboy disappeared, replaced by a hardened warrior, drilling her with a steely gaze.

Lu tugged on her hand, but his grip tightened. Her words ground out between clenched teeth. "I'm not playing any games."

His mouth firmed to a slash. "Why do you want to stay?"

Her mind flashed back to bodies floating in the bay then rocketed forward to Alfred, ducking for cover in the guardhouse. She shuddered and blinked hard, determined not to weep in front of this man. "I don't want to anymore." Her words scratched gritty in her throat. Would going home place Gran in danger? The uncertainty gnawed at her.

"Changed your mind kind of sudden."

She stiffened, willing herself not to shrink from his probing gaze.

"I consider that man a brother." His voice carried an angry fire she couldn't ignore. "You hurt him in any way and you'll answer to me. Understood?"

The warning seared red hot through her. "With his training, Jack has the upper hand."

His breath hissed between his teeth. "Yesterday, I would have agreed with you. I'm not sure I believe it, but…" his eyes narrowed.

She couldn't let him say the words. Denial kept her own wayward thoughts under control. "I would prefer to have *nothing* to do with him."

Liar.

Shut up!

Not a good time to argue with yourself, Lu. "He's the one that spouted nonsense about being God's gift to me."

Whit's mouth fell slack.

Good! The man was altogether too sure of himself. She looked pointedly at the hand holding her fist to his chest. "Now get your paws off me. You're not my type." Not that she knew what her type was anymore. Her track record was an utter shambles.

His lips wobbled. Beneath her fist, his chest vibrated.

"Are you laughing at me?"

He eased his grip, and she reclaimed her hand.

"No, ma'am. Want to be clear, you're not my type either."

Drawing in a deep breath, she turned away. Whit was out of line. *Big time.* Okay, so maybe he was right about the whole knight-in-shining-armor thing. But the closeness she felt for Jack was due to the danger he'd dragged her into and then rescued her from. Nothing more.

The light below flickered through the fluttering leaves. "Please hurry, Jack." The cool ocean breeze carried her whisper into the night. She hoped he'd found someone to talk to and would be back soon with good news.

"Stay put." Whit picked up the rifle and slammed the hatch closed.

Trepidation swirled through Lu. "Where are you going?"

"Ava should've been back by now."

"But, your leg. Maybe I should go find her."

"Won't take me long. If Jack shows up, let him know where I am." He disappeared into the night, rifle in one hand, crutch under the other arm.

Finny whined and scrambled to be let down.

"Are you thirsty?" Lu set her on the floor of the car. From the dark interior of the cat kennel, a pair of glowing eyes watched her. All around her the night was filled with the trills and peeps of the smallest inhabitants of the forest. The tangy wind brushed through the canopy.

Waiting for everyone's return, Lu busied herself repacking the tote and talking to the puppy and cat. The steady hum of a motor cut across her monologue. Ears perked, Finny stood on the backseat. A vehicle traveled down the mountain, headlights bouncing off rocks and flashing through foliage.

Relief swept through Lu, followed by a wave of trepidation. What if Jack was right and the light was connected to the rebels? Grabbing Finny, she slammed the door, extinguishing the interior light, and lunged for the bushes.

Too late.

The vehicle's high beams snagged her mid-stride. She flinched away from the brilliant light.

The passenger door opened. A man stepped out.

"Lucinda."

Her heart wrenched. *Esteban!* Blinded by the high beams, she hadn't recognized his white SUV. Revulsion scorched at the pit of her stomach. "You're here, thank goodness." Her words rang hollow. She leaned against the car to keep her knees from crumbling.

He studied her with cold flat eyes.

Pistol drawn, Rico walked around the hatchback peering in windows before opening a door on the far side. His voice carried across the roof. "Just a cat inside."

"Leave it." Esteban clamped a hand to her shoulder, squeezing cruelly.

Lu winced in pain.

"Where is your friend, Lucinda?"

"What friend?" She'd been on the floor of Jack's car when they'd left Ava's house.

He raised his hand to her cheek. "Do not play me for a fool." His fingertips left an icy trail across her skin.

"Ava isn't here."

He loomed over her. In the darkness, the white of his suit made him appear larger. "The man. Where is he?"

Which one? There are two. Thankfully, her mouth was cotton dry and the words didn't fly from her tongue.

Rico waved his gun at her. "Why are you here?"

"Running from the fighting in the city." She crossed one ankle in front of the other.

"Give me the dog then get into my vehicle." Esteban's eyes remained as frosty as his caress.

She shivered and hugged Finny close. She didn't want to go with him. The man standing before her wasn't the indulgent admirer she'd known these past two months. "S-She'll be better with me."

Stone faced, he waited for her to give him the puppy.

Lips trembling, she kissed the top of Finny's head and handed her over before climbing into the backseat of the SUV. Jack's "little woman" comment bubbled up through the fear and anger warring for dominance.

Anger won. Anger toward Esteban for being cruel. Anger toward Jack for recognizing what she had not. But mostly, anger with herself for being blind to Esteban's true nature.

Lu leaned her cheek against the smooth window glass, her mind a whir of questions as the SUV bumped down the road toward the light. Had Whit found Ava? Did he see her leave with Esteban? Would he think she'd gone willingly?

Well, didn't you?

Tears threatened to spill down her cheeks. Would Jack believe she was right where she wanted to be and abandon her? She had a stack of bad choices behind her. Perhaps God was justified in punishing her.

The source of the light Jack had gone to investigate consisted of two spotlights on a tall pole. Rico drove up to the side door of a metal building the size of a two-car garage. Several pickup trucks with the rebel insignia on the doors were parked nearby.

Lu clasped her hands together to control the shaking. Whatever was about to happen could not end well. *God? Are you here?* Rico opened her door and motioned for her to follow Esteban inside.

Heart beating double time and short of breath, she stepped across the threshold.

At the far end of the room, a noisy group of men gathered around a wooden crate with a colorful poster of a melon on the side. They wore mismatched combinations of military and civilian clothing. Only one man was dressed in a proper uniform complete with insignia. He oversaw the opening of the crate.

Another man broke away from the group and walked over to greet Esteban. He spoke in soft clipped tones and gestured toward the front corner of the building.

Lu's gaze followed the direction of his pointing finger. Her heart plummeted. "Jack!" She clapped a hand to her mouth. *What had they done to him?*

He sat on the floor, arms stretched high and wide with wrists bound to metal scaffolding. His head lolled forward, chin resting on his chest.

"You know him." Esteban seized her arm and led her to where Jack was tied.

Rico squatted and grabbed a handful of dark hair matted with blood. He jerked Jack's head back. "It's him. She left the club with him." He let go and Jack's head dropped at an odd angle.

"What happened?" A tremor ran through her voice.

Esteban's polished white loafer whipped out and kicked Jack's thigh.

She jerked, feeling the blow in her heart.

"You should be more careful choosing your friends, Lucinda."

"I...I..." She shook her head. "I didn't know him. He kidnapped me..." That was the truth. *He* had kidnapped *her*. So why did *she* feel like a traitor?

Esteban's hateful gaze flicked over her. "The men discovered him spying on this building."

Oh, God. Help. Don't let Jack die. He believes in you, God. She curled her hands into fists controlling the desire to claw Esteban's perfect features.

From the other end of the building shouts erupted followed by laughter.

"Stay here." Expecting her compliance, Esteban left her in the care of Rico.

Lucinda dropped to her knees. "Jack." Hands trembling, she stroked his cheek smudging a rivulet of half-dried blood. The muscles beneath her fingertips twitched. He was here because of her. She looked over her shoulder.

Rico sat close by on a metal folding chair. His pistol rested on his thigh. The men with Esteban pointed at Finny and laughed.

Several green melons were removed from the crate, followed by a weapon that looked much like those she'd seen in Billy Wilson's garage. A swell of approval from the men sent tremors through her.

One of them held up the gun and the others drew close. Their voices bounced off the walls in an unearthly commotion. The knot of men fell apart, moving away from the man with the weapon. Someone rolled a melon across the floor. It exploded in a short burst of automatic gunfire, the pink flesh spraying in all directions.

Lu recoiled and squeezed her eyes shut as bullets

ricocheted off the concrete blocks used as flooring, and pinged against the metal wall.

A guttural word mixed with the din. Surprise zipped through her. She looked at Jack.

Behind the dark fringe of lashes his eyes glittered blue.

Jack shook his head ever so slightly causing his headache to worsen.

The joy racing across Lu's features disintegrated into a frown. She clamped her mouth shut.

He inhaled slowly trying to keep his heart from exploding. Lu was here. With Duro. *Where on this forsaken island was McCord?* Sweat beaded across his upper lip.

Dead. The proof knelt at his side trying to be brave.

He should have stayed with them. Turned the car around and gone...where? He wrestled to think clearly. The situation was precarious, but not impossible. As long as he could draw a breath, nothing was impossible. A fragment of a verse from the book of Isaiah rose from beneath the layers of apprehension and pain.

"I will strengthen you and help you; I will uphold you with my righteous right hand."

Lord, I'm holding you to that promise. He had no choice. His hands were tied. Literally.

"How badly are you hurt?" Lu's whispered words shimmered between them. Head bowed, her hair hid her face from his limited view.

"Bad enough." He'd vowed to bring this woman home. Whether she wanted to go with him or not was irrelevant. He could only hope that faking unconsciousness would buy him time to form a plan.

The men opened a second crate and a wave of excitement rippled through the ranks claiming even the vigilant Rico's attention. Several small boxes were lifted out, followed by a rocket propelled grenade launcher.

Jack tightened the muscles in his shoulders and pulled at his restraints. "You know what's happening here?" Barely moving his lips, his words carried on a harsh breath. She had to understand behind Duro's gentlemanly façade crouched an evil criminal.

"They're mixing melons and firearms. A dangerous combination."

He accepted her sarcasm for what it was—an attempt to bolster a flagging courage. "Arms trafficking."

She sat so close he felt the truth rock through her.

Several men walked over to speak with Rico. Jovial because of the new acquisitions, they strutted and bantered, casting covetous leers in Lucinda's direction.

His captor had taken Ava's revolver as well as his knife, but he had his head and feet, and everything in between except for his hands. God willing, that was only temporary. As long as he didn't catch lead, he had a fighting chance.

A wad of money passed between Duro and the officer. The hustle of loading the weapons onto trucks removed most of the attention from Lucinda. Two hard cases hung back, gauging the wisdom of taking on Rico for a taste of the woman. They moved on when the choice became to go with their comrades or be left behind.

Doors slammed and engines revved. The soldiers pulled away in their trucks, leaving greater odds of survival in Jack's favor.

Esteban approached, holding Finny. His rings winked bright in the artificial light.

Showtime.

"Lucinda, stand up."

The air beside Jack stirred as she rose. He wondered how much longer he'd get away with his act.

"Now you know why I never told you about my enterprise." Duro reached out and stroked her cheek.

Jack wanted to rip his hand off.

"You're a smart man." Lucinda gestured toward the empty crates and scattered melons. "Why do this?"

He smiled. "A man has the best opportunity to make money doing the jobs others are afraid to do."

Lord, open Lucinda's eyes to the man's true nature.

She stepped closer to Duro. "Take me back to the club, Esteban."

Disappointment followed by red-hot fury swept through Jack. *Not what I wanted to hear, Lord.*

"In time, Lucinda. First we deal with your friend."

Jack had only a moment to brace himself for a well-aimed kick to his side. One of those was all he wanted to experience. He coughed and let his head drop back.

"Who are you?"

"A lost tourist?" Pain exploded through his ribs. He clenched his teeth to hold back a groan. He hadn't seen the second kick coming.

"What is Lucinda to you?"

Jack grimaced. "A job." He focused on Duro and not Lu's sudden intake of breath.

"Who do you work for?"

"Her grandmother."

Smack. The heavy rings stung his cheek. The metallic taste of blood flooded his tongue. Being bashed around by these amateurs was getting old fast.

"Stop. Esteban, please." Lu stepped closer. "He's telling

the truth. His name is Jack Conroy. My grandmother sent him for me."

Duro's hand shot out. He grabbed a fistful of her hair and twisted. "You have feelings for this man?"

Pain etched deep lines in Lu's smooth skin.

Murderous rage pounded through Jack. Only a steely grip on his emotions kept him from fighting the restraints.

She glanced at him then looked away. But not fast enough. The glimmer of tears pooled in her hazel eyes. "No."

The word cut Jack to the core. He should have expected nothing else. Survival mode or not, she had no feelings other than contempt for him.

"Then it will not matter to you that he dies."

Her face paled ashen and she breathed in short rough bursts.

Duro led her toward the door. "Not in here, Rico. I don't want a stain on the floor. That would be bad for business."

Lu stumbled in his wake, the erratic flip-flop of her sandals echoing in the building.

A wave of cold certainty washed through Jack. So here it was. The moment that determined who lived and who died. Lu had to live and he wasn't ready to die.

Chapter 19

A wicked sneer distorted Rico's full lips. "He wants her only a little longer and then," he caressed his knife with the tip of his thumb, "she will be mine to play with."

Hot rage exploded through Jack. Coarse words burst from deep within as he strained against his bindings.

Rico's booted foot lashed out, slamming Jack's right shoulder, ramming him backward. Bone crunched and agonizing pain shot from his shoulder to his hand as the ropes on his wrists held fast. A tingling jolt zapped the length of his right arm then—nothing.

He shifted to his knees, not understanding the absence of pain in his arm and hand, but welcoming it as he maneuvered into a defensive position.

Bloodlust infused Rico's olive complexion with a tinge of pink. Light glinted off the blade of his knife as it swept in an arc past Jack's left arm.

Jack braced for pain. His left arm dropped. He yanked it to his side. No spurting blood. The cord they'd used to bind him still braceleted his wrist. Nerves tingled and jumped, coming back to life from his shoulder to the tips of his fingers.

Another sweep of Rico's knife and Jack's right arm dropped. He fisted his hands. Only the left one responded. His heart floundered with confusion.

"Get up." Rico stepped back, his 9-mil trained on Jack.

Every muscle tense, Jack stood.

"Walk."

Playing the part of a lamb being led to slaughter, Jack stumbled toward the door. Something bumped his thigh. He glanced down. With each step his right hand slapped his leg. He bent his elbows. His right arm didn't move. Disbelief blew through him like a hot wind. Bile backed up in his throat, bitter as gall. With no time to assess the damage to his uncooperative arm, he swallowed back panic and concentrated on recalculating his next move. He stepped outdoors into the sprinkle of raindrops and stopped.

Rico shoved him between the shoulders with the flat of his hand.

Now.

Using the forward momentum, Jack planted his foot and pivoted, whirling around to Rico's rear. He latched onto Rico's weapon with his good hand and shoved it up. He struck out with his boot, connecting with Rico's leg. Bone snapped.

Rico cried out and sank to the ground, his leg at an awkward angle.

Jack staggered, his balance compromised by the useless arm. In control of Rico's gun hand, he braced his feet and twisted.

"I wouldn't do that Mr. Conroy." Duro held a subcompact 9-mil snug against Lucinda's temple. "Let go of him."

Jack's lungs pumped like bellows. Tremors ran the length of him as he struggled for control. He flung Rico's hand away. It hit the mud holding the weapon.

Time ground to slow motion as Duro aimed his weapon at Jack.

The mission isn't supposed to end this way, Lord.

Behind and to the right of Duro, muzzle fire flashed in the forest followed by a resounding crack.

Startled, Duro snapped his head around, his hand jerking up as he fired on Jack.

The bullet meant to kill him whistled harmlessly past his ear. Jack lunged. The chin jab he delivered landed slightly off mark, but was good enough to drop Duro.

Lucinda staggered back, her hand over her mouth.

Snatching up Duro's baby Glock, Jack spun to finish off Rico. But the goon lay lifeless; blood running in the rivulets of gentle rain.

The growl of an engine signaled new trouble. Whoever had shot Rico was coming in fast. "Move it."

"Jack, w-what...?" Lu shook her head, wiping rain from her eyes with a shaky hand.

"The shooter missed me once...not getting a second chance." Using her shock and confusion to his advantage, he pushed her toward the SUV.

Unresisting, she splashed through puddles, Finny bouncing and yipping at her heels. "But I think I know who—"

Headlights sliced through the silver curtain of rain. He pushed her to the muddy ground and took a defensive position at the rear wheel. Duro's weapon felt small in his off hand. How many rounds in the magazine? He thumbed the release, partially ejecting the magazine against his thigh. Brass gleamed through only half the windows. He'd make what he had count. Bracing his arm against the bumper, he lined up the fixed sights on the vehicle coming at him. It skidded sideways and stopped broadside to him. He blinked. *The hatchback?*

A bit of cloth flew out the window balanced on the top of a stick. "Jaaaack!"

He shook his head, sure the blow to his head had affected his hearing. *"Ava?"*

"Whit, too." Lucinda spoke close behind him. "I tried to tell you." She pulled herself onto her knees.

He leaned hard against the SUV prepared to fire, not ready to believe.

Ava clamored out of the car, waving Whit's crutch with his hat balanced on its tip. Whit limped into his line of sight carrying the old Sharps.

Jack lowered his weapon.

Whit claimed his hat and clapped it on his head. He thumped Jack's thigh with his crutch. "You're welcome."

"Thought you were dead."

"You keep saying that. Stop it."

"Jack." Lu's voice shook. Her eyes were locked on the ground beside him.

He looked down. His right hand dragged in the mud. A wave of panic crashed through him. He couldn't feel the wet dirt beneath his hand.

Whit muttered and leaned down to inspect the friction burns around Jack's wrist "Make a fist."

Jack gritted his teeth and strained every muscle in his body, willing his hand to do his bidding. "Can't."

Whit probed his wrist with a thumb. "There's a pulse. What'd they do to you?"

"Kicked my shoulder." Jack pulled in a deep breath, held it then let it out slow, intent on quelling the alarm growing in his chest. Whit's hand touched him, but he couldn't *feel* it. "Broke the collar bone, I think." *A minor setback. That's all.*

Whit pulled at the neck of Jack's T-shirt. "Bruised and swelling. Never heard a broken collar bone could leave an arm disabled."

"I'm *not* disabled!" There wasn't enough air on the planet

to fill Jack's lungs. He sat unmoving, staring at his arm as though it belonged to someone else.

"What is it?" Whit whacked Jack's good shoulder with the back of his hand. "Talk to me, Preach."

Feeling as though he'd been poleaxed, Jack looked up at his friend. "I can't feel anything. Not your grip on my arm, not the sleeve of my shirt. Nothing."

Whit's nostrils flared. He rose and hooked his hand under Jack's good arm. "Stand up."

Jack got to his feet and stood firm, though inside he reeled. His arm flapped at his side like a broken wing.

"Into the car." Whit motioned to Lu and Ava. "Back seat. Hustle it." He swung toward the warehouse and downed men.

The women pushed Jack toward the hatchback. Their pitying looks and mews of concern set his teeth on edge.

"I'm not useless. I have my other hand." Was the assurance for them or him? "I'm driving." Whichever one snorted would get his wrath as soon as he dealt with the terror crawling around inside his chest. They pushed him into the backseat before he had the wits to protest.

"Move over." Lucinda elbowed her way in beside him, her eyes looking everywhere but at him.

Cradling his limp right arm, Jack slid to the center of the seat. Pumpkin had been relegated to the floor behind the driver's seat. Lu climbed in beside him and wiggled for more room. He folded a knee and rested a boot on top of the cat kennel before shifting to give her a few more inches in the cramped quarters. Finny circled round and round on Lu's lap before settling down.

Out of breath, Whit fell into the driver's seat, water dripping from his hat brim. "Company's coming." He handed Ava his crutch and the rifle.

On the mountain, pinpoints of light flickered between the blowing, rain-swept leaves of the forest.

Jack sucked in a calming breath. "There's a road out the other side of this clearing."

Whit gunned the car's engine. The wheels spun, spitting pebbles and mud, before grabbing terra firma. Finding the road, he pushed the car to its limit on the ascent out of the valley.

Removing Finny's sling from around her neck, Lu swiveled to face him. She tucked a hank of wet hair behind her ear before holding up the colorful loop of cloth now limp with rainwater. "Use this for your arm." Her words wobbled and she cleared her throat. With each bend in the road, she rocked against him.

He focused, trying to feel the scrape of wet fabric or her warmth against his arm.

Nothing.

A flash lit up the car's interior followed by a deep boom that caused the car to shudder.

Lu jerked around and looked out the rear window. "What was that?"

A brilliant fireball set the valley aglow.

"Building's gone." Jack ground out the words. Flames licked into the night sky, high and bright, undeterred by the steady rain. "How'd you do it, McCord?"

"If I told you, I'd have to kill you."

Had Whit checked Duro? Leaving loose ends was bad business. If the blow to the chin hadn't killed the man, hopefully the fire would do the job.

"Esteban." Lucinda's whisper coursed hot through Jack.

"You aren't going back to the club."

She looked at him, eyes shining liquid. "I know." Hands shaking, she worked at the bulky knot on the puppy sling. "I can adjust the length for you."

The car turned a sharp corner throwing him against the car door.

Lu squealed with surprise, landing hard against his dead arm. Strawberry-scented hair curtained across his face, tickling his nose. Finny yipped and scrambled to right herself.

The car rounded another curve, and Lu's hand fumbled across his diaphragm before latching onto his good arm.

Something primal roared to life in Jack's chest with a blast so strong he looked down expecting to see a gaping wound. Instead, his gaze crashed into hazel eyes unfiltered and revealing concern that tamped their sparkle to a tarnished gold.

"Sorry." She pushed against him to sit up.

The desire to hook his arm around her and pull her to his side swelled through him. But the arm lay useless between them. The enormity of his situation chilled him to his marrow.

"Okay back there?" Whit's question seemed to come from far away.

"Peachy." Blood pumped fast and angry through Jack's veins. The effort to wrap his thoughts around an injury he couldn't categorize increased the aching in his head. He'd have to cope as best he could. Sam would provide the medical attention he needed when he reached stateside. Right now, his priority was to complete the mission.

Lu bent her head, working on the sling. Finny nosed around for a place to curl up before choosing his lap.

"I had to get him out of there." The soft words scraped hoarse with tears. Lu cleared her throat. "I wanted you to live."

Well, that was something. He was off her hit list for the moment. The car screeched around another curve, brush and tree limbs scratching the length of it. Lu braced to keep from falling against him. He ignored the coil of disappointment in his gut. "You're gonna kill us, McCord."

"You let Lucinda doctor your boo-boo and leave the driving to me, Conroy."

Ava chuckled. "I haven't had this much adventure in ages!"

Jack growled. "Don't encourage him." He turned to Lu. "Give me the sling." Her touch stirred up feelings in him better left at rest.

She scowled then threw it at him, hitting him in the chest.

He draped it around his neck. Holding the dead weight of his right forearm, he made a fumbling attempt to put it into the sling.

Without a word, she helped him work the fabric around his arm.

Fighting the sick feeling boiling through his stomach, he couldn't bring himself to look at her. He hated appearing less than capable of finishing what he'd begun. What if this was the end game? His last mission. Dread settled on his chest, making it hard to breathe. *Can't be.* But doubt, along with the familiar soul-deep prompting he'd been pushing aside for months, twisted through him. Would God remove his choice?

Finny poked him with her cold nose and looked up at him with worshipful puppy eyes, tail *pat-patting* his thigh. She was so white she appeared to glow in the dark. Jack rubbed beneath her chin. At any moment trouble could descend upon them. He had to get his head back in the game, pronto.

Now beyond the reach of the fire's bright glow, the darkness of the forest folded in on itself. The road ribboned out before them, its tenuous grip on the rugged terrain a constant reminder of its origin and purpose.

Reaching the mountain peak, Whit leaned over the steering wheel and scanned the starlit sky through the windshield. "Headed northwest."

Jack adjusted the knot of fabric at the back of his neck. "A lot of small bays on that side of the island. Part of a nature and marine preserve."

"My Reginald's yacht is moored in the nature preserve."

A profound silence like one that comes after a hard concussive blast, followed Ava's statement. Then Jack and Whit fired questions at her hot and fast.

"You have a boat?"

"Is it in the water?"

"Do you know where in the preserve?"

Her gaze flitted between them like a nervous butterfly, unsure where to land.

Jack punched Whit's shoulder to shut him up.

His teammate shot him a disgruntled look in the rearview mirror then locked his eyes on the road, and continued to drive too fast for the road conditions.

"Is the yacht moored at a marina?" He couldn't recall her saying how long ago her husband had died. Dry-docked or in storage wouldn't help them.

"Yes. There's a big pink flamingo painted on the building."

Seeing the rebels kill boaters and loot the yachts in Grand Bay, his initial decision to stay away from the waterfront had appeared the best course of action. Time to reconsider that choice.

Chapter 20

Lu scrunched her eyes closed, afraid of glimpsing the edge and the drop into black nothingness. Forget the rebel soldiers. Whit would kill them with his driving. The car slid sideways. Pebbles rattled along the undercarriage. The armrest dug into her ribs as the weight of Jack squished her to the door. The car surged ahead.

"Get off me!" She shoved him then froze, her hand pressing against his injured arm. Her heart plummeted. "Sorry." She swallowed back tears. She seemed to be forever apologizing to this man.

He turned his head, his lips only a whisper away from hers. "For what?"

"Your injury. It's my fault." She smoothed the fabric encasing his arm. "You can't feel me touching you?"

He gave one curt shake of his head. "Injuries come with the job." His features hardened, prepared to reject any expression of comfort.

"Well your job stinks." She pushed against his arm in a show of spite, angrier with herself and her own stupidity than with him. How had she missed seeing Esteban's sinister nature?

"You're a pain in the butt, you know that?"

Lu snorted.

"And not lady-like."

His comment brought her up short. Did that matter to him? "What of it? I tried to be the woman Esteban wanted." She huffed. "Look where that got me."

"Forget him." He shifted. "You be the woman God created you to be." He lifted his good hand and stroked her jaw. "I'm pretty sure that's not a chameleon."

She pulled away from his fingers and bumped his lips with hers. She jerked back.

He followed. "Be yourself, Lulabelle."

Her heart tripped as his words and lips brushed over hers. *Be yourself.* She lifted her chin, crossing that tiny distance between their lips. His mouth settled on hers with a sigh, warm and sure. For the first time in forever, she felt as though she was right where she belonged.

He broke the kiss, pulling back only a breath. "You're way better and more capable than you think."

Doubt and fear reared their ugly heads. She pushed at his chest. "You don't know anything about me." *You wouldn't be kissing me if you knew.*

"Wrong. I know you're gutsy." The car jounced as the front wheels thumped into a rut rocking him closer. "You handled that mess back there." He brushed a stray strand of hair from her cheek. "And I know you aren't naturally blonde."

"That's none of your business." He was crowding her emotionally as well as physically. She pushed him away, wishing she had the right to pull him close again, and this time, never let go.

Reluctant, he gave her space. "Just saying tha—"

A sharp coughing fit in the front seat was followed by Whit's voice rumbly with laughter. "Better quit while you still have one good arm, *amigo*."

Jack sat up. "Didn't your mama teach you it's impolite to eavesdrop on private conversations?"

"Just got your back. If you're interested, we're on a paved road now."

It was true. The tires hummed over smooth asphalt.

Jack raked her with a stormy gaze that promised they weren't finished.

She turned away, resting her hot cheek on the cool window, trying to calm the tremors racing through her. He'd almost been killed before her eyes, and he thought she'd done okay? She'd fought back a tsunami of tears upon seeing him bound and beaten. She'd managed to keep the contents of her stomach intact when Rico's chest splattered red, and he dropped to the ground. And she hadn't soiled herself when Esteban pressed a gun to her temple. If all that meant she'd "handled that mess", then hurray for her.

Shuddering, she wrapped herself around Finny who had crawled out of Jack's lap and into hers. Maybe if she held on tight enough, she wouldn't fly into a million pieces. Would Jack get the use of his arm back? Did Esteban die? Should she be afraid? Sad? Thrilled by the kiss they shared? A myriad of thoughts and feelings tumbled and rolled over one another in an emotional brew she stuffed deep inside. They weren't safe yet. There would come a time, and with it the opportunity, to turn into a wailing heap of humanity.

Darkness melted into gray dawn. A steady drizzle fell from the dark clouds boiling overhead. The cryptic sentences murmured back and forth between the men hardly counted as a conversation.

"This is it." Whit slowed the car and turned into the

parking lot of a small exclusive marina with a flamboyant pink flamingo painted on the side of the office. Located on a bay, the rain and rising wind stirred the surface of the water into heaving, foamy waves.

Following Ava's directions, Whit drove past docks with more slips empty than occupied. At this early hour when most residents should be abed, men hurried about making preparations to get underway. It was only a matter of time before the rebels lay claim to this quiet corner of the island.

"There it is." Ava pointed to a white yacht rocking in its berth on the far end of the dock.

Whit let out a long slow whistle and stopped the car. "Your husband had good taste."

Jack reached across Lu to open the car door. "Hope we can figure out the electronics."

Lucinda bailed with Finny in her arms, at once relieved to be out of the close confines of the backseat yet wanting to remain at Jack's side. The wind whipped her hair and clothing, propelling her along the dock past sailboats and cruising vessels. Salt spray mingled with pelting rain. Gulls bobbed in the choppy water and huddled on pilings, hoping someone would provide an easy meal. A strong hand clamped around her elbow.

"What are you running from, Lulabelle?"

"I wasn't running."

He guided her onto the finger dock where the yacht was moored. "Answer the question."

You. "I'm getting soaked." She relied on Jack's grip to keep her from reeling like a drunkard on the undulating boards. A glance over her shoulder confirmed Whit, carrying Pumpkin's kennel, and Ava weren't far behind.

Taking Finny, Jack jumped down to the swim deck at the rear of the boat. He set the puppy down and offered Lu his hand.

She ignored it and stepped off the dock. A rolling wave tipped the boat. She yelped as she pitched forward and landed against a solid wall of muscle.

"Got you." Clamping his arm around her waist, Jack steadied her.

Her heart pitched wild. Saved from the rough water, she was drowning in turbulent blue eyes.

Jack helped her through the transom door into the open cockpit then turned to help Whit bring Ava on board.

"Miss Ava." A young man dressed in a yellow rain slicker imprinted with the name of the marina, tromped down the dock toward them. Jumping into the cockpit, he unlocked the door admitting them to a well-appointed salon. "Didn't know you were coming. We would have had her ready for you." He opened the door of the electrical panel and flipped several switches. At once, recessed lighting dispersed the gloom. "Sorry to hear about Mr. Reggie."

Lu spun in a circle on the thick carpet, taking in the glossy teak trim and luxury accommodations.

"Come on." Jack ushered her through the galley to the carpeted steps of a short companionway.

"Where are we going?" She wanted to stop and peek into the closets lining the passage.

"To find you dry clothes." The artificial lighting emphasized the bruise on his jaw and the dark circles beneath his eyes. Her heart ached knowing she was the cause of all that had happened to him.

He steered her into the forward stateroom dominated by a v-berth. The close quarters and rocking of the boat turned her stomach queasy. Taking a deep breath to fight the nausea, she opened a hanging locker door. Bathing suits and beach cover-ups swayed on hangers in a kaleidoscope of color. Her stomach lurched and she closed the door with a bang.

Oblivious to her distress, Jack pulled out a drawer beneath the berth and dug around. "Here you go." He handed her a pair of gray leggings and a pink T-shirt that read: Keep Calm and Read On. "Change into these." His eyes narrowed. "What's the matter?"

Lu set Finny on the coverlet. "Nothing."

The muscle of his jaw knotted. "The trouble with lying is no one knows when you're actually telling the truth."

"*You* judge me?" Her indignation was unsustainable against a wave of vertigo making her head two sizes too big. "You insist on having your way whether by force or by guile. Why is it okay for you to use deceit, but if I do the same to *survive*, I'm a bad person?"

Anger simmered in his eyes, but she refused to look away.

"Yes I said I wanted to go back to the club. What would you have had me say?" Her chest heaved as she struggled to keep her stomach and emotions in check so the words didn't leave her mouth in a screeching vomit. "Gee, Esteban, I don't love you and maybe I never did, but can we be friends?"

"Is that true?"

"Is what true?" Her focus narrowed to her upset stomach.

"You never loved Duro?"

"We never…he never…" She rubbed her temples. Jack's assumption had been wrong. "There was never anything physical between us. I assumed it was the age difference."

He stepped closer, crowding her. "Tell me the truth, Lulabelle. Do you love him?"

"I thought I did."

"What changed? And don't tell me he's a bad man. Women love bad men all the time."

She wet her lips and his eyes followed the sweep of her tongue. Sickness boiled through her. "I met you."

His breath hissed sharp between his teeth. He grasped her jaw with his hand. "What are you saying?" His gaze flicked over her face, touching on each feature. "No deceit. Only truth, Lulabelle."

A tear slipped from the corner of her eye. He rubbed it away with his thumb. "I don't know what that is anymore."

He leaned closer, his gaze holding hers. "*This* is truth." His lips touched hers, light and feathery. He let go of her jaw and wrapped his arm around her shoulders, snugging her tight against his uninjured side. His heart pounded hard against her ribs. Her heart shifted to match the beat of his.

She pressed into him, tasting copper and salt on his battered lips. Warmth flooded through her. Emotions welled and she shuddered. Her head spun dizzily. A wash of perspiration bloomed on her skin, and she pulled away. "I'm gonna be sick."

"What?" He exhaled ragged.

She blinked, trying to merge the two images of his face. "I'm gonna—" The boat rolled and another wave of nausea crashed over her. She clapped her hand to her mouth gulping and breathing through her nose.

"Oh, no!" He spun her around and dragged her into the nearby head.

Falling to her knees, she leaned over the toilet. Her stomach knotted hard and she wretched with such force, tears wet her eyelashes. Jack's hand rested on her nape holding her hair out of the line of fire.

Several exhausting minutes later, she was sure her stomach had turned inside out. She sneezed and a tissue wiped her nose. Miserable, she rested her elbows on the seat and held her head in her hands, unsure if she'd finished.

"Not much of a sailor, huh?"

Her neck and cheeks heated with embarrassment. "I'm sorry." She sat back on her heels.

"Don't be." He stepped on the pedal at the base of the toilet.

The noise of the vacuum flush pounded through her head. Her stomach gave another sickening jump.

"Dry off and change while I check if Ava has something for seasickness."

The door to the bedroom slid shut. Lu stood clinging to the edge of the sink. The woman in the mirror had dark rings under her too big eyes. Her hair, tossed by wind and wet with rain, framed pale features. She swayed with the movement of the boat, willing the next bout of nausea to go away. Shaking, she entered the bedroom, stripped off her wet clothes, then dried off using a plush towel from the cupboard.

Once dressed, she tackled her hair with the hand-held dryer she found in the bathroom vanity. She was attempting to scrape a comb through the uncooperative mop when someone rapped on the bedroom door. "Come in."

"Take this." A tiny yellow pill rested in the palm of Jack's hand.

The thought of ingesting anything sent a ripple of objection through her tender stomach. Resolute, she placed the offering on her tongue and let it dissolve before swallowing. "How long do I have to wait for relief?"

"Lay down and close your eyes."

Functioning on landlubber legs, she fell onto the bed where Finny lay snoozing. Curling up on her side, she pulled the pup close. The steady vibration of the yacht's engines throbbed through the bed.

Jack sat on the edge of a small cushioned bench beside

her berth. Frowning, he fiddled with the colorful sling as though unsure what to do with his injured arm. Hoping for his sake the damage wasn't permanent, she let her eyelids drift shut.

"Tell me about the threatening phone calls you received in Kansas."

Whoa! Her eyes popped open. She stared at him, heart bumping against her ribs. "Now?"

"Good a time as any."

Hugging Finny, she tried to gather her wits. "What do you want to know?"

"How many were there?"

"Three."

"What was said?"

"Nothing the first time. Gran suspected it was a kid making a crank call. I answered the second time. He said, 'Keep your mouth shut.'"

"He?"

She hesitated. "The voice was deep."

"Keep your mouth shut about what?"

"Don't know." She sighed.

He rose, pulled a blanket out of the hanging cupboard, and spread it over her and the sleeping puppy. "You didn't notice the phone number when the call came through?"

"Phone is old. Pre-digital."

"And the third call?"

"The worst." She tugged the blanket up to her chin. "Said Gran could die," she whispered. "Next night after the fundraiser, Trent broke it off with me."

"The son of the mayor slash pawnbroker."

She didn't have enough oomph left to take offense with his comment. "Small town. Politicians serve for a stipend." Whatever he'd given her was turning her arms and legs to jelly. "Memories of a wonderful evening spoiled." She pouted when she thought about it.

A smile slanted across Jack's lips. "That good, huh?"

"For Ingersoll, Kansas." She snuggled deeper beneath the blanket. Her stomach settled and the gentle rocking of the boat lulled her senses. "Wore the perfect dress for a future politician's wife."

"High aspirations for Maudie Lavalle's granddaughter."

"Making fun of me?" She struggled to stay awake, but her body wasn't cooperating. Sighing, she gave up the fight.

Chapter 21

Jack rubbed his brow and studied her nestled beneath the blanket. Her hair fanned across the pillow, the roots a dark mahogany, the ends sunshine bright. Had she changed her hair color to be what some man wanted her to be?

She was a challenge. She'd questioned his deepest beliefs. Pointed out where he didn't measure up to his own standards, and still, his usual cautious nature vaporized in the heat of his desire for her. This woman called to his heart like none other ever had.

The memory of her kisses warmed him. Granted, his timing had been impeccably poor this last time. He ran his finger over the small heart on her temple then tucked the blanket around her and left the room.

An assortment of canned goods cluttered the galley's counter. Ava knelt on the floor, plundering another cabinet.

Letting her know Lu was resting, he left the salon and climbed the steps to the enclosed bridge. Whit stood at the helm speaking to the young man from the marina.

Jack glanced over their shoulders at the console. The vintage yacht had the original electronics. For their purposes, simple was good. He left the bridge intent on running recon on the rest of the boat. Stepping up on the non-skid surface of the portside deck, he held the rail with his good hand. A four-foot swell thumped the boat against the dock. Taking the yacht out in this weather wasn't an ideal plan, but with God's help, this would be a short run around the top end of the island.

"Could you calm the sea, Lord?" In a quiet voice he added, "and at the same time my heart that's filled with fear." Though he'd refused to dwell on his injury, fear had found a foothold. To continue to do the job he'd been trained to do, he needed to be fully functional.

I'm calling you to something new.

The voice burned through him hotter than ever. "I don't *want* something new." His words scattered on the wind. He'd spent years training to be one of the best operators on any team. He'd left the Rangers for something new when he felt God calling him to SeaMount. Using his skills as a civilian had been the balm his war-weary soul needed. Why change *again*? He was content.

Yeah, right. He'd never been so unsettled in his life, and it had begun long before meeting one small, sassy woman.

He leaned into the wind, relishing the sting of wind-driven rain and salt spray. He didn't know what to do with his feelings for someone so ill-suited for him. She pushed away anything to do with God, but at the same time was seeking Him. It was as though she wanted to believe, but was afraid, so she fought Him at every turn.

Hadn't he been doing the same, fighting God's call to something new for months? His right arm was as good as dead. Had his choice been removed? His chest squeezed tight making it hard to breathe. He'd demanded truth from Lu, but wouldn't look it in the eye himself.

"Preach!"

Jack looked over his shoulder.

Whit stood in the cockpit leaning on his stick, looking up at him through the rain.

With gut-wrenching realization, Jack stiffened. If he turned around to walk back, the rail would be on his right side. He'd be unable to hold on. The heat of embarrassment flamed through him. *Idiot!*

Gritting his teeth over his own stupidity, he slid one booted foot behind the other, backing his way toward the steps. Waves bounced the boat sideways. The rail pulled on his hand. He tightened his core muscles and hunched low to maintain his balance. Toppling over the railing would be the ultimate humiliation.

At the small of his back, a hand grasped his belt. "Step down."

Jack felt for the step with the toe of his boot. "Don't need a *mother*."

"You need someone with sense following you around telling you what to do." Not letting go until both Jack's boots were on deck, McCord stepped back. "Go inside."

Toe to toe with Whit, Jack roared, "This is *my* mission. I call the shots."

"Crazy talk." McCord shook his head. "I don't argue with cripples."

Jack bellowed and launched himself at McCord, delivering a bone jarring body slam.

On impact, Whit stepped back. He closed both arms around Jack in a reckless bear hug. "That all you got?" He pushed Jack away.

The bench seat caught Jack behind the knees. He fell back banging his head against the wall of the cabin. He scrambled to his feet, the pitching deck and useless arm making it hard to find his balance. Rain sluiced down, dripping from his hair, impeding his vision. He swiped at his face, fury making it hard to think straight.

Crutch abandoned on the deck, Whit bent low favoring his leg. A smirk played across his lips. "Com'on. Let's get this over with."

Rage screamed through Jack. "You think this is *funny*?" He clenched his fist.

"A gimp and a crip going at each other? Oh, yeah. I could sell tickets."

"Stinking politically incorrect, you know that?" Jack gulped the wet air, looking to right his world. "My arm's *temporarily* out of commission."

Whit's smirk slid away. "It's giving you a belly full of angst and clouding your thinking." He widened his stance and motioned for Jack to come closer.

Jack eyed McCord, wanting to deny the truth. But truth was his anchor. "I'm not gonna fight you." Wavering, he fell back onto the bench seat. "But, don't underestimate me, McCord." It was a pitiful attempt at saving face.

"Last thing I'd do. I know what you're capable of. Even short a wing."

Jack rested his head against the cabin, gulping and trying to bring his breathing under control. The roof's overhang didn't protect him from the blowing rain. For the first time he spoke his fear aloud. "What if it's permanent?"

"You'll deal with it and move on." Whit took up his stick. "No sense worrying. You have a job to finish." He turned his back on Jack and headed for the cabin door. "Any brains at all, you'll come in out of the rain."

Jack let him go without a word. The bluster of the wind and the pelting of the rain matched the storm raging inside him. Anger because the mission had fallen apart. Because

God had allowed it to happen. Because he'd chosen to ignore the gentle promptings from God.

"You have my attention, Lord." Weary, he stood. He'd do his best to finish this mission and turn the outcome over to God.

He stepped inside. Ava stood in the galley working at the counter. She pointed a butter knife at him. "Go change, dear. Reginald's clothes will be big on you, but you'll be dry."

Taking the steps down into the master suite, Jack found McCord, already dressed in khaki slacks and a Hawaiian shirt. "Spiffy."

"Wait till you see what I left for you." Whit sat on the end of the bed pulling on his boots.

Jack ducked into the head. Undressing was a one-handed wrestling match. He gritted his teeth against the pain radiating through his shoulder and up his neck. His right arm was a lifeless object to be handled with care. Grabbing a towel, he caught a glance of himself in the vanity mirror. His stomach knotted sickly, but he refused to look away.

A dark bruise stained his chest and shoulder. He touched the pulse in his wrist. Would the injury get worse by not having immediate medical attention? Taking two painkillers he found in the medicine cabinet, he toweled off, tossed his wet clothes in the shower on top of Whit's, and exited the head.

Whit's voice and Ava's laughter drifted through the closed door from the galley above. On the bed lay a knife in a sheath with a clip. Whit's boot knife. Jack smiled and started ransacking the drawers and closet. He found a green knit polo shirt with pink horizontal stripes and a pair of soft khaki chinos with an elastic waistband. Reginald hadn't believed in dark colors. He'd have to carry Duro's baby Glock like an old-time street narc. Hopefully Ava had elastic bands to wrap around its grip to keep it from slipping out of the waistband of his pants.

He discovered a cache of scarves in a plastic shoebox in Ava's closet. Pawing through them, he pulled out the most sedate. Impatient to be on his way, he wrangled with a pair of socks, clipped Whit's knife in place, and jammed his feet into his boots.

He stopped cold.

The laces had him beat.

Grabbing the scarf, he climbed the steps into the salon, taking care not to trip on the trailing laces.

"'Bout time you showed up." Whit sat at the dinette booth, coffee mug in hand and Rico's Glock in front of him. A map lay open on the table. Ava had pulled rain slickers and life vests out of storage and piled them high in an overstuffed chair.

Jack sat on the end of the dinette's bench seat.

Leaning out beyond the table, Whit looked Jack over, from the untied boots to the scarf tossed over his shoulder. "Need help dressing, boy?"

Jack mouthed an impolite word and flicked the scarf at his friend. "Make yourself useful."

Whit snorted coffee and coughed. "Do tell. Heard Rangers can do anything with one hand tied behind their back."

"You really are a——." A rustling noise cut him off.

Lucinda stood at the top of the steps. Wrapped in a blanket, her bare feet peeked out the bottom. Deathly pale, she looked shaken.

"What are you doing up?" Jack stood, taking one step toward her before remembering his untied laces.

"I…had a bad dream…" She combed a hand through her hair, flat on the side where she'd fallen asleep. "I thought you were dead."

"Ha!" Whit slammed his mug on the table. Coffee spilled over the rim. "*Finally!* It's not *me* bein' accused of dyin'."

Confusion slipped across Lu's face as Ava wrapped an arm around her shoulder. "Ignore the men, dear. I'll make you a cup of tea."

"Why don't you help Jack finish dressing?" Whit sipped his coffee. The mug did little to hide his smile.

Lu's gaze held Jack's then moved to his arm, the scarf on the table, and his untied boots. The blanket slipped from her shoulders to the sofa.

Heat crawled up Jack's neck and set his ears on fire as he took a seat. Holding his arm in place, he waited for Lu to adjust the royal blue scarf hand painted with pink hibiscus blossoms. Her closeness set all his senses on alert. He breathed in her scent, strawberry now overlaid with the tang of salt and mustiness of her clothes.

"This is a pretty scarf." Lu smoothed the folds over his elbow.

"A gift from Reginald." Ava stood at the small electric stove.

With care, Lu knotted the swath of silk at the back of his neck.

Jack lifted one booted foot. Kindergarten had been the last time he'd asked anyone to tie his laces.

Without hesitation, she placed the sole of his boot against her leg above her bent knee, tightened the laces, and tied a bow. She did the same for the other foot in short order.

"Look at those pretty bows." Whit leaned his elbows on the table.

Meant to keep him angry enough to stay in the fight, Jack let the harassment slide. "When do we leave?"

"There's another boat leaving soon. We'll follow him. Channel is tricky. In this weather I could miss a buoy." Whit swirled the coffee in his mug. "Don't want to run aground and sink before we get started."

The teakettle whistled and Lu joined Ava in the galley to fix a cup of tea. Some of the color in Lu's cheeks had come back, but she wasn't her usual feisty self. She'd seen too much.

"You keep on looking at her like that, I'll be thinking whatever's happening between the two of you is for keeps." Whit leaned back in his seat.

Jack shifted his gaze to Whit. "Not now. Maybe never."

"That hungry look says different."

Shaking his head, he studied the map. They were farther from the second PZ than he'd thought. Waiting to leave worried him, but he agreed with Whit's reasoning. They didn't know the bay. They barely knew how to run the boat.

Ava set out plastic bottles of water on the low glass-top table in front of the sofa. Lu followed with a cup of tea and a plate of crackers spread with peanut butter, her nose wrinkled with distaste. Her stomach wasn't up for anything solid. What he was about to tell her wouldn't help to settle it.

"Come here, Lulabelle. You should know where we're to meet the team."

"Why?"

He didn't want to answer the question. The way events were unfolding, she needed all the information he could give her. "If anything happens to us," he waved his thumb between himself and Whit, "you and Ava are to head for the beach." He could only hope she'd do this and not return to Duro.

She stood beside him, not saying one way or the other if she would follow his instructions. The team would take her and Ava off the island then come back to find him and Whit. On the map, he pointed out the bay where the launch would be waiting. "Get there and the men will do the rest."

Lu looked at the map. "Men like you?"

He placed his hand on her shoulder and swiveled her round to face him. "You have a way of trusting the wrong people."

A blush of pink colored her cheeks. "I thought Esteban loved me." The distress in her voice caught Finny's attention. The puppy bounced at her feet asking to be held. Lu complied and sat on the sofa.

"Of course you believed he loved you, Lucinda." Ava took a seat beside Lu. "Just look at Finny."

All eyes shot to Finny, curled in a contented ball on Lu's lap.

Ava took a napkin and placed a cracker on it. "A man is very much in love when he gives a woman that many diamonds."

Chapter 22

Jack snapped to attention. "Diamonds?"

Eyes wide and questioning, Lu stared at Ava. "What diamonds?"

Ava chomped on her cracker and chuckled. "Those sparkly stones on Finny's collar, dear. They aren't paste, you know. Almost a caret each."

Lu shook her head in disbelief, clutching Finny to her chest. "They can't be real."

Jack moved to stand in front of her. "Remove the collar."

Fingers trembling, she undid the buckle and held it up. In the artificial light, the stones glinted bright.

Taking it, Jack studied the strip of pink leather with a single row of stones spaced evenly apart, each in a gold setting. Running his finger over them, he counted twenty. He huffed his breath on them. The fog cleared at once. A chill ran down his spine. He slapped the collar, stones down, against the tabletop. Pressing, he pulled his hand an inch before lifting it. Evenly spaced scratches marred the glass.

Whit let out a low whistle.

Lu looked up at Jack. Distressed, she held out her hands palms up. "I didn't know."

"Did Finny come with the collar?"

"Yes."

"Some of the new expensive fakes pass the scratch test." Taking the knife from his boot, he pried the prongs from one of the stones and placed it on the map. The print was visible through the stone. He exchanged an uneasy look with Whit.

Ava drank from her water bottle and set it down. "I don't know why he didn't tell you, Lu. Diamonds always earned my husband brownie points."

Whit leaned forward. "And which husband would that be, Miss Ava?"

"All of them, dear." She smiled and winked. "One pair of earrings Ellison gave me had to be kept in the bank vault. I didn't care for that."

The puppy looked from one human to the next, big-eyed and anxious to please. The perfect little package to ensure the stones wouldn't be lost.

A shout was followed by the thud of running feet.

Jack dropped the collar on the table. Weapon in hand, he stepped to one side of the salon door. Whit dove for the other side holding Rico's weapon.

The young dockworker appeared at the window and banged on the door. "They're leaving."

"Be right out." Whit thrust his weapon out of sight. "Rain gear and life vests, ladies. *Now*." A gust of wind curled a corner of the map when he opened the door to go to the bridge.

Lu sat unmoving, staring at the collar. She appeared smaller, as though she'd crumbled in on herself.

Jack held her cold hand in his and rubbed his thumb across the back of it. "Lu, it's time to get ready." He pulled her to her feet wishing he knew what to say to take the hollow look from her eyes.

Ava sorted through the pile of slickers and personal

flotation devices. She held up a blue raincoat. "Lu, this one should do."

She rubbed her eyes with the heels of her hands and joined Ava.

Jack scooped the diamond into his half empty water bottle. With the tip of the knife, he removed the others from the collar and did the same with them.

"Here you go, Jack." Ava held up a rain poncho.

Pocketing the collar, he placed the water bottle on the table and pulled the poncho over his head. Helpful hands tugged it down his back and over his injured shoulder. He turned to say thank you, and Lu met his gaze, her hand resting over his pounding heart, the air between them thick with unspoken words.

She turned away to take the life vest Ava held. Lifting it over his head, she threaded the strap beneath his injured arm and snapped the ends together. She frowned. "It's not the best fit."

He shrugged, forcing himself to pull away. "Better than no protection."

Lines were tossed aboard. Frustrated working with one hand, Jack secured them as best he could. The yacht eased away from the dock. He hauled in the fenders he could reach from the cockpit. The others would have to stay out.

He climbed the steps to the bridge. Whit stood at the helm, legs braced wide. They followed in the foamy wake of a much larger boat. In the chop and roll of the sapphire water, the channel markers bobbed in and out of sight.

Jack hung onto the grab bar overhead. "Why set diamonds on a dog collar?"

McCord glanced his way. "Why leave them with the girl? He'd want them someplace he could access fast."

"She worked for him at the club. He'd know where to find her."

"She has legs." A smile played across his teammate's lips. "Nice ones, too."

Jack's attention jerked to the man beside him. A possessive streak snaked through him.

With a look of wide-eyed innocence, McCord kept talking. "Your woman could walk away with the stones. Doesn't seem the safest way to hold business assets."

Your woman. The words rang loud in Jack's ears. Words he couldn't deny—to McCord or himself. Truth was an inconvenient taskmaster.

To the lull of the windshield wipers whisking away rain and salt spray, he reviewed what he knew, which was precious little. Lu's surprise had been genuine. If the stones were currency for business dealings, Duro would want to keep tabs on them.

Vessels were stacked up tight and jockeying for position to go through the hurricane barrier that protected the bay. They bobbed on the fringe of the flotilla.

Whit muttered under his breath. "You praying?"

Jack sank into the seat beside him ready to give as good as he'd gotten. "Your first rodeo, cowboy?" Whit hated cows. He was a horseman.

McCord shot him an irritable glance. "Shut up and pray."

"Touchy." Jack closed his mouth and opened the gates of his heart.

The raw power of the wind, swept white spume off the crest of the heaving waves. Whit worked to counter the drift toward a public dock and boat ramp.

Jack played with the knob on the marine radio, passing several crackling bandwidths to find the one the team would monitor.

"Preach to Red Dog." In the stormy atmosphere, the speaker hissed.

Jack repeated his call and this time received an answer.

"This is Red Dog." Static snapped across Caleb Fallon's response.

"On our way to the revival meeting." He gave their location and signed off.

Portside, more boats crowded close, competing for a position. Uneasy with the wait, Jack pulled Finny's collar from his pocket. The boat rocked hard. A surprised yelp spun him around in the chair.

Lu stood on the steps. Her pale face peeked from the confines of a too large life jacket. Before he could move to help her, she dove for the bench seat and leaned back against the wall.

"What are you doing up here?" He wanted to reprimand her and at the same time hug her close.

"Needed air." She gulped in great droughts. "Took another pill."

"So soon?"

"Was thinkin' about what you said." She blinked, trying to focus on the collar in his hand. "All makes sense." Her words slurred around the edges.

"What makes sense?"

"He always wanted to know where I was." She looked down at her hands. "Thought it was cuz he loved me." The wistful disappointment and shame in her voice tugged at his heart.

"Some men are jerks, Lulabelle. They don't know when they have a good thing."

A derisive huff was her only answer. He wished he hadn't said a word.

"Idiot!" Whit's frustrated bark was followed by a surge of power. "Where'd you get your license?" A small race boat leaped the crests of the waves too fast for the crowded conditions. It passed on their portside.

"I sneaked away with Finny sometimes." Lu wiped a hand across her sweating brow. "He'd always find us."

Jack's gut bottomed out. Every place they had been, Duro found them. Every time he'd had a plausible explanation. Rico was a tenacious tracker. Simao betrayed them for money. But what if it was something else entirely?

Moving to sit next to her, he bent the collar between each empty setting. Where the leather folded back on itself after looping through the buckle, he felt resistance. "Hold it." He handed the collar to Lu and pulled the knife from his boot. Using the tip, he lifted the stitching.

"What're ya doin'?" Her hands were steady, but the second pill, so close on the heels of the first, was too much medication for her small stature. It was making her loopy.

Metal glinted. Goose bumps prickled up his arms. He opened the layers. Sandwiched in the small channel between the stitching, a small computer chip glittered. He dug it out and held it up.

Whit glanced over his shoulder and whistled. "Look what you found, *amigo*."

"What's it?" Fear tinged Lucinda's words.

"My guess, the latest in tracking devices." Jack turned it over.

"Pitch it overboard, Preach." Whit didn't turn away from the helm.

Jack descended the stairs to the open cockpit where the rain drenched him in a matter of seconds. Not knowing if

Duro was dead or alive had come back to haunt them. Holding the rail, he flung the chip into the waves.

A high-pitched whine cut through the throbbing idle of the surrounding boats. The race boat circled and came at them fast. Jack glanced toward the bridge. With the traffic jam on the portside and the public dock not far off the starboard, Whit had little room to maneuver.

There was a pop. The air crackled close to Jack's ear and set his heart thundering. They were under fire.

Lucinda stumbled down the steps from the bridge.

He caught her with his good arm and sank to the cockpit floor. "Lu?" Had she been hit? Manhandling her, he checked for blood.

"Shtop tha…" She pushed his hand away.

Her indignation halted his exploration.

Another pop had him drawing his weapon.

She pulled back. "Don' shoooot."

"Listen to me Lulabelle." He leaned close, demanding her attention through the haze of the drug overdose. "Get in the cabin with Ava. Stay away from the windows."

Crack. A chunk of fiberglass exploded off the corner of the cabin. He glanced up at the bridge where Whit was doing his best to control the yacht in the panicked scramble of boats surging around them. Against the wind, he pried the cabin door open and pushed her through.

Crawling to the stern, he took cover behind the dinghy. The race boat weaved in among the other vessels drawing closer. Four men sat in the cockpit of the boat. Against the dark water, the white suited figure was easy to spot.

Duro.

Bullets whiffed by shattering cabin windows. A scream pierced the air, setting Jack's heart to double time. He returned fire, providing cover for Whit who was fighting to move the boat out of the log jam of smaller vessels. He seemed to be maneuvering the yacht closer to the dock.

Jack breathed in spurts. Up against the pilings they'd be cornered. Squinting, he peered up at the bridge wishing for headpiece and mic. He clambered across the cockpit, the bulk of his PFD making movement uncoordinated. Releasing the clasp, he stripped it off. In a hail of automatic fire, the windows of the bridge disintegrated. Sharp bits of glass peppered him as he popped off another round.

One of the men dropped. The race boat pulled away.

He slammed his back against the sidewall. Overhead an alarm squealed. His nostrils flared, catching the scent of acrid smoke. He lunged for the steps leading to the bridge.

"Get the women off!"

Whit's bellow turned Jack back. The stern bumped the dock, and he fell to his knees. They were sitting ducks. He had no time to second-guess Whit's plan.

Yanking on the door, he dove through and landed beside the dinette. The women huddled at the bottom of the master suite steps. Finny peeked out from beneath Lu's bright orange PFD. Ava held the kennel, the big cat moaning with indignation.

"Let's go."

Ava pulled the drug-befuddled Lucinda up the stairs.

Shouts rose from the cockpit.

Jack spun as Manuel Mingau stepped through the open door.

The boat pitched, and Lu stepped in front of Jack's drawn weapon. He thrust her out of the way. Mingau's weapon remained trained on her, ripping Jack's heart in two.

Duro stepped into the salon, his suit peppered with charred spots. Half of his face was covered in a messy field dressing.

Digging for the calm he needed to see this through, Jack dropped his weapon, focusing to hear over the rush of the blood pounding through his veins.

"Esteban." Lu's voice cracked.

"Take a good look at me, Lucinda." With each word Duro's rage grew. "I crawled as far as I could before the explosion. The fire destroyed everything I'd worked for."

Her indrawn breath dissolved into a soft sob. She clamped her trembling hand over her mouth.

Duro's exposed eye drifted over to Finny. "Such a pretty little thing." He snatched her from Lu and held her up. "The collar. Where is it?"

"Let the women leave and I'll show you where the collar is." Beneath Jack's boots he could feel the gentle vibration of the twin engines. Was Whit at the controls or was it one of Duro's men?

The arms dealer faced Jack. "You will pay for what you have done to me." His eye snapped with hatred.

Pumpkin yowled like a tormented soul in the depths of Hades.

Duro signaled Mingau. "Shut that animal up."

"He wants to be let out." Ava held the kennel protectively beneath her arm.

Mingau snatched it from her grasp, tossed it on the chair, and released the door latch. Claws unsheathed, Pumpkin leapt out and landed on his chest.

"Aagh." Mingau reeled back, falling over the glass table, and going down.

Jack twisted and kicked Duro's injured side. "Lu! Go. Go, go, go!"

Duro fell to the couch, cursing and groaning with pain.

Ava grabbed Lucinda's hand and ran for the door.

The pup in Duro's grasp squirmed trying to break free.

On his back, Mingau screamed at the cat. He brought his gun up.

Shoulder on fire, Jack kicked the gun from his hand. It clattered down the master suite steps.

Mingau staggered to his feet, clawing at the cat stuck to his chest. With one last hiss, Pumpkin released his hold and dropped to the floor, leaving bloody spots on the front of Mingau's shirt.

Face red with rage, Mingau lunged at Jack.

Jack dropped low and came up beneath him. They fell through the open door grappling, Jack cursing his bum arm. Mingau landed a glancing blow to his jaw.

A streak of orange flew by as Jack gathered his feet beneath him and rose. Finny's frantic bark cut through the fog of the fight. The pup stood between them making a racket.

Mingau came at him swinging. Jack blocked an uppercut. With an arm out of commission, he followed through with a vicious kick to the side of his leg. The rolling deck saved Mingau from a broken knee. Jack shifted, rocking to the balls of his feet on the heaving deck.

Murder in his eyes, Mingau rushed him. The stern dipped in a trough throwing them over the transom door to the swim deck below.

Jack's injured shoulder took the brunt of the fall. The edges of his vision darkened as pain speared his chest and neck. Mingua's weight pressed him to the deck. He thrust his legs up and closed them in a scissors hold around his opponent's waist.

Mingau threw his weight to the side, toppling them into the water, taking a frantic Finny with them.

Cold water closed over Jack. Mingau's grip slipped from his shoulders to search for another hold. Praying they wouldn't come up under the boat's powerful propellers, Jack lifted his knee and used it as a wedge between them. They broke the choppy surface, coughing and gasping for air.

"Out of the water."

Through blood and seawater, Jack looked up.

Duro stood in the cockpit of the racer with a weapon trained on him.

The yacht bumped against the dock. Engines silent, it rocked wildly in the waves.

Something bumped the side of Jack's neck. He twisted and came face to face with Finny, paddling hard to keep her nose above the choppy waves.

Spitting out a nasty stream of Papiamentu, Mingau pushed him toward the racer.

Defeat grinding hard in his gut, Jack swept the puppy up. He couldn't leave her. A hard scissor kick carried him to the sleek boat. He dropped Finny over the side. Hooking his good arm over the gunwale, he pulled up and slung his leg on board. Wet clothes clung to his skin, restricting his movement. He fell into the boat, pain stealing his breath. Scrambling to his knees, he scanned the public dock. Had Lu escaped? He didn't see her. *Lord, let her get safely home to her grandmother.*

"Where's the collar?" Duro's hand was wrapped around Finny's neck. Wet fur plastered to her body, the shivering pup was the size of a small river rat.

Jack reached into his pocket. He was seasoned enough to know handing over the collar wouldn't save the puppy's life. He held it up. The empty prongs earned him a kick in the gut.

"Where are the diamonds?"

Jack's chest tightened.

The driver, dressed in the mismatched uniform of a rebel

fighter, spoke to Duro. The arms dealer dropped into the front passenger seat. Mingau sat behind the driver staring at Jack, malice in his dark eyes.

Jack spit blood from his mouth. The boat slammed from the crest of one wave to the next, sending shooting pains through his chest and shoulder. He'd failed his mission. Had McCord's life been spared? If Lu and Ava made it to the PZ, the team would take them off the island. Then they'd come after him. They would haul his sorry self off the island—dead or alive.

Chapter 23

Whit helped Ava cross a strip of sand to the parking lot where cars crowded every inch in a silent traffic jam. In their wake, an unhappy Pumpkin picked his way through the coarse beach grass.

Lu followed, struggling to think clearly around the haze of medication and the adrenaline coursing through her veins. *Esteban.* He had been a frightening shadow of the polished man she'd known. His one exposed eye revealed the depth of his hatred. What would he do to Jack?

She lunged and grabbed Whit's flapping shirttail. "You can't leave him." Her tongue obeyed, but her voice held a shrill note. She gulped back a sob. Where was Finny? Her arms felt empty without her little pup snuggled close to her side.

He whirled around, and she ran smack into his chest. Taking a step back, she looked up. His face was contorted with rage.

"Retreat is *not* in my vocabulary. I promised him I'd take *you* to safety." He spun and moved on, his stick kicking up sand.

When Lu left the cabin with Ava, Whit had scooped each of them up in turn and tossed them over the side of the boat onto the dock. She had no time to reconsider obeying Jack's order to go.

Whit motioned to a small wooden bench. "Wait here."

Legs wobbly as cooked spaghetti, she sat with a thump. The rain had stopped, and the late afternoon sun was burning a hole in the cloud cover. With shaking hands, she unbuckled her life vest and set it aside, along with her rain gear, then helped Ava with hers. Holding a miserable Pumpkin in her lap, her friend looked done in.

Lu looked over her shoulder. A tremor ran the length of her. Would she ever see Jack or Finny again?

An engine fired and tires crunched over crushed seashells. A battered sedan pulled up in front of them, and the passenger door swung open. Whit leaned across the console. "Get in."

Lu helped Ava into the back before falling into the seat beside him. "You're stealing a car?"

"The owner is in a boat headed for safety."

Lu shook her head. She wasn't a poster child for being good, but she'd never stolen a car. What would Jack say? She didn't realize she'd asked the question aloud until Whit answered.

"He'd spout 'thou shalt not steal'. Then he'd take it."

She shrank back into her seat, her mind not clear enough to muddle through the paradox of what men like Jack and Whit had to do to complete a mission at any cost. She jammed her knuckles against her lips, remembering Jack's kiss. For a few fleeting seconds she felt as though she'd found where she truly belonged. A tear brimmed and trickled down her cheek. *By force or by guile.* What if he'd only pretended to have feelings for her? He was good and honorable. She couldn't say the same about herself. A pain speared through her heart.

Whit stopped the car at a crossroad. Turning left, they'd be headed toward the beach Jack had shown her on the map.

The other men would be waiting to take them off the island. If they turned to the right, they would circle back around to the more populated end of the island. That road was the shortest way into the city.

"He wants you safe." Whit took the left turn.

Lu twisted her hands together in her lap. Of course, Jack wanted her safe so he could take her home to Gran. She sat up straight. "We have to go after him."

Sharp green eyes snapped with disbelief. "*We?*"

Lu swallowed hard around the lump in her throat. "I can't leave him here."

"Why not?"

The harsh question raked along her nerves. She had to know if the powerful emotions rocking through her were real. Jack was willing to die for her. How could she not take the risk to help him? She had to know what he meant when he said, "this is truth" and then kissed her. She didn't understand her feelings enough to explain them to anyone, least of all to Whit. He'd trounce on her feelings in a second, leaving her heart more bruised than it already was.

"He promised to take me home, and I'm holding him to that promise." She bit her bottom lip hoping Whit didn't see it tremble.

His mouth gaped. "Is *that* all you got? Because he made me promise to finish the job if he couldn't." Whit adjusted the set of his hat. "We can leave Jack's rescue to the team. They have the skills and the resources."

"They could be too late." She leaned toward him. "Do they know where *we* are?"

His throat worked but he didn't speak.

Her heart dipped hard. Surely the boat radio worked. "Whit, do they?"

"Preach radioed we were on our way." He didn't look at

her. "The console and radio got to shot up before I could transmit we'd run into trouble."

"How long will it take us to get to them?" Urgency coursed through her. "They have to take us—me—to safety before they can return to search for him." She sat forward. "I know where Esteban took him."

Green eyes narrowed. "Where?"

"The club."

His thumbs drummed the steering wheel into submission. "You're sure?"

She'd never let herself dwell on the room upstairs and the muted noises the loud music didn't cover. When she asked about it, Esteban had given her a plausible explanation. She'd chosen to ignore her doubts rather than face what she knew in her gut. "I'm sure."

The coastal road heading for the city was quiet. There were no tourists in rental cars traveling too fast. There were no locals riding bikes and burros. The tires of the sedan splashed through the puddles of two villages silent as ghost towns. A stray goat and clucking chickens seemed to be the only residents.

From the backseat came a gentle snore and the continuous rumble of purring as Ava and Pumpkin settled in for a much-needed nap.

Tension rolled off Whit as they left the villages behind. "Don't like it."

Relieved they hadn't run into any trouble, Lu looked at him out of the corners of her eyes. "What don't you like?" If Whit had too many doubts he'd insist on turning around and going back.

195

"No rebels. No government forces." He shook his head. "One of them should be out here, if for no other reason than to stake their claim so the other guy doesn't."

Lu twisted her fingers together in her lap. The quiet that only minutes ago appeared good, now felt ominous.

Brief patches of open water were visible through the low growth of trees and scrub. Whitecaps frosted the deep blues and greens of an ocean stirred by the passing storm. A silver-lined cloudbank hid the face of the sun, its golden rays fanning high into the atmosphere.

Rolling through small villages, Lu's nerves stretched taut. The streets were silent as ghost towns. They passed two technicals parked on the side of the road. A fire glimmered on the beach below. They were on the outskirts of the city before they saw civilians outside their homes and businesses cleaning up and salvaging what they could in the aftermath of the fighting.

Avoiding the main roads, Whit followed Lu's directions to the club. Dread blanketed her. What if they failed to get to Jack in time?

The setting sun peeped from behind a low cloud, shedding an eerie pink light on the buildings. In the backseat Ava stirred awake, rested from her nap.

"Go slow past here." Lu pointed to the entrance of the back alley Jack had raced along carrying her over his shoulder.

Manuel's van was parked next to the motorcycle shed.

Driving to the end of the street, Whit pulled the car into a public lot. "Both of you wait here."

"I'm going with you." Lu reached for the door handle. A hand twice the size of hers and many times stronger covered her fingers.

"You. Stay. Here." He emphasized each word as though she didn't have the ability to understand English.

"But—"

"I take you into this and Jack'll skin me alive."

She loosened her grip. "What are you planning?"

Whit studied the street. "You said he'd be upstairs?"

"Yes." He *had* to be here.

How do you know?

Hating the voice in her head filling her with doubt, she stared at Whit.

"Keep the car running." He pointed at Lu. "You're driving. We'll be in a hurry."

"This is suicide." She couldn't keep the incredulous sneer out of her voice. "You are one man going in alone." She pointed at his crutch. "And not very well armed at that."

A lopsided grin split his face. "Don't worry. I'm not taking the crutch." One foot out the door, he swiveled to look in the back seat. "Wish me luck, Miss Ava?"

Ava's smile wavered. "You need prayers not luck, Whit McCord."

"I'll take as many of those as I can get." He had the audacity to wink before exiting the car and slamming the door. He limped away without his crutch.

"Ava, I'm going into the club."

Ava's eyes widened.

"Take the car and go wait at the edge of the city. We'll meet you there." Lu hesitated. "If we don't show up within the half hour, head for the place Jack showed us on the map." Ava would have to drive through the remote villages by herself. Lu pushed the fear aside. They'd come through and been fine.

That may not be the case going back.

Shut up!

As though reading her mind, Ava patted her shoulder. "I'll send Jack's team back for you." She climbed into the driver's seat. Pumpkin jumped up on the console and rubbed against her shoulder. "If I get there, help will be on its way."

Lucinda smiled at the feisty woman sitting next to her. She wasn't sure how she would have survived the last few days without Ava's friendship. "I love you Ava Endicott Smythe Fairfax Meriwether."

"I love you too, dear." They exchanged a hug that included a miffed Pumpkin.

Lu climbed out and waited for Ava to drive away before crossing the street and walking in the direction of the back alley.

A technical pulled up beside her. The men seated in the bed of the truck whistled and called out lewd comments. The hair on her arms stood on end. These men were now the law.

The window on the passenger side rolled down. A young man dressed in a uniform shouted a suggestive slur inspiring more idiocy from the peanut gallery in the back.

Lu forced a laugh from between lips stiff with fear and waved a hand as though she appreciated his comment. She'd learned early on at the club not to tell the men they were jerks or to go home to their wife or girlfriend. To her relief the truck sped away.

Cutting between buildings, she hurried to Manuel's white van. The double rear doors were unlocked. Pulling down on the handle, she swung one open. Blood smeared the floor. A tremor quaked through her. She backed away. Were they too late?

Refusing to give into her terror, she ducked inside the motorcycle shed. Her bike sat to one side, an emergency key in a small magnetic box hidden on the frame. It didn't take but a minute to find a second larger bike Whit could manage with his injured leg. The key was tucked in a saddlebag pocket. Leaving keys in the ignitions, she ran for the back door of the club. Whit already had too much of a lead on her.

Entering through the backdoor, Lu held a hand to her chest to calm the frantic beating of her heart. She paused at the kitchen and breathed in the familiar tang of spices. One by one her former co-workers stopped what they were doing and stared at her. They had never seen her rumpled and without makeup.

"Is Esteban here?"

She heard muffled shouting from the room overhead.

Uneasiness filled the room as everyone wordlessly returned to their work, filling platters and prepping dishes. They refused to acknowledge what was happening upstairs as she had done in the past.

She stepped back into the hall. Where was Whit? Climbing the stairs, she struggled to control her breathing. At this rate, she'd hyperventilate and pass out. On the top step, she leaned against the closed door and listened.

"Tell me what you did with the diamonds."

Esteban. His voice was cold and demanding.

She heard no response other than what sounded like an open-handed slap.

"Manuel, show him how skilled you are with your knife."

Tears blurred her vision as she backed down the stairs. On the bottom step, hands closed around her waist. She almost peed her pants.

"You better have a good reason for being here." Whit's furious words hissed close to her ear.

"They're using a knife on him." The words were half whisper, half sob. "I can get E-Esteban and Manuel out of there."

"I'll go in and kill them."

She didn't doubt Whit meant every word. "I have a plan." Before he could protest, she jabbed her elbow into his solar plexus and lunged from the stairwell. Running down the hall, she passed the kitchen and stepped into the open barroom. A few of the regulars sat at a table in the corner. As she walked past, Roberto clamped his beefy hand around her forearm.

Her reaction was swift. She kicked him.

Surprise changed to anger burning in his eyes. He opened his mouth to speak.

Lu snapped her hand up, palm out. She had to look a fright because he stopped and glanced at his friends. They stared at her in shock. She leaned down so not one would miss a word. "If you want to live, get out."

She straightened up, her voice sugar sweet. "Let me clear your table." Gathering up all the paper napkins, she snitched the red votive cup containing a burning candle. Walking past the small service station she grabbed more napkins and two oil cruets. She paused at the men's restroom and looked back at the men staring after her before entering.

Plugging the sink she dumped the oil in the basin, threw the paper napkins on top, and lit them on fire with the candle. Exiting the room, she left the door ajar. She pulled the handle of the firebox as she walked past. The banshee scream of the alarm hurt her ears.

The men scrambled to leave, tripping over chairs and each other in their haste.

Dodging tables, Lu crouched behind the service station. Footsteps pounded down the stairs. Manuel and Esteban ran past her hiding place, drawn by the smoke at the far end of the room.

Slipping into the hall, she bumped into Tito. Snatching the pitcher of beer from his hands, she ran for the stairs.

Chapter 24

"Aah!" Jack clamped his lips shut. *Waterboarding?* Was he strong enough to control his thoughts and not panic? A hand on his shoulder shook him.

"Jack, wake up." Manuel's voice had changed to Lu's voice.

His gut plummeted. His mind had already slipped off the rails.

Someone yanked on his bindings.

They're tight enough, already. He'd tell the scumbag if he could get his jaw to work.

The bindings loosened, and the arm he could feel swung to his side, prickling painfully with the unhindered circulation of blood. His fuzzy mind scrambled to figure out what came next. He blinked away rivulets of moisture running from his hair and into his eyes.

Lucinda's face wavered before him.

Lord, help. They gave me a hallucinogenic.

She dipped away. Someone played with the cuff of his pants. *You have my knife.* She appeared again, in front of him.

"Come on, Jack. Let's get out of here."

"Wha…" She looked and sounded so real, but it wasn't her. She was safe. He had to believe that.

"Jack." A hand cupped his stinging cheek.

He executed a fumbling grab and missed. Tightening his core muscles he expected another blow to his gut. None came. He went with it, not letting his confusion slow him down. He leveraged his legs and lunged.

"Jack!"

Mingau had shrunk...was smaller...and softer. An arm slipped around his back.

He looked down at Lucinda tucked up beneath his shoulder. She'd been there before. "Lulabe—"

"Yes, Jack. It's me. You need to help us. Walk." She moved. A hand prodded his back.

"Yer on th'boat..." His words were thick but his feet moved, one foot in front of the other.

"Not without you, Jack."

"Head screamin'."

"It's the fire alarm."

"Fire?"

"I set it."

"You hate fire."

"Yes, but I'm thinking maybe I love *you*."

His brain spun. Had he already cracked? He'd rather hallucinate this conversation than feel the pain of whatever torture Duro was doling out. He guessed it had to do with fire. Smoke caught hot and dry in the back of his throat— maybe he was dead. He'd expected to go to heaven.

"Hustle it up, you two lovebirds."

Whit! Jack lurched forward. Strong arms caught him. *The team had come.* He stumbled and fell forward ending up across wide shoulders in a fireman's carry. "Duro?" The name sputtered from his lips.

"Slipped past me. Took out Mingau." Whit's voice was strained.

A cool wind washed over Jack, taking some of the smoke with it as he rocked to the rhythm of Whit's limping hustle.

Jack's boots hit the ground.

Lu's hands were on him. "Lift your leg over." He reached for her.

"Climb on the bike, Preach." Whit's voice rumbled in his ear.

He staggered. Whit kept him from doing a face plant. He settled on the seat that was too low for his height. His dream Lulabelle brushed past his knees. One bounce and the bike fired up. The vibration of the engine and her close presence flowed through him. He leaned to the side trying to look into her eyes. "Gotta be heaven."

"You're not dead yet, Jack. Quit talking and wipe that silly grin off your face."

He did what he'd wanted to do for days. He wrapped his arm around her and rested his cheek on her temple. "Tiny."

"Shush up, mister. I'm trying to rescue you."

"'Kay." He slumped closer trying to find a position that didn't hurt. Blood ran down his neck from the nick behind his ear where Manuel had chosen to begin carving on him.

She did some fiddling. When he felt the fabric of his shirt tug across his back, he realized she'd secured his bum arm. He tried to see what she'd done, but she pushed him away with her elbow.

"Shouldn't you be praying or something?"

He had to think about that. Didn't know if he had to pray in heaven. Didn't matter if she disagreed. He was in heaven. Somebody placed his feet on the pegs. The motorcycle whipped forward and he hung on, the cool air blowing the cobwebs from his mind. The end of a scarf tickled his neck. He recognized his flowery sling. It was wrapped around Lu's throat.

A horn honked. A technical passed them headed in the opposite direction. Familiar buildings flashed by. Hair the color of sunshine caressed his cheek. The last bit of mist cleared from his brain and painful clarity struck him.

"Lu?"

"Are you with me?" She yelled at him over her shoulder.

"I'm on a mo'cycle...with you." His mouth had trouble working.

"Riding off into the sunset, Jack."

He looked over his shoulder and set his sights on Whit following at a distance. "You set a fire?"

"A smoky one in the sink."

There were holes in what was taking place. "The team?"

"On the beach."

His heart flipped. Only McCord and Lu came for him. "Ava?"

"In the car, headed toward the beach. Getting you out took longer than I expected."

He struggled to wrap his hurting head around what she was saying. Where was Finny? Last he remembered Duro had placed the pup on a stack of boxes. Her fluffy white face and black eyes had been a focal point for him. Had they picked up on that? "Finny?" he choked out.

Lu let go of one handle. She covered his hand with hers and shifted it a little. The knit fabric of her shirt stretched over a lump. It moved beneath his palm. His heart pinged all the way to his toes. He let out the breath backed up in his chest.

"She okay?"

Her hair brushed his cheek as she nodded in the affirmative.

Thank you, Lord. Lu would be devastated by the loss of her pup. The road passed beneath the tires in a blur. He'd be a stiff mess soon. Wrapped around Lu, he wanted to do nothing more than close his eyes and enjoy the moment. Maybe dream about the future. Did they have one together? To get off this island alive, he had to stay alert. The future would have to take care of itself.

Give it to me, son.

The hair on Jack's arms prickled. The Holy Spirit had prodded him along for many years now, but this voice was different. Had called him "son". That meant... Jack glanced up, unsure what he'd see. Maybe a hand coming out of a cloud or a pillar of fire.

"God?" Not a blasphemy but the name of the Holy One. The One he most wanted to understand.

"What?" Lu turned her head. Her ear brushed his lips.

"God's talkin' to me." In his arms, she stiffened.

"What'd He say?"

"Gotta give Him somethin'." A whole bunch of somethings. His bruised pride. An arm that didn't work. A woman who had somehow found her way into his heart.

"I hate to butt into a conversation between you and God, but can you excuse yourself long enough to help me watch for the road up ahead?"

He wanted to laugh but it would hurt too much. He just held on and did as she asked. "Left."

She nodded her understanding, probably figuring he and God would resume their conversation. She leaned low around the corner.

He bit his tongue. She was reckless, this Lulabelle of his. She would keep him on his toes, if he had any left after this ride. Beneath his arm, she tensed and slowed the bike.

A car he didn't recognize was pulled off the road near a thicket of bushes. "Who?"

Lu sat stiff.

A diminutive woman stepped out of the brush carrying an orange cat and a honkin' big purse.

Ava.

Lu slumped. The bike wobbled. Jack dropped his boots to the ground helping her balance.

"Hefe!" Simao followed on Ava's heels.

Lu slid from the bike and stopped short.

Jack blinked, sure his mind was playing tricks on him. She'd tucked his slack hand into the side of her pant's waistband. The pain in his face was no match for the amusement rocketing through him, causing him to grin like a fool. "Wish I had feelin' in my hand." He couldn't help but stare where his fingers rested on her hipbone.

"If you could feel anything, your hand wouldn't be there." She pulled on his sleeve and dislodged it, letting his arm drop to his side.

"Cruel woman."

Whit dismounted and limped over to help him off the bike. "This isn't how I planned it." He looked at Lu, a scowl furrowing his brow. "She doesn't follow orders."

Leaning on his teammate, Jack lifted his leg up and over the bike, getting off with a stumbling step. "Never will."

With a napkin he'd grabbed at the club, Whit applied pressure to the nick behind Jack's ear. "You're not seriously considering getting mixed up with her, are you?"

Jack shrugged and touched his arm. Until he knew the extent of the damage to his arm, he couldn't answer the question. Besides, hadn't he just given the whole mess over to God?

"Simao and I are waiting for you." Ava beamed. She wrapped her free arm around the boy. "I found him walking out of the city."

The boy looked up at Jack, all hopeful eyes.

Whit growled with impatience.

A rustle in the bushes snapped both men to full alert.

Angelina stepped from the bushes.

Jack pointed to the bulging pockets on the boy's shorts. "What you got?"

The boy's hands dropped to protect his treasures. "Things we need."

"What things?"

Simao shuffled his bare feet and remained silent.

"We have to go." Whit prodded Ava toward the car.

Forcing himself to work through his pain, Jack held out his hand and spoke in a commanding '*hefe*' voice, "Empty them."

Head down, the boy unloaded his pockets. A pack of gum, granola bar, cell phone.

Jack's heart jumped and landed hard against his hurting ribs. He pressed the phone to his palm with his thumb and let the rest fall to the ground. "Into the car, Simao."

The boy peeked up at Jack then grabbed his sister's hand and ran to the car.

Jack turned to follow and stumbled straight into Lu's arms.

The evening breeze carried the growl of a vehicle approaching from behind. Whit opened the driver's door. "Let's go."

Lu's arms dropped away leaving Jack hollow with disappointment. Moving slowly, he climbed into the car, riding shotgun. Pushing buttons on Simao's stolen phone, Jack listened to it ring while Lu squeezed between the front seats. Taking off Ava's scarf, she looped it around his neck.

"Your nickel." Caleb Fallon, a member of the SeaMount team answered.

"Preach here."

"You missed the revival." There was relief with a veneer of annoyance in Fallon's response.

"Yeah, tell me about it."

"Say location."

Jack recalled what he'd seen on the maps. "Seven miles out of the city."

Ava spoke up from the backseat. "We're four miles from Canna Bay."

He relayed the information.

"Copy that." There was a pause and then Fallon continued, "We'll make the extraction there."

Jack pressed the end button. "New plan. Canna Bay." Trying to control the amount of pain he inflicted on himself, he shifted so Lu had better access to his arm. "Must have started to move down the coast when we didn't show up."

"Second team could cover the PZ." The only speed limit Whit was minding was the one he set, which exceeded everything posted along this stretch of the coast. Hitting the outskirts of a village, he didn't slow. "Came through here earlier and saw two technicals. Keep an eye out."

The trucks were still there on the side of the road. The men were gathered around one. The whine of the car's engine drew their attention.

Whit sped past. "They'll follow."

In the passenger side mirror, Jack watched the men jump into action. Both trucks were soon on their tail. They had less than two miles to go. "Ladies, get down."

Lu and Ava pushed the children to the floor and then scooted down in the seat, upsetting Pumpkin who'd been napping on Ava's lap.

Jack called Fallon. Time to give the man some specifics. The vehicles behind them gained ground.

"Red Dog."

"Coming in hot."

"Of course you are."

"I have my package and then some."

There was a pause. "Some *what*?"

"Older woman and McCord."

"Copy that. Need a medic?"

"Me. And McCord." Smiling hurt but he couldn't stop. "Women and kids are okay."

The cool monotone, every-thing-is-under-control voice cracked. *"Kids?"*

"Two of them." He pictured Fallon chewing on that.

"You got yourself a *family*, Preach?"

He looked over his shoulder at Simao and Angelina on the floor playing with Finny. His grin grew wider. "Complete with dog."

The silence from the other end was deafening. Voice strained, Fallon asked, "How big is the dog?"

Jack laughed. For all the pain it caused him, it felt good, too. "Smaller than the cat."

The connection went dead.

He hit the End button. "Fallon is rearranging his seating chart."

"Persnickety." Whit pressed the gas pedal as the car crested a hill and left the pavement to land with a jarring thump.

Jack sucked in his breath, determined not to be a wimp and groan. The ocean came into view stretching to the horizon. Below them the pure white sand of the beach glowed.

"Where are they?" Whit's gaze shifted between the road and the rearview mirror.

Jack scanned the coastline ignoring the wide expanse of

beach. "Bear right." A cart path led to the other end of the dunes. The land rose in a gradual incline forming a ridge high enough to provide cover for a rescue launch in the water below. Following well-worn ruts through the rough beach grass, Whit drove between boulders and stunted sea grape bushes. Taking a sharp turn at the top, he jammed on the brakes beside a large boulder.

The front and back doors on the passenger side were pulled open by two heavily armed men crouched in the shadow of the rock.

"'Bout time you showed up." Logan St. John glanced at Jack's abused face and makeshift sling. He shoved his own side arm into Jack's hand and moved back.

Jack bailed out, Whit on his heels. "Women and kids in the back."

"Got them." Ethan Thomas handed Whit a weapon then unceremoniously hauled everyone out of the back. His dark mahogany face split into a tense smile as a bullet pinged off the trunk of the car. He scooped up Angelina and herded the others over the crest of the dune as Whit and St. John lay down cover fire.

The tip of Pumpkin's tail disappeared over the dune just as Jack took a knee behind the back wheel.

The truck following them halted about one hundred feet back. Fire flashed from the muzzle of an M16. The rapid *tat-tat* bounced across the hillside. Jack joined the others in returning fire.

Boots scuffed in the dirt, and Whit landed beside him.

"Get out of here, Preach."

"Think I can't hold my own?" Jack took aim at the gleaming headlights and fired. They shattered leaving the hill awash in the low light of the moon.

"Don't be a hero. Get to the boat."

In Jack's peripheral vision, a white ball bounced from the car. "Finny!"

"Leave her." A spat of gunfire jerked Whit's attention back to the job at hand.

Spooked, the puppy ran in the wrong direction.

"Cover me." A volley of rough words rang in Jack's ears, as he hunched low and followed the puppy. He scrambled for cover behind a rock he wished was a great deal bigger. Every painful inch of him screamed *idiot*. "Finny. Com'ere, girl."

Confused, she stopped.

Behind him, St. John joined McCord, calling him every kind of fool. Ignoring their smear on his parental origins, he jammed Logan's weapon into his waistband and held out his hand. "Com'on girl." He enticed her with little kissing noises.

The ploy succeeded in getting the puppy's attention, as well as ramping up the abuse from the men protecting his backside. Another juicy smooch and she ran to him, all fluffy fur and flapping ears. He clamped her beneath his good arm like a football and waited for an opportunity to retreat.

As one, Whit and Logan let loose with suppressive fire.

Stumbling, Jack left his cover and ran for the car. Bullets kicked up sand around him. His feet felt heavy, and he couldn't move fast enough. A bullet seared across his ribs. He fell in a clumsy roll. Trying to protect the pup from being crushed, he inflicted more agony on himself. Another bullet spit sand in his face. One more roll and he fell behind the car. Before he could yank his legs out of sight, a bullet burned through his calf.

"Get to the boat." Whit didn't look his way. "We'll finish up with these yahoos."

Jack didn't have any argument left in him. Blood, wet and sticky, oozed down his side and leg. Pushing through the pain, he focused on getting to the launch. He staggered and pitched forward, his leg not working right. Leaning against a boulder, he caught his breath before crawling over the crest of the grassy dune. Below, the dark silhouette of the waiting launch broke the glimmer of the water. He slid down the unstable sand dune, stumbled across the narrow beach, and splashed into the stinging cold water holding Finny high. Determined not to die by drowning this late in the game, he kept his head above water.

Hands closed around him.

"Hold steady." Ethan half-carried, half-towed him through the water to the side of the launch.

Logan's twin brother, Gabe, had the motor idling. Caleb held an M16 trained on the crest of the dune, waiting for Whit and Logan to come over the top.

Jack handed Finny up to Lu.

Ethan tightened his grip and tossed him over the gunwale.

Falling headfirst into the launch, he sprawled at Lu's feet. The boat rocked and Ethan climbed in.

Caleb lifted his weapon. "Here they come."

Whit and Logan rushed in low.

Jack struggled to his knees. He pressed close to Lu. "Get down." Everything faded to gray. He blinked to clear his vision, unable to hear her response through the cotton blocking his ears.

Whit and Logan hit the water at the same time the silhouettes of four men appeared on the moonlit ridge. Ethan and Caleb fired.

Too exhausted and weak to keep his weapon high, Jack lowered it. Accidentally shooting a member of the team would be frowned upon.

Whit rolled into the boat followed by Logan. Loaded to the max and sitting low in the water, the launch still had plenty of power as it pulled away from the coastline. Caleb and Logan continued cover fire, until the launch was out of range for the men on the beach.

Shuffling for space, Whit scooted up next to Jack. "*Whooee.* That was close." He punched Jack on the shoulder.

Jack gritted his teeth against the pain pounding through his body. A gray mist clouded his vision.

Caleb leaned close and sniffed. "The teetotalin' preacher-man smells like a brewery."

Hair flying in the wind, Lu shouted over the roar of the boat's motor. "I dumped a pitcher of beer over his head to bring him around." Her words froze the action on board. A wave of laughter swelled into hoots and foot stomping, adding to the already unbearable roar in Jack's ears.

"Bunch of hyenas." Jack's words came out garbled.

Caleb jumped on him like a flea, hands everywhere yanking at his clothing. "You're hit." He eased Jack back on the floor of the boat. "Why didn't you say something?"

Pain ripped through Jack as the boat porpoised from one wave to the next. Behind him, paper tore and someone applied pressure to his side. He should tell them to look at his leg, too, but the words wouldn't form on his tongue.

Lucinda looked down at him. He blinked hard, trying to bring her almond-shaped eyes into focus.

"Jack. Stay with us."

He wanted to tell her he'd be okay. Just hold his hand because maybe he loved her, too. But his lips and tongue wouldn't co-operate, which was probably a good thing because for some reason he shouldn't be saying that to her. He was tired. Too tired to talk. He needed to close his eyes for a minute...

Chapter 25

"Jack?" Lu placed a hand on his shoulder. "Is he dead?" She didn't recognize her own voice, so raspy and raw.

Whit joined Caleb. "Nah. He's too ornery to die." Together they worked over Jack, discovering the wound to his leg. Whit yelled to the men in the front of the launch. His words sailed past Lu on the wind. "Hit. Bleeding."

IV tubing and a bag of fluid materialized from the front of the boat.

She scrunched her eyes shut and hugged Finny tight. "God, please don't let him die." Praying came easier when scared spitless and out of options.

Whit bent over Jack's leg, knife in hand. He sliced the pant leg open to the thigh and peeled the cloth back. Ethan and Caleb helped him roll Jack so a pressure bandage could be applied to his calf. She caught only the occasional word they spoke but enough to know they were praying as they worked on their fallen comrade.

Time moved too slowly, and it felt like forever before the motor on the launch idled back and the boat slowed as they pulled alongside a dimly lit dock where a cluster of armed men awaited them. One man stood apart from the others, the wind tugging at his loose fitting shirt and pants.

Dock ropes sailed through the air. The boat engine went

silent. Curt words were spoken low and urgent. Over the slosh and roll of the water, the distinct *whap-whap* of rotor blades beat the air. Ethan handed the children and Finny up to the waiting men. Ava was next with Pumpkin.

Lu shook her head in refusal. "I'm staying with him."

"Not possible, little lady." Ethan gathered her and Finny into his arms. Ignoring her screech of protest, he tossed her into the waiting arms of another equally large man.

She wrenched to get away and he let go. She fell to the wood planks. Her bottom stung on impact.

The men handed a stretcher down into the boat. Thankfully, they were gentler with Jack. She scrambled out of the way as they lifted him from the boat and ran to the waiting helicopter, ducking low beneath the spinning blades.

"Where are they taking him?" The men melted into the darkness, leaving only the two children, Ava, and the lone man on the dock.

"He'll get the best medical care."

The gravelly voice caught Lu's attention. The man's face was crisscrossed with old scars. A full mustache dressed his upper lip.

"Come with me." He included Ava and the children in his command.

Following him, they trooped off the dock and up a stone walkway where palms, banana trees, and anthurium danced in the breeze casting a patchwork of moving night shadows.

The helicopter lifted off and Lu's chest ached. The lights and the whining throb faded in the distance. She wiped away tears before following Ava and the children indoors.

They huddled together in the airy front entry like the war refugees they were. Lu pushed damp hair away from her face. Surrounded by a soft neutral palette echoing the colors of the sand and sea, the peaceful villa was a welcome respite from the terror of the last few days.

The man beckoned them to follow him to the dining room where a light meal was set out. Eyes wide, Simao and Angelina climbed up on chunky teak chairs. Their host wasn't as old as Lu first thought. Something terrible had happened to him, leaving him scarred and limping.

"Who are you?"

"Sam Traven."

"The SeaMount Agency?"

He nodded.

"Jack's badly hurt." She couldn't let go of her worry.

"You're tired, Miss Lavalle. Have a bite to eat and then rest."

"When will I see him again?"

He ushered her to the table. "I suggest you begin your meal before the men come in or there will be nothing left for you to eat."

Flatware clattered as Ava wrestled Simao for a spoon. "That doesn't belong in your pocket, young man."

Lu didn't want to eat. She wanted answers. "Jack said he would take me home to Gran." His promise had become monumentally important.

"Much has changed, Lucinda. The mission began as a simple extraction. It's now more complicated." An aura of power surrounded Sam.

She shook her head, as though she could deny his words. "I want to go home."

"Esteban Duro has connections to your hometown."

The blood drained from her head in a terrifying *swoosh*. Lightheaded, she groped for the table and lowered herself into a chair. "No."

Pouring a glass of cold water from a pitcher, he handed it to her.

Her hand trembled and the rim of the glass clacked against her teeth. "Is Trent involved?"

He stopped to think before speaking. "We don't have all the answers yet."

Lu set the glass down and clasped her hands across her stomach, hoping to press the sick feeling away. Her sleepy hometown, where *nothing* ever happened, was now a hot bed of intrigue.

Ava dug through her purse and pulled out a plastic water bottle. "You'll want these." She handed the bottle to Sam.

He accepted it turning it over and over before looking at her puzzled.

Ava clapped her hands together. "Jack didn't think anyone saw him do it, but *I* did." She pointed at the bottle. "Look close. He hid the diamonds in there."

Like an electrical shock, Lu's nerves tingled to her toes.

"I grabbed it when we ran. Couldn't leave those beauties behind."

Sam lowered the bottle. "They're evidence."

"Better to be held in an evidence locker than be guzzled down by a looter."

Lu sucked in her breath. "Ava!"

Her friend shook her head. "I have no illusions. If the rebels don't loot my yacht and home, the island people," she glanced at Simao and Angelina, "will make use of them."

A door banged open and the tramp of booted feet announced the arrival of the team. They filed into the dining room, filling it with their powerful presence.

Ethan sat across from the children, his gaze never leaving them. Whit slipped into the seat next to Angelina. The twin brothers sat across from each other, eerily alike in looks and mannerisms. Caleb was the last to enter the room, casting an intent gaze around the table, he sat at the far end.

Sam said grace then took his seat at the head of the table. A man of Asian descent served bowls of savory soup accompanied by crusty bread. Talk was nonexistent as everyone concentrated on eating. The silence magnified the quiet *tink* of spoons against bowls and the clatter of butter knives.

The peacefulness grated on Lu's nerves. She set down her spoon. "Will Jack live?" Tears welled in her eyes, and she quickly wiped them away. She tossed her head back, daring anyone to pity her.

Whit set his butter knife aside, his green gaze unwavering. "We had the best tools and training available for field first aid." He glanced at Sam then back at Lu. "The rest is in God's hands."

Jack wrestled to push back the darkness threatening to swallow him. Something pressed into the crook of his arm. A band tightened above his elbow. He jerked to get away, but his weak defense did nothing to dislodge the pressure, which melted away after only a few seconds. A needle pricked his arm and once again he sank into the black abyss of oblivion.

Lu stared out the window of the private jet. Puffy clouds glowed in the bright morning sunlight. Far below, sparkling white caps laced the blue expanse of the ocean. The whine of engines accompanied her swirling thoughts. All of them led back to Jack.

According to Gran, love was a choice. Heat crept up her neck and cheeks. Falling in love was easy. Maybe too easy. Could she *choose* to love? Jack was a man of integrity. So much so, maybe he wouldn't want anything to do with someone like her. She touched her lips, remembering his kiss. Had it meant anything to him? The unanswerable question surfaced frequently in her mind.

She ran her fingers through Finny's shining coat. Upon waking this morning, the pup had been beside her on the bed, clean and fluffy with a tiny pink bow clipped to the fur of one ear. Discovering Finny had been taken from her room and returned without her knowing was a tad unsettling.

Stealing a covert glance at Sam Traven, she pushed back the impatience streaking through her. She'd awakened ready to confront him, only to discover Finny was cleaner than her. A detour to the rose marble shower became an adventure in luxury, beginning with jets of water streaming at her from all sides, and ending with shampooing and conditioning her hair three times with the expensive toiletries provided.

A swell of good-natured jeers rose from the group of men playing checkers at the other end of the private jet's cabin. From conversations she'd overheard, the other agents were concerned about Jack, too.

Removing a small tube of hand cream from her pocket, she applied it liberally. In her search through the bathroom vanity looking for a hair dryer, she'd found a small fortune in brand new lotions and makeup. She'd used what she needed then stepped into the bedroom to find the bed made and clean clothes set out. Finny sat in the middle of the puffy spread, wagging her tail and smiling a goofy doggie grin.

Yesterday's clothes had disappeared. She had no choice

but to dress in the lavender slacks and plum-colored knit tunic top. They fit perfectly, adding to the freaky feeling running rampant along her spine. The sooner she was on her way home to Kansas, the better.

A red banknote with a picture of Romanesque architecture fluttered in front of her face, pulling her from her reverie. She batted it away as Whit fell into the seat beside her. "What's that for?"

"Figured your thoughts were worth more than the proverbial penny." His lopsided grin slipped into a grimace as he stretched his leg.

"And a euro is worth *sooo* much more in *Kansas*."

"Ohhh." He waggled his fingers in front of her nose. "*Somebody's* grumpy."

The man was a full-fledged loony bird. Lu turned back to the window, hoping he'd catch on to the fact she didn't want his company.

"Sam just received the latest word on Preach."

She whipped back around, heart pounding. "He's alive?" Sam refused to give her any news this morning before they left the island. Granted, time had been short, but he could have told her *something*. It would have saved her from vacillating between mourning Jack as dead and hoping—and even *praying*—that he lived.

Whit nodded.

Her heart jumped with joy, then crashed as he continued to stare at the floor. "What aren't you telling me?" The words caught in her throat.

He looked at her, the lines of his face etched deep. "He's stable and will recover from the bullet wounds and broken collar bone."

Whispering a quiet "thank you", she exhaled the breath she hadn't realized she'd been holding.

He rubbed the palm of his hand against his thigh. "His arm is a different story."

Jack was alive and recovering. She clung to the news. "What's wrong with his arm?"

"It's useless."

"I know that." She leaned forward, glaring at him. "What's the medical diagnosis?"

Lips drawn tight, he looked at her. The bleakness in his green gaze shattered her composure, leaving her trembling all over.

"It's a lateral traction injury."

She shook her head. The words were a medical mumbo-jumbo buzzing in her brain.

"The arm was stretched. It's like a nerve amputation with the skin and, fortunately for Preach, the artery and veins miraculously still intact."

She closed her eyes. "C-can the doctors fix it?" She looked at him, not wanting to believe the worst.

Whit leaned toward her, probing her with an intense look. "If they can't, will you run the other way?"

Lu's fingers curled around the arm of the chair. Jack had been injured because of her.

Whit looked up with a disgusted huff. "There's another one leaving the island half *loco*." Ethan hovered out of hearing range. Without a backward glance, Whit stood, brushed past the big man, and joined the rest of the team.

Lu didn't have time to wonder whom else came off the island crazy. Ethan settled into the chair Whit vacated, a frown furrowing his brow. The man was huge, even by the standard set by the other men on the SeaMount team. Broad shoulders and legs as wide as tree trunks, she wondered how he found clothing to fit.

"Hi." Lu's tentative greeting went unnoticed. Her bottom still hurt from being tossed around the night before.

His wide hand swallowed up the cushioned armrest. "Tell me about Simao and Angelina." The melodious soft drawl was at odds with his size.

"Simao was on the pier the day it blew up. He followed us out of the water. I told Sam all I know."

He looked at her, and she wished he hadn't. His tortured gaze cut a jagged hole in her heart.

"Tell me, please. I want to know everything."

Lu leaned back against the headrest. "Simao led us to a soup kitchen run by a man who had been a business acquaintance of Ava's husband." Lu wondered how Ava was doing. She'd chosen to stay at the villa with the children while Sam searched for any living relatives they might have on the island. "The little rascal is a world class pickpocket."

She shared all she knew in just a few minutes. She waited for a response.

He sat quiet, unmoving.

Had he fallen asleep? She turned to look at him. His eyes were open and he appeared to be staring into space at something she couldn't see. Lu turned away feeling as though she'd interrupted something private. Snuggling Finny close, she stared out the window at the clouds. Not long after, Ethan rose and left.

"A cold ocean breeze whipped Lu's hair across her neck and shoulders. Holding Finny close to keep the pup warm, she stared up at the monolithic yellow building laced with white gingerbread and bathed in the late afternoon sunshine.

The men were removing gear from the van that had met them at the airport.

"Home sweet home." Whit bumped past her and jumped up onto the loading dock where a large overhead door yawned open. He glanced at Lu, an easy grin on his lips. "Take care to mind your manners. Aggie is a stickler for that stuff."

Caleb nodded in agreement. "She runs a tight ship."

"No swearing allowed." Logan slid a hard equipment case onto the dock.

Gabe tossed up a soft duffle. "She's not fond of pets, either. Had to find Corkscrew another home."

Lu clutched Finny tight. Would this Aggie person tell her she couldn't have Finny here?

Their driver, Charlie, approached from the other side of the bus. "He was a snake." Ruffling Finny's ears, he added, "And ten feet long."

"He was quiet." Gabe chucked another bag onto the dock. "Didn't bother a soul." The defense of his former pet earned him a duffle in the face.

"Com'on, Lucinda." Charlie headed for a set of cement steps on one side of the dock.

The honeybees stirred, and there was a whole lot of buzzing beneath her ribs. Following him up the steps to the service entrance door, she took a deep breath, willing them to settle down.

The brightly lit hall opened into a small foyer dominated by an open stairway curving up to the next floor. Across the room, a wall of windows framed a gym outfitted with heavy-duty equipment. Other doors opened off the foyer including one leading to a wide deck, but there was no time to explore. Charlie was already halfway up the wide sweep of stairs, talking as he went.

"This time of day, we'll find Aggie on the side porch." He glanced back at Lu. "She'll provide what you need."

Lu nodded. What she needed was a ticket home, but that wouldn't happen anytime soon. At the top, she stepped into a sitting room. Wishing she could sink into one of the overstuffed chairs and warm up in front of the small blaze crackling in the beach stone fireplace, she raced to keep up with Charlie.

He crossed the room and opened a door to a covered porch overlooking an herb garden and green house. Beyond that, beach grass swayed in the breeze coming off the rough and tumble ocean.

"Aggie? Lucinda's here."

A puffy mint green jacket occupied the bulk of a rocking chair. On top of the jacket's upturned collar sat a pink and yellow knit hat, its pom pom loose and swaying with each rock of the chair. The top of the hat reached only as high as the middle of the chair back. The toes of comfortable black shoes similar to the ones Gran wore, barely reached the boards of the deck. The woman was about her own height.

The buzzing in Lu's stomach eased. She stepped in front of the chair. Dark eyes peered at her from the narrow space between cap and coat collar.

"Sit." Clothing muffled the single word.

The door closed, signaling Charlie's retreat. Shivering in the September wind, she sat in the chair next to Aggie.

"So you're Preach's woman."

Shock rippled through her. "Well, no. I mean... I'm not..." Thoughts scattering on the sharp wind, she shut her mouth, the only alternative to blathering.

"Colder than on the island, I expect."

Lu wrapped her arms around a trembling Finny. "Yes."

The green-gray water of the Atlantic Ocean and cutting wind was a sharp contrast to the soft tropical breezes and deep turquoise of the Caribbean.

"You'll need warm clothes."

"My money is in the bank on the island." Though she couldn't see enough of Aggie to determine her age, the shoes and tremor in her voice were clues that she was up there in years.

"Sam will get it for you." A mittened hand waved dismissively. "But not to use for clothing, mind you."

"Thank you." Rigid with cold, Lu hoped she had warmer clothes soon.

The capped head swiveled toward her, dark eyes snapping. "You're what Preach needs."

Lu's heart flipped. She wanted to see him so badly it hurt. "Have you talked to him?"

The corners of Aggie's eyes crinkled. "Not yet." She rocked faster and looked at the horizon where the sun had begun to descend. "Not yet."

The door to the porch swung open.

"Honey, I'm home!" Whit burst through the doorway, shaggy blonde hair blowing in the wind. His long stride ate up the distance between him and Aggie. Sweeping the woman from her chair, he wrapped her in a bear hug. Over her head, he winked at Lu. "Didn't we tell you she was a tyrant?"

Aggie boxed his ear with her mittened hand. "You did nothing of the sort, Whit McCord. Put me down."

Still grinning, he did as she asked.

Wisps of gray escaped her skewed hat. She looked at Lu. "What did they tell you?"

All the tension drained from Lucinda. "To mind my manners, not swear, and you don't like pets." And she'd swallowed all of it whole, like a pelican stealing fish on the pier. "You don't mind having Finny here?"

Aggie clicked her tongue and shook her mitten at Whit.

Lu was sure there was a finger in it pointing straight at him.

"Bring the puppy inside. She needs a coat, too." Aggie pushed Whit aside and walked to the open door. "You live in a barn, McCord?"

He snatched her cap off by the pom pom. "Not anymore, but old habits die hard." The hat dangled from his hand.

Lu wondered how many times he'd yanked on it for the pom pom to be so loose.

Aggie's entrance into the sitting room created happy chaos. Surrounded by the men, the only thing visible was the tight gray bun on the top of her head. In this place the men called home, they'd created a family with Aggie at the heart.

Lu collapsed into a chair close to the hearth. Gabe added logs to the fire. Jack missed this homecoming. Was he okay? Other than what Whit told her on the jet, no one had said a word. Would he want to see her knowing he'd lost the use of his arm on the mission to bring her home? Chest tightening, she held back the sob that threatened to be her undoing. *She would not fall apart in front of all these men.*

Finny stretched up and licked her chin. She smoothed her hand over the pup's head as she studied her surroundings. Pots of tiny pink orchids sat atop each small side table. She stroked a leaf.

"They're real." Gabe took the seat across from her. "Sam has a thing for them."

"They're beautiful. This place is beautiful."

Gabe nodded. "It's a replica of the original Victorian hotel that sat on this same bluff. He demolished the original down to the ground and resurrected it with all the modern amenities."

"Lucinda." Charlie came out from behind what, in another era, would have been the registration desk, and stood in front of her. "Sam wants to meet with you."

"Now?" The pace of events left her little time to catch her breath.

"Come with me."

Every gaze in the room followed her as she walked past a baby grand piano to the hall. On her right, she caught a glimpse of a fancy dining room set for dinner.

"In here." Charlie opened a door and stood aside for her to enter.

She stepped in and halted. The room's glossy dark paneling reflected the light cast by brass wall lamps. A cream sofa and rich red leather chairs faced a fireplace flanked by a wall of bookcases. A man-cave for the affluent male.

"Come in, Lucinda."

Sam's gravelly voice pulled her attention to the opposite side of the room. He sat at the head of a conference table with another man at the foot. He motioned for her to take a seat.

Pool table get nixed for a cherry conference table? She bit her lip to keep from blurting out her thoughts and sank into the chair Charlie held for her. At least they kept the wall-mounted flat-screen TV. From beneath her lashes, she stole a glance at the other man. Physically intimidating like all the agents she'd met, this man's face was an expressionless mask.

Sam frowned at Finny, not speaking until after Charlie left the room and closed the door. "Meet Gray Kerr."

Cool gray eyes studied her.

"Hi." She held his gaze for a moment before turning to Sam. "Why am I here? May I visit Jack? Please." *Make nice, Lu.* "When can I go home?" She was babbling.

"When the FBI, ATF and Homeland Security say it's time."

Whoa! "The Feds?" Her gaze ricocheted between the two men.

"Until then you'll stay with us."

Had Jack talked to Sam? She gripped the edge of the table. "Does this have to do with the threatening phone calls?"

"Yes."

"Is my Gran alright?"

"She's being protected. I can't give you specifics, but you're a witness so you're under our protection."

Trembling, Lu stared at her blurry reflection in the glossy tabletop. She shivered and pulled Finny closer.

"You are not to have contact with anyone in your hometown or on the island. Understood?"

"Does Gran know I'm here?"

"Your grandmother knows you're safe."

She breathed a shaky sigh. "Thank you."

Voices murmured outside the door followed by a *tap-tap* before it swung open.

"Andi, *no*."

A child bounced into the room followed by a blond woman. "I'm sorry." The woman snagged the little girl's hand and looked at Kerr with a sheepish smile. "Sorry."

Lu glanced at him and did a double take. The man's inscrutable expression had transformed to a wide grin and twinkling eyes. Even Sam had relaxed with the entrance of the pair.

Kerr held his hand out, and the woman walked over to him. "Sophie, meet Lucinda." His arm curved around her waist. "Lucinda, this is my wife, Sophie, and that," he nodded toward the little girl edging closer to Lu's chair trying to see Finny, "is my daughter, Andi."

"What's your dog's name?" Andi flung a braid over her shoulder.

"Finny." Lu didn't know where to look—at the couple so obviously in love or the little girl peppering her with questions.

"Is it a boy or a girl? Will it get bigger?"

"Andi, stop." Sophie looked apologetically at Lu. "Give Lucinda space." She addressed Sam. "Aggie says dinner is ready."

Sam gathered up the papers before him. "Well then, we're done here. Wouldn't want to upset the boss."

His deadpan expression left Lu unsure if he meant what he'd said or if he was teasing.

He rose from his seat. "Lucinda, have dinner and get a good night's rest. In the morning, you may visit Jack at the hospital."

Her heart bumped against her ribs. Standing, she clung to the table, afraid her knees wouldn't support her.

Sophie touched Lu's shoulder. "We're staying for dinner. Come sit with us. I know how intimidating this place," she speared her husband with a look, "and *these men* can be."

Chapter 26

Jack fought his way through a gray mist. He lay on his back, his ribs cinched tight. A soft beeping noise accompanied a whisper of movement at his side.

His heart kicked into high gear.

Opening his eyes a slit, a blur of white moved through his field of vision. Someone touched his arm. He struggled to formulate a counterattack on the person keeping him bound and drugged. He couldn't hang onto a thought long enough to piece a plan together. The gray mist pulled him under once more.

His mind was clearer the next time he surfaced to consciousness. He lay still, listening and assessing the danger. Steady beeps and a soft *hiss* came from close by. The sounds were familiar, but he couldn't place them.

"Open your eyes, Preach."

His pulse jumped. *Sam*.

He rolled his head to the side. A tube pressed against his cheek. Sam's scarred face came into focus. A warm wave of relief rolled over Jack followed by annoyance at being in a hospital bed. He tried to sit up. His breath ramped to short gasps. Hands pressed him down. A male nurse stood next to Sam. Big and bald, the guy was a dead ringer for the character on a bottle of cleaning solution. Just needed an earring. He held a bag of clear liquid in his hand.

"Stand down, Preach, or you'll leave no choice but to put you under again."

Jack pressed back into the pillow willing himself to relax. He shook his head, or at least he tried. Whatever Sam saw must have communicated his panic at being sent off to lala land again. The nurse left.

"Do you remember the team extracting you and Lucinda from the island?" Sam's gaze bore into him.

Lucinda. The name opened the floodgates of Jack's memory. Impressions and pictures flashed through his mind like movie clips on fast forward. He tried to speak around his cotton-coated tongue, but the words came out an unintelligible mumble.

"She's at SeaMount if that's what you're asking."

Relieved, Jack sipped water through the straw in the glass Sam offered. Aggravated by the tubing clipped to his nose, he started to lift his hand to remove it, only to discover his hand was tucked tight beneath the bed sheet. He grunted his displeasure. Sam's obvious amusement at his predicament ticked him off more. Working his left hand free, Jack peeled back the crisp white linen. Starting at the top with the nasal cannula, he ran through a quick assessment.

The muscular nurse reentered the room to stand inside the doorway, arms crossed.

Jack rolled his eyes to Sam. "Where did you get that guy?" His speech was clearer this time.

Sam ignored his question. "You ready to listen?"

No. But ignoring the obvious wouldn't change a thing. "Yes."

"Two gunshot wounds. A crease along the ribs and one through the calf of your leg. Broken collarbone and heavy bruising to your chest and shoulder. You'll have headaches from the knock on your head."

Memories rushed back. He looked down at his right arm encased in a sling. "My arm…" He tried to move his fingers. Nothing. His gaze rocketed between his arm and Sam. "Did they fix it?"

"Not sure they can."

His heart jumped wild in his chest, causing the incessant beeping to speed up. Sam's words rocked through him like a concussive blast. *No.* His fight response kicked in. With his good hand, he tried to push away the sheet and rise from the bed. "What about surgery? Rehab. Would take time, but I can do it." His breath rasped in the back of his throat.

The nurse stepped toward the bed, but Sam stopped him with a wave of his hand. "Listen to me, Preach."

Panting, Jack paused. Sitting up only halfway, he stared at his boss. "Use your resources. *Get my arm fixed.*"

"I'm not God."

The statement hung between them. Unmoving, Jack kept his eyes on Sam.

"Your injury is to the nerves. The blow to your shoulder tore the nerves."

The regret in his boss's voice burned hot through Jack. He glanced down at his arm, now skewed at an odd angle beside him. "What are my odds?"

Sam shook his head. "They may be able to repair some of the damage, but your arm will never again be fully functional."

Jack's stomach spasmed. He gulped back the bile rising in the back of his throat.

"You had no arterial damage so there's no urgent need for amputation."

The words echoed in Jack's ears. He sank back onto the pillow, staring straight ahead, seeing nothing. *God! Why did this to happen to me?* The silent scream filled his mind. His career as an agent ended here.

Caught up in the fear-filled thoughts rattling through his head, he gripped the sheet he lay on with his good hand, needing an anchor. How many times had he talked to the other men, telling them God was their anchor? He'd been so sure and steadfast in his belief. *Why did You allow this?*

Even as the question echoed loud through his thoughts, the many times he'd pushed aside the Holy Spirit rolled in on him. Anger seared through him. *Did you have to take my choice away?* He buried his fingers in his pillow, yanked it from beneath his head and flung it across the room. He slammed his hand against the bed rail. Once. Twice. Three times.

Only then did he realize Sam had left the room. The nurse stood inside the doorway.

"What are you looking at?" Anger warred with panic. "You here to see the freak show?" He pinched the bridge of his nose. If God thought this would force him to follow some divine plan, all meek and mild, God had another think coming!

He glanced up. The nurse stood over him, arms crossed. "Get out." He didn't need someone gawking at him as his world fell apart.

"No."

The man's white short-sleeved shirt was embroidered with the name *Gene*.

"Then make yourself useful, *Gene*. Send me back to

oblivion." He forced the words past the tightness in his throat.

"No." The man had the audacity to step closer. "Better to face the truth."

Truth. Jack's high-pitched laugh bordered on hysterical. *Oh, that's priceless.* Even his penchant for truth had come back to bite him. His right arm lay lifeless in a sling. "I'm right-handed."

"Was. Now you're left-handed."

Jack growled. "And that's supposed to make me feel *better*?"

"It's only the truth."

There it was again. *Truth.* "I've heard about all the truth I can stomach for one day."

Gene shook his head. "You haven't begun to face the truth. Life goes on, but it will be different. You'll adjust."

Jack stared at him. *I'm stinking wrestling with God here. Give you one guess who's gonna win, but it won't stop me from fighting. Not yet, anyway.*

"You may not believe it now, but it's true."

"And you're an expert on this?" The question was edged in bitterness.

Gene bent his left knee and planted his white shoe on the bedside chair. He pulled up his white pant leg to reveal a titanium prosthesis.

Jack stared at the high-tech knee and lower leg.

"The answer to that question is yes, I am an expert on this." Slipping his foot to the floor, he looked down at Jack. "We don't always get to choose what happens to this earthly body, but we do get to choose our response to the change." He leaned over Jack and straightened the linens Jack had ripped aside. "Eventually, everyone will shed this fragile shell of bone and flesh." He looked straight at Jack. *"Everyone."* He stepped back. "You and I have lost a piece sooner than most. It's our constant reminder that eternity begins in *this* life."

Shifting the small heart-shaped ivy topiary from one hand to the other, Lu wiped the palm of her hand against her new jeans. Caleb stood next to her, staring at the numbers of the floors as they ticked by. The elevator eased to a halt, the motion rolling her already sensitive stomach. What if Jack refused to see her?

She stepped off directly into Whit's path.

He caught her by the elbows. "Didn't know you were coming in today." The much abused hat he'd worn on the island had been replaced by an ivory cowboy hat.

"Sam said I could." Other than in her room, she didn't have a moment to herself. She'd had an escort from the time she'd left her room and bumped into Logan sitting outside her door. Sam wasn't giving her any opportunity to defy his no-contact order with Gran or anyone else.

"You sure you want to go in there?"

She tipped her head back and looked him in the eye. "Yes."

"Why?" He crossed his arms, throwing Caleb an irritable glance.

Caleb shrugged and stepped back.

Her heart skipped a beat as she dragged in a deep breath. "I love him." There. She'd said it. Itching to remove the skeptical look from Whit's face, she clenched her hands together and glared at him.

"You fall in and out of love real easy."

How could she convince Whit he didn't need to protect his friend from her?

Licking her lips, she backed up a step. "Before meeting Jack," her throat hurt as she forced the words out, "I wanted to know what a relationship would do for me. This time it's different." She stepped around him surprised he let her pass. She didn't have all the answers. Maybe she never would.

His eyes were closed, giving Lu a moment to study him. A butterfly bandage covered the cut behind his ear. The bruise on his jaw had faded to green. Heart aching, she sighed.

His eyes opened.

"Jack." The longing to touch him drew her into the room. His silence gave her hope. "I wanted to come sooner, but Sam wouldn't let me." Setting the ivy on the bedside table, she devoured him with her eyes. He'd acquired these wounds rescuing her.

"You shouldn't be here." His chest rose and fell. "Go."

"No." Her gaze followed the slope of his shoulder traveling down his sling to his limp hand. She bit her lower lip to stop the trembling.

"I don't want your pity." Anger tinged each word.

Tamping down the sorrow for his loss, Lu gripped the bed rail. If he wanted a fight, she'd give him one. "Good. Because pity isn't any part of what I feel right now."

Rough and stormy, his gaze held hers as though daring her to feel the brunt of his rage.

Before she could chicken out, she clasped his left hand in both of hers. She refused to let go when he tried to pull it from her grasp. "Hear me out, Jack. I'm sorry this," she nodded at his right hand, "happened. And though I feel it's my fault, guilt and pity won't heal it."

"You're hoping for forgiveness?" The words were a snarl.

Was she? "M-maybe." The ache in her chest grew. "The truth? Yes."

He looked away, not speaking. She refused to give up her hold on his hand. After a minute he turned his head on the pillow. "The truth is, my job is..." his voice cracked, "*was* dangerous. This isn't the first time I've come home from a mission injured. Goes with the territory."

"A territory that is no longer yours?"

He tried to snatch his hand away.

She held on.

His chest expanded and contracted in heavy gulps of air, eyes glinting dangerous and untamed.

A tear slipped down her cheek, but Lu refused to give up his hand to wipe it away. She cleared her throat. "I have something to tell you."

"Say it, then leave."

"I love you." The words flowed along with the tears and the fear she'd been holding back. "I love you, you thick-headed man." She stopped, shocked at her audacity.

A muscle twitched at the corner of his mouth. "My arm will never be right again." His voice roughened with emotion. "May come a time I have to have it amputated."

"I didn't fall in love with your arm. Nice as that arm is." She continued to cling to his hand. "And I didn't fall in love with you."

His eyes glittered blue beneath raised eyebrows.

The words weren't coming out right. She wanted to be completely truthful and was making a hash of it. "Actually, I did."

"Which is it? The truth, Lulabelle." His eyes were a storm-tossed blue barely containing the flood of emotion boiling up inside him.

She shook his hand in frustration. "What I'm trying to say is I've had a lot of bad luck *falling in love.* So I'm *choosing* to love you." He'd found a place in her heart so deep he was embedded permanently. "You rescued me from myself."

His throat worked, but he didn't speak. He turned his face toward the ceiling.

She leaned over the bed. Tenderly kissing his cheek, she whispered in his ear. "Whatever you do, wherever you go, I want to be with you."

"Do you understand what you're saying?" The quiet intensity of his words matched hers.

A longing like she'd never experienced before imparted the courage she needed to go on. "Probably not all of it. But I'm willing to learn, preacher-man."

He rolled his head on the pillow to face her. His lips brushed against hers. She stayed still, feeling his breath on her face and the warmth of his lips. He dragged her hand across his chest and pressed it to his damaged arm. "I won't chain you to a lifetime with this."

She made sure he felt her smile against his lips. "It's *my* choice. One of several choices I'm making. I'm also trying to understand the whole God thing. And I'm praying. God never answered my prayers as a kid when I asked Him to bring my dad home. Maybe He had a good reason. I'm willing to try again."

His hand came up and cradled the back of her head. She shivered as his fingers threaded through the hair at her nape. He pulled her closer till his lips clung to hers, demanding and desperate. She pressed close, willing to weather the storm at any cost. The hospital room faded away. Nothing existed but Jack and her desire to show him how much she loved him.

He withdrew and settled back on his pillow, the anger still there in the lines of his face. "It's good that you're praying, but choosing to love me…that choice may not be yours to make."

She was drowning in the turbulent blue of his eyes, going down for the last time and not caring. "You can't order me not to love you, Jack." She pulled away. Eyes blurry with tears, she left the room.

A hand closed around her elbow. Through her tears she recognized the outline of Whit's Stetson. He steered her toward the elevator where Caleb waited. "You did good in there."

She wiped her nose with the back of her hand. "Then why do I feel so awful?"

Chapter 27

The day had only begun and Jack was already tired of looking at the ceiling and arguing with God. He rolled his head to face the wall of windows where the horizon glowed gold and pink with the rising sun. On the sill, bright balloons from Gray and Sophie's three girls floated above a grinning teddy bear vase filled with flowers. Beside it stood the heart-shaped ivy Lucinda had brought him two days ago.

"I'm choosing to love you."

The woman could give a man a heart attack. The words left a mark on his heart. He wanted to accept her declaration, but what did he have to offer her? Seemed so easy on the island, half out of his mind with pain. Would this be another prayer of hers that went unanswered? Would it be because of God's will or because of his own rebellion and stubbornness?

The reality? His plans had dried up and turned to dust. And God's plans...well, he didn't know what God had planned. Wasn't sure he wanted anything to do with God's plan. How could he pull Lu into his fight with God?

Victory over life's challenges is found in joyful submission to the will of God. Arrogant of him to preach that from the pulpit. How did the rest of that sermon go? *We may not understand God's purpose, but giving Him control is where we find our happiness.* Anger boiled hot in his gut. He fisted his hand and banged the bedrail, not doubting for a minute that he would eventually surrender. But not yet. Right now, he wanted to be mad!

A whisper of movement came from the direction of the door. He didn't bother to turn his head to see who entered. He didn't much care. He'd had his fill of helpful people dressed in medical uniforms. More to the point, he was fed up with Gene. More than a nurse, the man pushed him through physical therapy without a bit of sympathy.

"You ready to rock and roll?"

The low words whipped Jack's attention to the door. His gaze crashed into McCord and the St. John brothers standing behind him.

"You ready to blow this clam hut?"

The sticky pull of tape stretched the skin on Jack's hand. "What are you doing?"

"You're not using this." Whit removed the cannula. Slapping a wad of gauze over the site, he taped it down and applied pressure. "Time to get dressed."

Logan dumped sweatpants and a hoodie sweatshirt that zipped on the foot of the bed. "Hustle it." All business, they hauled him to his feet and snatched off the hideous hospital gown.

Pain meds dulled Jack's wits and reaction time. Happy to have his naked butt covered, he didn't fight as they wrestled him into the pants. "The doc releasing me?"

"Not that we know."

His head spun trying to track the movement of the men around him.

Whit pulled the sleeve of the hoodie up his good arm, they wrapped it over his sling and zipped, leaving the empty sleeve flapping. Gabe tapped on his foot. Leaning against

Logan, Jack lifted it. A sock slid on and his foot was shoved into a waiting boot. They went through the same routine with his other foot.

Gene entered the room. Everyone froze. He took each man's measure. "Care to tell me what's going on?"

Whit stepped forward. "We were cleared to take him out for a few hours."

Easy-going smiles all around were Jack's tip off. Nothing of the sort had been granted though a general murmur of agreement traveled through the room.

"I have to confirm this." Gene included every man in his sweeping gaze. "Will take me at least fifteen minutes to get verification." He left the room without a backward glance.

The twins dove into action, one at each boot yanking and tying laces. "Let's go."

A wheelchair materialized and they pushed him into it. They rolled him into the hall and past the nurse's station where Gene stood with his back to them, busy on the computer. Whisking him onto the elevator, the silence and tension within the unit seeped into Jack's befuddled brain. He was at the center of a mission. He *was* the mission. They were busting him out.

The elevator doors slid open. They moved out through the exterior door to a waiting black SUV.

"Where are you taking me?"

Whit opened the back door. "You're gonna be our dummy."

That didn't sound so good. Before he could protest, he was pulled from the chair and pushed into the backseat. Seated in the center, a St. John brother sat on either side of him. "Whose idea is this?"

"Mine."

Jack looked up. The rearview mirror reflected cool gray

eyes. His heart did an odd little flip. *Gray Kerr.* "I should have guessed." The man's propensity for bending rules had resulted in being relegated to 'team trainer'. Not that he minded. Head over heels in love with his new wife and her three daughters, he didn't care that his wings were clipped.

"We're going climbing. Figured you'd want to come along." The corners of Gray's eyes crinkled.

Jack shook his head. "Can't climb. Can't get myself rigged."

Riding shotgun, Whit glanced back over his shoulder. "Don't worry about it."

Okay. Time to worry.

The hospital entrance disappeared from view. A mix of fear and anticipation fizzed beneath his skin. He didn't know where they were going, but he knew these men. They were his brothers. Whatever they had in mind, down to a man, they were safety-minded.

The gravel road wound up the mountain. Ground water seeped from the mossy layers of minerals and granite rising above the road on one side. Ferns clung in the narrow crevices. At the top of the hill the road widened and ended as a gravel parking area. Gray pulled alongside another SUV.

Ethan stood at the back of it, knee deep in the duffle bags that held the new climbing gear Sam brought in before Jack took off for St. Beatrice.

Jack climbed out on shaky legs.

One of the packs lay partially open, revealing a rolled plastic stretcher. The 'dummy' comment now made sense. He stepped back. "No way I'm doing this."

Gray and Whit blocked his retreat. The clink of

carabiners accompanied the click of cobra buckles as the St. John boys adjusted and tightened the webbing of their harnesses.

"Yep, you are." Whit gripped his arm, a smirk on his lips. "We're going to rescue you."

Gray stood on Jack's right. Probably holding his other arm, though he couldn't feel it. "You're still part of the team."

"Not for long." Jack dug in his heels. "You can do this without me."

"Sam hasn't released you yet." They forced marched him to the end of the railing. For years, people had ignored the safety of the handrail and worn a narrow footpath in the dirt sloping a short distance before coming to the edge of a sixty foot drop. People like them.

Ethan was busy rigging the anchor straps to old growth trees shading the parking lot. Gabe worked with him laying out lines and pulleys.

Whit grinned wide. "While you were lying around, we've been practicing with all this fancy stuff. Don't you want to see it in action?"

"No." He had no doubt they'd been using the equipment, learning the capabilities of each piece. The problem was *he* hadn't been a part of it.

Logan approached with the stretcher and proceeded to unroll it so it lay flat.

"Lay down." Gray prodded him forward.

Jack went into a full-blown sweat from head to toe. He planted his boots. "Oof." Without warning he landed on the ground. He kicked out, hitting Logan's thigh with a glancing blow. He twisted, too weak and protective of his injured arm to fight effectively.

Gray and Whit forced him onto his back, the smooth

plastic of the litter beneath him. Continuing to struggle, they moved the length of him fastening buckles and tightening the webbing so the sides curled around him making movement impossible. Someone tipped his boot toes up and secured the last straps in place.

Gray's face popped into Jack's line of vision. "We'll carry you to the edge. Whit's getting rigged and gonna go down at your side. If you bang against the rock, blame him." He tucked a soft stabilizer around Jack's head and neck. Giving Jack's shoulder a double tap, he stood.

Anger and more fear than he'd care to admit burned in his gut.

Whit bent over him, harnessed and ready for action. "All set?"

Jack glared at him. "What do you think?"

A wide grin broke across Whit's face. "You make a mighty cute package."

Jack didn't try to bite back a coarse response as Whit set about double-checking fasteners.

Gray grabbed a handle. "There are rules against swearing in this outfit."

Manning the other handles, Whit and the St. John brothers lifted on Gray's count.

The blue sky disappeared behind an orange, red, and yellow kaleidoscope of foliage. Rocking between the men, Jack fought back panic. The voices of the men became a murmuring background noise as he concentrated on the racket in his head. His muscles ached with tension.

They set him down on uneven ground. The men moved back and forth over him, running the slings and gathering them into a carabiner above him in preparation for lowering him over the edge.

"You praying?" Whit attached the litter to the haul system. Gray stood next to him running a safety check.

"You have no idea." Jack ground the words out.

"Well, don't go calling down the wrath of God before we get you to the bottom." Whit double checked the rigging and his own rope then grasped the center handle at Jack's side. "Here we go." He backed up, Ethan and Gray helping to guide the stretcher as he walked over the edge.

It bumped against the lip of the cliff, wobbled, and then Jack hung in space.

His breath dammed in his chest. He stared up through the straps angled above him and into the limitless depths of the blue sky. Facing his Creator with every ounce of helplessness one man could feel. *You ran me to ground, Lord. I want to fight though I know I'll lose.* The verse from Jeremiah came to mind. "*I know the plans I have for you, plans to prosper you and not harm you, plans to give you a hope and a future.*" His stubborn heart bled hot with rebellion, as he lay suspended from the sheer face of granite.

"Doing okay?" Whit's voice broke through the racket between Jack's ears.

"Yeah." His throat, constricted with emotion, hurt to talk.

"Stop holding your breath and relax. We wanted to try a vertical rescue first."

First? His armpits were swimming.

"Gray eighty-sixed the idea."

As cliffs went, the team had tackled higher ones, but this was the first time he'd been unable to do anything for himself.

Whit called out to his left and Gabe answered.

The St. John brothers were coming down on either side using the new fall arrest devices to control the descent.

Moving past the tops of the trees and into the canopy, the

sun glowed through leaves burnished by the cold autumn nights and warm days. The litter dropped off a knob on the face of the cliff and rocked. His muscles jerked tight in response. Brush crackled. Boots thumped.

"We're here." Whit eased the foot then the head of the litter to the ground and signaled the men at the top. "Still okay?"

"Get me out of here." The sweet green scent of broken grass and torn leaves wafted past. Boots thumped to the ground behind him. At his feet, brush crunched and twigs snapped. Gabe thrashed in the bushes, muttering a few choice words.

Whit leaned over him and smiled. "Ready to go back up?"

Jack clamped his lips together. They had him and they knew it.

Whit's finger dug into his neck.

"What're you doing?"

"Not getting worked up; are you?"

Jack focused on the edge of the cliff high above his head where Gray and Ethan kept watch over the anchor strap and safety lines. The men around him switched to ascenders and checked the connection of the slings.

In too short a time, Whit signaled Gray and Ethan. The litter lifted off with a slight swing. The men got it under control and began the return climb.

If he thought time crawled going down, it stopped on the return trip. He had to trust the bunch of them.

Do you trust them more than Me?

Jack's heart contracted with a stabbing pain. *Yes.* In this moment, as the stretcher scraped against a rough outcropping of stone, he trusted the men around him more than he trusted his future to his Heavenly Father.

The truth left agonizing stripes across his soul. *Forgive me.* Those two words cracked the hard shell encasing his heart, relieving some of the pressure squeezing his chest. *How do I go on without my arm? How do I change who I am?*

Surrender.

No! Surrender is not a Ranger word! But, hadn't he been the one to tell Gray that the hardest thing men like them had to do was give up control to God? Easy to say when it wasn't *your* life being torn apart. He was on the losing side of this battle, but he'd been trained to fight to the bitter end.

The litter bumped and skidded on the grass at the top of the cliff. Whit bent over him, checking and inspecting, changing up the slings. The men were talking to one another, but Jack didn't listen as the battle in his heart and head raged.

They tipped him over the edge.

He yelped. His heart banged against his ribs. He dangled in a vertical position, staring across the treetops to the mountain on the other side of the valley. Several trails wound their way to the peak.

A verse from Psalms filtered through the defiant need to win the battle. *"...he guides me in paths of righteousness..."* All God wanted for him was right and good. Values that were in lockstep with the creed he'd lived by his whole adult life. He wasn't surrendering to an enemy. He was receiving new orders from the One whose rank surpassed all others.

He dropped lower, and the trail disappeared amid the blue-green of pine trees and the brilliant reds and oranges of maple trees.

"How're you doing?"

"Gray?" With his head immobilized he hadn't realized the men had switched positions.

"Doing okay?"

Jack licked his lips. "No."

"You should'a said something up top." Whit's fingers pressed his carotid artery.

"Not that. Well, it is, but not entirely." He heard a boot scrape on the rock.

Gray swung out in front of Jack. Cool eyes studied him. "We got your back, Preach. Whatever comes of your injury, we got your back."

The remnants of the armor encasing his heart crumbled and fell away. He didn't have to do this on his own. He wouldn't lose his bond with these men. They would continue to anchor each other, providing a safety net for any brother who stumbled or fell along God's chosen path.

They lowered him to the ground and undid the slings and straps holding him in place. The tightness in his chest melted away. Whit and Gray helped him to his feet. He looked up the sheer face of the cliff. "You were right."

"Yeah?" Whit unhooked his line. "About what?"

"Rescuing me." Finding a rock, Jack took a seat.

More ropes sailed over the edge. Whit and Gray took up the ends and positioned themselves for a standing hip belay. The St. John brothers leaned out over the top. In perfect L-shape form, they walked flat-footed to the halfway point where they tied off and proceeded to turn so they were head down.

His teammates didn't question or badger him as he sat silent and watched them go through the training exercises. He'd never again feel the rush that came with the physical challenge of carrying out missions. He'd be a fool to think he wouldn't miss the surge of adrenaline or the camaraderie. But what awaited him could be just as incredible if he opened his heart to God's plan.

"I'm not going back."

Sweaty and in good spirits, the other men paused in packing up the gear.

"What's that?" Whit exchanged a look with Gray.

"Take me with you to SeaMount." This taste of freedom whetted Jack's appetite for more. Ignoring pain and exhaustion, he forced himself to stand straight and not wobble. "I can do rehab there."

Holding a coiled rope, Gray stepped up to him. "What about your injuries?"

"You weren't worried about them this morning."

An uneasy shuffle rippled among the men.

"Sam can hire someone. I don't want to go back to those four walls." Jack held Gray's hard stare for a long minute before the other man nodded.

"Help us load up, then."

Unable to stop grinning, Jack lifted the lightweight litter already rolled and stuffed in its nylon bag. He tossed it into the back of the SUV on top of the other gear. He was going home.

Jack followed Whit and Gray up the steps adjacent to the loading dock and into the building. He'd find some mega-strength painkillers then locate Lucinda and talk some sense into her about *choosing* to love him.

"About time you all got back." Sam stood in the doorway to the left of the gym, toweling off after putting time in at the lap pool. His gaze flicked over Jack and travelled to Gray then Whit.

Unwilling to let them take the heat for his decision, Jack stepped forward. "I refused to go back to the hospital."

"Figured you would." Sam looked up to the top of the sweeping stairs.

Jack followed his gaze. Surprise snapped through him.

Gene stood at the top, arms crossed.

Jack wheeled around in time to see Sam disappear into the men's locker room, his voice drifting back to the incredulous men.

"Took you all long enough to haul him out of there."

Chapter 28

A train of waves boomed ashore, sending a spray of sea foam high into the air to be caught up by the wind and tossed onto the beach and dunes.

Lucinda stood on the deck, the wind's damp cold fingers pulling her hair and tugging her jacket. The air was heavy with the brisk tang of the ocean. She breathed it in and tasted the salt on her lips. If she stood out here long enough, maybe she would grow numb from the cold and not feel the hurt that arrowed through her each time she thought of her visit with Jack. She'd laid her heart bare to him, and he'd all but rejected her.

God, do you care? Is Jack just another man who will hurt me?

Stuffing her hands into her coat pockets, her fingers bumped the small Bible she'd found in her room. She pulled it out and dropped into the closest deck chair. Finny, dressed in a green coat, jumped up onto her lap.

She'd always considered the Bible a book old people read for comfort. Finding a man as self-reliant as Jack using the scriptures to shape his life was a surprise. If someone as strong as him needed the Word of God, how could she go through life without at least looking to see what the Bible had to say?

She flipped to her bookmark, the wind ruffling pages.

"While we were still sinners, Christ died for us."

The verse plucked uncomfortably at her heartstrings. She hadn't lived a life that was beyond reproach, but the word "sinner" made her cringe. She didn't like that word. Then there was the unconditional love displayed by Christ when he died for everyone. A gift like that was hard to accept.

She leaned back in the chair. Her experiences with love always held disappointment. Would God's love be different? What if she blew it? Would He stop loving her?

The deck door slid open behind her. Charlie approached.

"Sam wants you in the Club Room."

Her heart skipped a beat. Sam had shared nothing with her about the investigation since that first meeting the evening she'd arrived. She rose, tucked the Bible in her coat pocket, and followed Charlie into the hall.

Her gaze crashed into sultry blue eyes. *Jack!*

Breathless, she stood rooted in place. His eyes darkened and his soft smile set her pulse on fire. "I didn't know you'd been released from the hospital."

His arm rested in a real sling, and he walked with a cane. An odd little smile played across his lips. "Only just got out."

"That's great." She wanted to throw her arms around him, but held back, unsure how he'd respond.

Behind him the door of the Club Room opened.

"Preach. Lucinda. Please come in." Sam stood waiting for them.

Jack stepped aside and let her pass.

Whit sat at a table in front of windows framing the turbulent ocean. She settled on the edge of the seat Sam indicated. Jack sat at her right. Finny chose Whit as her keeper for the meeting and stood on her back paws to push at his leg.

Beneath the table Lu clutched her hands together. In her tummy, the honeybees were busy.

Sam rocked back in his chair. "Lucinda, you're leaving for Kansas late this evening."

"You're sending me home?" She glanced at Jack. His hand slid over hers and squeezed, sending her heart into a wild tumble. His gaze was shuttered, neither fire nor ice, giving away nothing of his thoughts. Uncertainty ran jagged across her joyful heart. This is what she'd wanted, so why did she feel her heart being torn in two?

"Whit is going with you."

Jack jerked. "No." He didn't remove his steely gaze from Sam. "This is my mission to complete."

"You aren't fit for this duty."

Duty? She didn't know which stony-faced man to look at. "Would someone please tell me what's going on?"

Jack ignored her question. "It's all set up?"

Sam's voice grated rough. "All that is left to do is pull off the sting."

A sting? She knew what that was, sort of. A cold wave of trepidation annihilated the bees in her belly leaving her empty at the core. "Wait." Dragging in a deep breath she leaned forward and looked at each of the men in turn. She glared at Sam, determined to get the words out before she thought better of it. "I'm tired of being yanked around."

She heard a squeak from Whit's end of the table. The noise must have been Finny. Whit wasn't a squeaker. "Tell me what is going on." The words scraped her throat, as sharp as crushed glass.

Sam leaned forward in his chair. "Once you're on the jet, you'll be filled in." He shook his head. "You'll be met at the airport in Kansas City." He glared at the two men. "I'm not happy about this, but I'm not the one running the op."

Lu's breath whistled between her teeth. She hadn't wanted to believe Trent could be connected to Duro. But...a sting? *Oh, God, help.*

"They want Finny there, too."

"Why does she have to be there?" Lu didn't try and soften the belligerence in her voice. Jack's warm hand closed over her knee. She jumped, cracking her shin against the center leg of the table. The heat of a blush traveled up her neck and cheeks. She refused to look at him.

A smile tipped Sam's heavy mustache. "On the jet, Lucinda. You'll have all your answers once you're on your way and not before." He nailed Jack with a dark look. "Suppose you're intent on displaying your intestinal fortitude?"

A smile ghosted across Jack's lean face. "It's mine to finish."

"Try this on." Jack stood in front of Lu, a white vest in his hand.

Her head still spun from the speed with which preparations for the trip had proceeded. In the end, Sam insisted not only Whit go with them, but also Gene. He would see to Jack's healing wounds. Aggie helped her pack and saw that Finny's needs were met. Curled up at Whit's feet in a plush yellow bed, she slept unaware she was forty-thousand feet above the earth.

Lu took the vest. "It's heavy."

"It'll stop a bullet."

Her heart dropped to her toes along with the vest. "There'll be bullets?"

Jack picked it up. "We need to be prepared." He helped

her slip it over her head and showed her how to adjust the side closures to fit her small frame. Only once did a hint of frustration lace his voice as he tried to help her with his one hand.

She tugged at it. "Makes me feel fat."

Sticking his hand in his pocket, he looked her up and down. The heat in his eyes rooted her to the carpet. He still hadn't said anything about her visit to the hospital. She kept silent for fear of ruining the unspoken truce between them.

"Should feel safe. It'll go under your clothing." He led her to a lounge area at the opposite end of the cabin. The artificial lighting did nothing to soften the lines of fatigue bracketing his mouth.

"Federal agents are meeting us at the airport." He set aside his cane and looked down at their entwined hands. "They have proof Trent was involved in the illegal purchase and sale of firearms."

His words ripped through her. Her breath caught in her throat. "I didn't know."

"You wouldn't be here if anyone thought you were involved." He squeezed her hand and let go. "Promise me one thing, Lulabelle."

Her heart bumped hard. She'd missed hearing him call her that silly name. "What?"

He circled his arm around her, pulling her close. "Promise me you'll do exactly as instructed by the agents."

She slipped her arms around his waist and looked up at him. "I'm a little scared."

One side of his mouth tipped up. "It's okay to be a little scared." An undercurrent rippled through the clear blue of his eyes. "Just promise me you'll follow the game plan." His voice broke. "I can't lose you."

"Okay." Her heart thudded heavy. She touched his jaw. "I can't lose you, either."

"You won't."

"But...you're willing to die for me." She shuddered. "That totally frightens me."

His steamy gaze tracked across her features before he covered her lips with his.

She clung to him, his musky scent invading her senses, making her lightheaded while the honeybees danced in her tummy. She pressed closer, needing to feel the warmth of him. Needing to show him how much she loved him, because words only seemed to get in the way.

He pulled back. "Why don't you rack out. Tomorrow will be a long day." Helping her undo the vest, he lifted it over her head. He hesitated, a longing in his eyes. "Stretch out here. I'll join Whit up front."

Dazed, she sank to the leather sofa and watched him limp away, leaning on his cane. How was she supposed to sleep after that kiss? Holy cow! She'd never experienced a kiss of that tummy-tingling magnitude. Not from *any* man.

Trent and Esteban.

Her thoughts careened back to earth and reality. They didn't measure up to Jack in any way. Dread sickened her stomach. The two men were in the same business. What were the odds? Elbows on her knees, she held her head in her hands, and stared at the pattern in the carpet. Trent was a criminal, and she had almost married him. What about the threatening phone calls? Jack hadn't told her everything.

She looked up and watched him sit not so gracefully in the seat next to Whit. Though he wouldn't admit it, his injuries had taken a toll. Even if she couldn't sleep, maybe he would.

Kicking off her shoes, she stretched out on the couch. She had a long night ahead of her.

Jack settled into his seat. Things were moving so fast he hadn't talked to Lu about what she'd said in the hospital. Truth be known, he was uncertain what to say, so he'd kissed her instead. She'd felt right and perfect in his arm. There was something about her that made him feel complete. He wanted her—outspoken, klutzy, and irreverent—she belonged with him forever and always. But should he tie her to his side when he had no idea what his future held? Did she understand what she meant when she said she chose to love him? Did *he* understand? Would he be strong enough to let her go if she changed her mind?

"She okay?" Whit spoke from beneath the hat tipped over his face.

"So far. Doesn't know all of it yet."

"When you gonna tell her?"

Jack just grunted and adjusted the sling at his neck.

"Chicken."

"Shut up, *cowboy*."

Whit's hand struck out, slugging Jack's bad arm.

"Hey!"

Whit shot up, his hat tumbling down his chest and onto the floor. "I didn't think…"

Jack rubbed his bicep.

Whit's gaze zeroed in on his action. "Did you feel that?"

"No. Surprised me."

"Yeah. Well." Whit picked up his hat and slapped at imaginary dirt. "That's why I should be the one going in with her, *not* you."

"Think I can't do the job?"

"I think everyone will be so busy trying to protect your numb bits—and that includes your brain—the mission may be compromised." He slammed back his chair and crammed his hat over his face.

Withdrawing a small prescription bottle from his pocket, Jack popped a Ranger candy in his mouth and waited for the mega dose of painkiller to work. He had to be the one to tell Lu the truth. Once she got her equilibrium back, she'd blow like an ammo dump.

Chapter 29

The squeal of tires hitting asphalt roused Lu from a restless doze. She rubbed her eyes, gritty with fatigue, and glanced to the front of the cabin.

Esteban!

Her vision tunneled as she grabbed the edge of the couch to keep from pitching forward. Dressed in a white suit, Esteban stood at the front of the cabin talking to Whit and Gene. Her heart raced. She breathed in short painful gasps. His back was to her. Had he seen her? She tried to stand, but fell back on the sofa, dizzy. Did Jack know he was here? A strangled whimper escaped her lips.

He turned.

Shock jolted through her.

Jack?

Motionless, she stared at him.

He approached leaning on his cane, his suit so similar to those worn by Esteban. Finny trotted at his heels.

"Lucinda." He was back to the formality of using her full name.

"Why are you dressed—" Her voice deserted her.

He dropped to the sofa beside her, his lack of expression frightening. She swiped hair from her eyes and with trembling hands reached for Finny. "There are facts you

260

haven't told me." The accusation hung in the air between them.

His hand moved as though to meet the other, to crack his knuckle. He frowned. "All I can offer you is the truth."

Heart thumping, she cuddled the puppy close. "Then answer my questions truthfully. Leave *nothing* out." She didn't try to keep the hard edge from her voice. Anger and shame had been her bedfellows for the last five hours. Combined, they'd created a combustible brew looking for release. "Trent was taking me to St. Beatrice for our honeymoon. Coincidence?" She could barely get the words beyond her tight lips.

"No."

"I saw guns in Billy Wilson's garage. Is he a part of this?" Her voice rasped.

"A straw buyer. One of several working for Ingersoll." He paused as though weighing his words. "The pawn shop is the perfect cover for laundering the money."

"The phone calls to Gran?"

"Billy Wilson's doing. The Feds believe Trent was truly concerned about your welfare so he broke off the engagement."

She pressed her lips together unimpressed by Trent's belated concern. He'd been cold and calculating, and she'd been infatuated and naïve.

He continued. "A change in plans on this end called for a change in plans on Duro's end so he sent you to the island alone. How did you and Duro meet?"

Her mind whirled with the implications of Jack's question. "He came in for lunch every day at the hotel." She tugged on the sleeve of his tropical weight jacket. "It was hard to miss the suit." She paused. "One day, he asked me to join him. He told me about the job at Paradise."

Understanding swept through her. "*That* wasn't coincidental either."

"No. No more than Finny's collar with real diamonds was an accident. You and Finny were to be mules bringing diamonds into the states to pay Trent for the weapons. Diamonds are easily laundered through the pawn shop."

The anger Lu had been holding back flared hot. She sprang from the sofa, sending Finny tumbling to the floor. Panting as though she'd run miles, she stood stiff with fists clenched at her side. "Trent used me. And I was *stupid* enough to believe he wanted me for who I was. I was so proud to be his fiancée." A second thought followed close on the heels of the first. "And *Esteban*! He used me, too." She stopped and shook her head. "I really know how to pick them don't I." Self-loathing left a bitter taste on her tongue. "So let me be sure I understand. My honeymoon would have been a business trip to…to…arrange an arms deal. But Billy Wilson became a loose cannon, and they had to switch it up. Esteban would come to the States with me and Finny, carrying the payment in diamonds?"

Jack stood. "We don't know if the original plan called for Duro to accompany you and Finny home."

"How would Trent get the guns to Esteban?"

"South America has porous borders making it easy."

Her face paled. "The guns in the crates at…" She pointed at his arm. "Did those come from Trent?"

"No. Duro uses several suppliers."

She huffed and hooked a stray swatch of hair behind her ear. "Why are you dressed like Esteban?"

"The ATF, with the help of the NSA, had intercepted Ingersoll's communications with his contact on the island."

"Who?"

"Manuel Mingau."

Her stomach rolled over. "Trent knows nothing about...?" she gestured toward his arm.

Jack shook his head. "From what was gleaned from the exchanges, he and Duro have never met. Nothing has happened or changed, as far as Ingersoll is concerned. A meeting has been arranged at the pawn shop." He looked uncomfortable for a moment.

"What aren't you telling me?"

"Even after Manuel Mingau was no longer a factor, the agents continued to listen."

Her frown morphed into wide-eyed shock. "He's dead?"

"Yes."

Lu sat with a thump. *Is Esteban alive?* She pushed the thought away, afraid to ask, needing to be able to concentrate on the task before her. Finny hopped into her lap, dishing out forgiving kisses. "What's my part?"

"Ingersoll has been adamant you accompany Duro." Jack raked his hand through his hair. "I think he's worried about you, and this is his way of insuring you get home safely."

She huffed and waved off his words, dismissing his attempt to soften all she'd heard. "He should have thought about that before he set me up! What do I have to do?"

He looked at her with narrowed eyes as though trying to read her thoughts. "As you can see, I will play the part of Duro. You will be with me so Ingersoll can see you're alive and well, then you're to get lost."

"What about Finny?"

"Ingersoll expects payment." He reached into his pocket and pulled out a pink collar decorated with a single row of sparkling stones. "She'll be with me."

Lucinda buckled the collar around the puppy's neck. "They aren't real, are they?"

"No. But they're good fakes." He looked at his watch. "Time to change your clothes."

Heart pounding, she handed Finny to him and went into the well-appointed bathroom where a change of clothes hung along beside the ballistic vest. She stripped to her undies and slipped the vest over her head. She pulled the side bands tight as Jack had shown her, and then pressed the patch of tiny nylon hooks into the soft looped fabric square. Running a hand down the soft shell of the protective barrier, she shivered. The vest could be all that stood between her and death.

She dressed in the aqua pantsuit, pulling the tunic over her head rather than deal with the tiny pearl buttons running the length of the back. The cotton fabric flowed soft and loose, concealing the lines of the vest. White flats with brilliant aqua gem clip-ons finished the outfit. She touched up her makeup with trembling hands before opening the door.

Jack stood on the other side waiting for her. "Does it fit okay?"

"I look like I belong in a harem."

A sensual smile ghosted across his lips, tempting her to disregard caution and fling herself into his arms. *Arm.*

She held up a foot and let the light catch in the gemstones. "Are these real or fake?"

"Have to ask Aggie." He hooked his arm around her waist, his hand wandering as he nudged her forward.

She glared up at him. "You're checking to see if I'm wearing the vest."

"You bet I am."

Sitting beside Lu in the back seat of the car, tension hummed through Jack. The high-end, full-sized sedan ate up mile after flat Kansas mile under Whit's steady hand.

Jumping into the middle of an ongoing mission with nothing more than fragmentary orders made Jack twitchy. Taking Lu in with him might drive him over the edge of sanity. He shifted in the seat, wanting to gather her close. *Nothing* could happen to her. Hadn't he promised to bring her home safely? What would her grandmother do if she were hurt? What would *he* do?

On the horizon, a brown dust cloud haloed a tractor pulling a drill as it cut furrows and dropped seeds for the winter wheat crop. To the south, pumpjacks nodded in the fields, a testament to the discovery of oil in the region. Almost overnight sleepy farm communities had been transformed into boomtowns.

In the town of Ingersoll, the federal agents had used the influx of strangers to their advantage, getting lost in the crowd and going about their work unnoticed. The lead agent, Bob Edwards, met them at the airport.

Lu stared out her window, breathing shallow and fast with an occasional deep shuddering sigh. Earlier he'd coached her through breathing exercises to manage the adrenaline rush. Whatever ran through her head now was getting her worked up again. She'd be a danger to herself and everyone else if she didn't get it under control.

She wasn't sharing her thoughts so he could only speculate, and everything he came up with made *his* gut crank over with fury. If anyone had a big score to settle it was this small woman sitting next to him.

Grain elevators broke the flat line of the horizon. Soon they passed the sign welcoming them to Ingersoll.

"Doing okay back there, Preach?"

Jack fingered his earpiece, glanced in the rearview mirror at Whit and nodded. Both of them were wired and being monitored by the Feds.

He leaned across the seat and took Lu's cold hand in his.

She turned to him, eyes glazed and far away. "Will Gran be alright?"

"Your grandmother won't be anywhere near the pawn shop."

"You don't know Gran. If she caught wind of this..." Her voice trailed off.

"Gene is with her."

Her gaze sharpened. "He's a nurse."

Jack tipped his head toward her. "Don't underestimate the man."

She checked on Finny lying quiet in a soft blue carry kennel, then turned back to the window, once again silent.

"We have you in sight." Agent Edward's voice in Jack's earpiece was accompanied by a crackle of static.

Whit's instructions were to drop Jack and Lucinda at the front door. Duro would have wanted to make an entrance. Ingersoll may or may not know this so Jack was to stay in character.

A right hand turn at the Farm Bureau and a left at the John Deere dealership, and they were in front of a tan stand-alone cinder block building. Black security bars were barely visible behind the gaudy signs plastered on the windows. Following the town's ordinance for angled parking, Whit nosed the car to the curb and killed the engine.

Game on.

"Remember, Lucinda out first, Duro exit same side."

The agents running this op wanted Trent distracted and watching her for those precious few seconds. He understood the plan; that didn't mean he had to like it.

She stepped from the car hitching the strap to Finny's kennel over her shoulder.

Jack's protective instinct rebelled. He followed on her heels fighting the urge to yank her back into the car.

Amped on adrenaline, she started to rush across the sidewalk to the door.

Praying he didn't fall on his face, he hooked his cane over the wrist of his bum arm and snaked his other arm around her to slow her down. "Smile, Lulabelle."

She looked up at him, her lips bent in a stiff grimace, which was no smile at all.

Time for an emergency action.

Curling her tight to his side he bent down, hiding her face from the view of anyone in the shop, and claimed her lips. Her squeak of surprise made his heart thud slow and hard. Ignoring the kissing noises Whit was making in his ear, he nibbled her bottom lip before lifting his head. He smiled and prodded her forward. "Don't trip on the curb."

She did.

He caught her.

"Why'd you do that?" Breathless, she held tight to his arm, her dazed eyes bouncing between him and the storefront where a neon sign flashed PAWN.

"I needed a good luck kiss."

"You don't believe in luck." Her voice trembled and her step faltered.

"It'll be okay, Lulabelle. Greet Trent, give me Finny, and move on to look around." Jack slid his hand to her back trying to convey a calm he was far from feeling.

With only a few feet to go, the door opened with a jingle. An unshaved man dressed in greasy green twill work pants and shirt stepped out onto the cracked sidewalk. Spying Lucinda, he stopped.

"Hello, Billy." Her voice rasped.

Jack went on alert unsure what she'd do.

Giving Billy a cold shoulder, she looked up at Jack, eyes smoldering with seduction.

His belly bottomed out on a wave of desire. He could do nothing but endure the sweet agonizing payback for the kiss he'd sprung on her.

Pushing her through the door, he smiled at Wilson, fighting the urge to plow a fist into the man's soft gut in retribution for the trouble he'd caused Lu.

To the right of the door, a garden tiller and ancient lawn mower filled the floor space beneath a wall display of shovels and rakes. A squeal from behind the sales counter followed by the *clump clump* of shoes yanked his attention to the back of the store.

A dark haired woman Lucinda's age raced toward her with arms stretched wide. "*Luuu,* I've missed you!"

"Hi, Abby." Lu got swallowed up in an exuberant hug.

Monitoring the greeting between the women, Jack let his gaze travel the store. The first sweep turned up no one. On the second pass, a man stepped from behind a spinner rack of DVD's. He approached Jack with his hand outstretched and a politician's smile plastered on his face. "Trent Ingersoll." An awkward moment passed before he noticed the sling and realized his mistake. He dropped his hand to his side.

Jack hid his immediate dislike behind an easy grin and an accent he pulled out for occasions like this. "Esteban Duro."

Before the animated Abby could drag Lu to the opposite side of the store, Trent claimed her attention. "Lucinda. It's good to see you."

Lu looked down at the toes of her shoes but not quick enough to hide the fireworks flashing in her hazel eyes. "Hi,

Trent." Her fingers curled into Finny's soft fur, and the pup moved restlessly. She looked briefly at the guitars on the wall behind the display cases filled with jewelry and coins. "You've added another display case."

He ran his fingers across his neatly combed bangs and puffed his chest. "A lot of new business in town because of the oil."

Lu wrinkled her nose as though smelling something offensive. "Lots of men arriving in town down on their luck, and you're here to help until they find a job."

Ingersoll's smug smile widened, missing the sting in her statement. "And find housing. That's a big need. Can't build houses fast enough." He gestured toward a wall of power tools. "Hoping maybe some of the guys coming in will decide working in the mud isn't for them." His gaze sharpened. "Did you enjoy your time on the island?"

The guy should know when to shut up. Jack stood quietly, prepared to jump in should Lu need him.

She tossed her hair back over her shoulder and shrugged. "Yes. Well, except for the *war and the dead people*." She cut short the sarcasm, pulled out a high wattage smile, and beamed it on Jack, giving him the itch to kiss her again. He settled for putting his arm around her waist.

She stepped close and leaned against him. "Esteban treats me *very* well."

Not damming the desire surging through him, strong as a tidal wave, Jack looked down at her. "Spoiling you gives me great pleasure." He was playing a part, but the words rang true to his core. He wanted that privilege.

She gulped, a fervent sparkle in her warm honey eyes.

"Ooh." The breathy sigh came from behind Lucinda. "That's *sooo* romantic." Abby clasped her hands together, a dreamy look on her face.

Another heavy sigh echoed in Jack's earpiece followed by a masculine voice attempting falsetto breathiness. "*Sooo romantic.*"

Someone needed to rein in Whit.

Jack winked at Lu. "Give me your puppy and go choose a trinket from the jewelry case. Mr. Ingersoll and I have business to conduct."

For one moment Jack feared she would insist on staying at his side. But Abby took the bait, pulling Lucinda toward the jewelry case, jabbering about the pieces they'd received since her departure.

In the back corner behind the exercise equipment, a middle-aged couple argued over a set of stereo speakers stacked next to a rack of long guns secured with a chain.

Ready to get this show on the road, Jack settled the strap of Finny's kennel on his shoulder and nodded toward the gun rack. "I'm assuming *those* are not what I'm here for."

"No." Ingersoll's thin smile didn't reach his eyes. "I have much nicer items to show you in the back."

Cane in hand, Jack followed Trent into the back office area and through a steel door to the warehouse portion of the building. Rows of metal shelves held tagged items taken in as collateral on loans. In the far corner, beyond the maze of shelves, a table was set up and draped with a floral bed comforter lumpy with items hidden beneath it.

"This is a sampling of what I have for you." Trent fingered the cloth. "You have the diamonds?" Perspiration trickled from his hairline.

Jack patted Finny's kennel, noting Ingersoll's nerves were getting the better of him. "As we agreed."

"Good. Good." He flipped back a corner of the comforter to reveal several small handguns.

Jack stepped back. "Not what I'm here for."

Fumbling with the fabric, Ingersoll peeled the spread off the rest of the way.

Jack's gut zinged.

A MAC-10 lay on the table alongside an AK-47 and an M4 carbine.

Chapter 30

"What about this one?" Abby held up a diamond tennis bracelet. "It came in yesterday. One of the motorhands bought it downtown to take home to his girlfriend in Georgia. She sent him a Dear John letter before he could get back there."

Lu slipped it on and rocked her wrist back and forth for Abby's benefit. She removed it and pointed to a silver heart necklace set with diamonds and aquamarines. "How about that?"

"I *love* that one!" Abby pulled out the tray and lifted it by the delicate silver chain. "Turn around."

Lu lifted her hair off her shoulders and swung around. The bell on the door jingled. She looked up and froze in place. Billy Wilson's malevolent stare raised goose bumps on her arms.

"Look." Abby stepped in front of her holding up a hand mirror, breaking the line of sight between Lu and Billy. "That goes great with your outfit."

Lu touched the necklace with trembling fingers. "It does."

A floorboard squeaked.

Billy stood directly behind Abby, his mean little eyes boring into Lu. "You come back with that highfalutin' boyfriend of yours," he pointed at the toes of her shoes, "flashing jewels and thinking you're better than the rest of us."

Abby heaved a sigh and twirled around, taking the mirror with her. "Oh, for pity sake, Billy. Shut up and go look at the tools or something. We're doing girl stuff here." She turned back to Lu, flashed a brilliant smile and hurried back behind the counter. "There's a matching set of earrings."

Without Abby's presence between them, Billy's hatred rolled over Lu in a hot wave. Refusing to be intimidated, she turned to look at the earrings. She felt the heat of him on her back as he stepped closer.

"Why'd you have to come back?"

Every hair on the back of Lu's neck stood on end. Trapped between the display case and Billy, she cast an irritated look over her shoulder. "Back off."

"You can't order me around." His hand shot out and closed around her arm.

"Hey!" Her heart slammed against her ribs. She pivoted trying to wrench her arm free from his grasp. She sidestepped, but he hung on. "Let go!"

"Somethin's not right." Spittle sprayed from his mouth.

She'd given him a chance. Bracing her feet, she struck out with the heel of her free hand. Pain shot up her arm.

"Aggh." Billy reeled. Bent double, he held both hands to his face.

Lu stepped back. Fear blocked her hearing, and the scene before her played out in slow motion.

"We'll take the speakers." The couple stepped up to the end of the counter and plunked them down in front of Abby, startled into silence.

"Why you..." Billy straightened. Blood ran from his nose

coating his lips and hands. The veins in his temples bulged with rage. He lunged for Lu.

She wheeled to run, but his fingers tangled in the fabric at the back of her tunic. Several buttons let go. Wrenching around, her breath stuck in her chest. Her vision tunneled to the gun he held in his hand. Terror rocketed through her. He pressed the muzzle behind her ear. Paralyzed with fear, she struggled to breathe.

"Everybody, back off." Billy's harsh snarl had the desired effect.

The couple latched onto Abby, pushing her behind them as they backed away.

Billy yanked on Lu's tunic.

Her breath caught in her throat. Tears blurred her vision.

Grabbing the neck of her exposed vest, he shook her, and then pulled her backward toward the door leading into the back of the store.

The vest cut into her stomach and underarms. Hot tears trickled down her cheeks as she stumbled along in reverse on legs stiff as fence posts.

Help me, God. The back room was empty. The pressure on the vest let up. Before she could react, he pushed the steel door open and shoved her into the warehouse. Did Jack have time to make the deal? Was Trent in custody? Dare she try and reach something—anything—on the shelves to use against Billy?

His hot, rank breath burned across her cheek. The gun made it hard to think of anything else. How could this be happening to her again? Heart knocking, she stepped beyond the end of the shelves.

"Ingersoll!" Billy's voice shrieked in her ear.

Trent turned, holding Finny.

Jack's sharp gaze knifed through the fear blanketing her.

A look of deadly intent masked his face. Could she buy him time?

Chest heaving, she dragged her eyes away from Jack and aimed her pent-up venom at Trent, standing before her in silent shock. "Tell Billy to get his filthy hands off me." She ignored the tremble in her voice. "And to put his gun away."

Trent dropped Finny, pocketing her collar.

Jack spoke, his voice low and deadly. "I don't like complications, Ingersoll. Get him under control."

"Somethin' ain't right." Billy waved his gun between Jack and Lu. "She's wearin' a bulletproof vest."

"I protect what's mine." Jack's cool voice cut Billy off. "Get him out of here, Ingersoll."

Face red and twisted with anger, vitriol spewed from Billy's mouth. Finny yipped and he lashed out at the pup with his foot.

Rage rocketed through Lu. She rammed her elbow against Billy's gut. He lifted his pistol taking aim at Jack.

"No!" She lunged, arms spread wide. *"Jack!"*

His eyes widened.

A force slammed between her shoulder blades, pitching her hard against him. Pain exploded cutting off her breath. Darkness edged her vision. Jack's arm wrapped around her, and they were falling…

Jack clutched Lu to his chest letting his back and shoulder take the brunt of the fall.

Shouts echoed and chaos erupted as federal agents took down Ingersoll and Wilson. Where had they been a minute ago? He rolled, sliding Lu to the cool cement floor. She lay on her stomach still as death, her top and vest streaked crimson.

He jackknifed to his knees sick with terror. *"Lu!"* He yanked at her clothing, alternating between cursing his useless hand and praying. Why hadn't the vest worked? *Don't let her die, Lord.* He had to stop the bleeding.

A hand rested on his shoulder. He shook it off. "Medic. Get a medic. She can't die."

Someone grabbed his wrist and applied pressure. He jerked back, ready to bodycheck the idiot trying to stop him.

Green eyes. Jack blinked. *McCord.*

"…not hers. You hear me, Preach?"

He shook his head, heart thundering in his ears.

"The blood isn't *hers*."

Jack looked down. The words echoing in his head and heart. *The blood isn't hers.* He dragged in a deep breath. "Who—?" He choked.

"Wilson's. She popped him a good one in the nose."

Relief warred with rage in Jack's aching chest as he recalled Wilson bloodied and pushing a terrified Lu into the warehouse.

Whit stepped over her and squatted across from Jack to check her pulse. "Wind knocked out of her. She'll be a hurtin' unit." He grasped a side tab on the vest and pulled.

The sound matched the tearing of Jack's heart. He lifted the edge of the vest. She had the beginning of a massive bruise created by the energy of the strike. "Maybe a broken rib or two." He stroked the hair from her cheek. "Lulabelle." He leaned over her, wanting to breathe for her, not daring to move her and risk a punctured lung. A droplet of moisture beaded on the tiny heart on her temple. He wiped it away only to have another follow. The tears were his.

She wheezed. Her eyelids drifted up and down, then

popped open. Her gasp was followed by a groan. Fear blazed in her eyes.

"You're safe." Jack lifted her head from the cement, cupping her cheek in his hand. "Lay still. You may have a broken rib."

"You 'kay?" Her breathy question tore at his heart.

"Yes, you little fool." He wanted to laugh and cry at the same time. "You shouldn't have done that."

Her lips tipped in a half smile. "My turn to save you?"

He shook his head. "We aren't keeping score." The commotion around them settled to a dull roar. In the distance an ambulance wailed. He didn't have long before they'd whisk her away. He leaned down and kissed the corner of her mouth. Those soft lips had lied and sassed and challenged him to face his own demons. He'd stopped running from God. Maybe it was time to stop running from this woman.

"Preach." Whit tapped his shoulder. "Let the EMT's have at her."

He lifted his head and allowed Whit to pull him away. Heart in his throat, he called Finny. Lying on the gurney, she looked tiny as a child. They pushed her out the door to the waiting ambulance. He followed, not wanting her out of his sight, feeling like a piece of himself was being torn away.

"Com'on." Whit whacked him between the shoulder blades. "Let's get our part in this mess over with."

Chapter 31

Jack set Finny down on the cement patio. Sitting here in the warm Kansas sunshine, surrounded by pots spilling over with purple and pink petunias, he needed to crack his knuckles in the worst way. He had to settle for rubbing his sweaty palm against his jeans.

The screen door banged. Lu's grandmother stood at the top of the short flight of steps, carrying a tray loaded with cookies and a pitcher of iced tea.

"Let me help with that." He stood and hesitated, cursing under his breath. *One hand and a cane.* A flush of embarrassment crept up his neck. Leaving his cane hooked over his chair, he took the few steps necessary to retrieve the pitcher and set it on the table at the center of the patio.

"Thank you, young man." She set the tray down and took a seat. Sunlight polished the silver of her short curly hair.

He dropped to the edge of his chair, thankful he hadn't embarrassed himself by falling face first into her petunias.

Peering at him from behind thick lenses, she smiled. "Thank you again for bringing Lucinda home."

"You're welcome, ma'am." He was sweating like a sixteen-year-old.

"Please, call me Maudie."

"Yes, ma'...Miss Maudie." He glanced toward the second floor of the white farmhouse.

Maudie poured the tea. Ice cubes clinked against tumblers decorated with bright flowers partially obliterated by years of scrubbing. "She'll be down soon. A cookie?"

Jack took the offered oatmeal cookie and hesitated, unsure if he should eat it or wait for Lu. His Ranger training hadn't taught protocol for taking tea and cookies with grandmothers, and he was in a poor frame of mind to improvise.

He hadn't seen Lu since she'd been taken from the scene in the ambulance. After the chaos at the pawnshop was cleared and he and Whit debriefed, they'd hightailed it for the hospital only to discover she'd been released.

She suffered a cracked rib and didn't require a hospital stay. He wouldn't rest until he saw her and could see for himself how she was doing. If she didn't come down soon, he'd go up after her. He wasn't leaving without saying goodbye...and a few other things he couldn't think about at the moment if he wanted to carry on a conversation with the elderly woman who meant so much to her. "How is she doing?" He had to know.

Her grandmother thought for a moment. "Changed."

His stomach flipped. She'd faced life-altering disappointments and danger. He placed the cookie on the napkin set in front of him. "How?"

Holding her tumbler in a hand gnarled by the demands of hard work, Maudie took a sip. "She's quiet."

Jack stared at his tumbler. A bead of moisture dribbled down the glass to pool on the table. A numbing blast of cold dread spread through him. He'd tried to shield her from the worst and failed. She'd need to be monitored for post-traumatic stress. If her sudden quiet were a harbinger of social withdrawal, she'd need counseling. Maudie's voice pulled him from his thoughts.

"...found what she's been looking for." She harpooned him with a speculative look. "Has that got anything to do with you?"

Jack cleared his throat and sat up straighter. Maybe coming here hadn't been the best idea. "I...I... Excuse me?"

She leaned forward her voice a shocked whisper. "Who would have suspected Trent of running an illegal business from his father's shop?" She tsk tsked and sat back. "Never liked the boy, but Lu had her heart set on him for all the wrong reasons. I couldn't convince her differently." She looked at Jack expectantly.

Unsure how to respond he took refuge in agreeing with her. "No ma'am. I imagine not."

"You're of a different caliber. She can be a handful. Just like her mother." Maudie plunked her glass on the table. "You'll be good to Lucinda?"

The unexpected change of subject left Jack with mental whiplash. "Yes, ma'am." What had she told her grandmother? Sweat trickled beneath the collar of his shirt.

"That's all I ask. She deserves happiness." Maudie took a cookie and bit into it.

The screen door squeaked.

Jack's heart leapt in his chest.

Lu stood stiff on the top step, dressed in jeans and red T-shirt. She'd pulled her hair back in a ponytail. Fatigue rimmed her eyes, but her lips were relaxed in a half smile. He had to remind himself to breathe as he rose from his chair. "I couldn't leave without seeing you."

Holding the railing she took one careful step after another. "I'm glad you came." Gingerly, she sat down at the table and helped herself to a cookie. "Gran, you bake the best oatmeal cookies." She played with a crumb on the table. "What will happen to Trent and Billy?"

"Jail time." Jack didn't want to waste time talking about the local yokels. Whit and Gene had taken off on an errand and would no doubt be back soon.

Maudie pushed back her chair and stood. "Lu, would you mind taking Uncle Everett cookies and a thermos of tea?" She hurried off to prepare the snack, leaving them looking at each other. They'd been through a horrific experience together and now, thrown into the calm of everyday life, a wall of awkwardness had gone up between them.

She rose and Jack followed. He fumbled for words. "Must be nice being home."

"Yes." She frowned. "You changed clothes."

He looked down at his black T-shirt and twill pants. "Couldn't stand another minute in the suit." His heart bottomed out. He'd been dressed like Duro.

She smiled up at him. "It's okay, Jack. Those clothes weren't you."

"These aren't me either. I'm still figuring out buttons and zippers."

"I've been afraid to ask," she looked away, "about Esteban." She licked her lips. "What happened to him?"

"When we left the island he was still alive." He was glad he could be honest with her, though knowing the man was still among the living made his gut coil. Duro was not the type of man to forget.

Maudie came out of the house and stood on the top step. "Here you go."

Lu claimed the thermos and a small brown paper bag. Side by side they walked along the gravel laneway lined with Burr oak. The air was heavy with the scent of animals and freshly tilled soil. Rocks and grit crunched beneath their feet. Finny followed close on their heels.

"I—"

"You—"

They both stopped talking.

Lu blinked. "You first."

Jack shook his head. "Ladies first."

She sighed. "It's good to be home."

"You don't sound so sure." Relieved she wasn't asking more questions about Duro, he needed to hold her, feel the warmth of her, vibrant and alive.

The lane led to a barn, its red paint weathered to the color of old bricks. At its foundation, the heads and backs of several chickens peeked above a depression in the dirt where they scratched and fluffed.

A sad little smile wisped across her lips. "Gran's right. I've changed."

"You were listening." His heart ached for her.

"Yes. You sounded like you were facing a firing squad. So I came down to rescue you—again."

"Cheeky wench." He tried to lower the volume of his voice, but he was sucking in droughts of air looking for release. "You could've been killed."

Her chin jutted out, and her upturned face pinked with defiance. "But I wasn't. And I'd do it again if I had to."

That's not what he wanted to hear. He herded her toward a wooden bench set back in the shade. Finny followed, skittish of the hens bathing in the dust.

Setting his cane aside, he dragged her onto his lap. She came willingly, placing her uncle's snack on the bench and winding her arms around his neck. His nape tingled where her fingers brushed then curled up through his hair.

Taking care not to cause her more pain, he wrapped his

arm around her waist. Kissing her was the only way he knew to block out the image of her lying on the warehouse floor with blood on her clothing. The gold flecks in her eyes sparked a firestorm that raced wild through his veins, melting what little resistance he had left. Drawn together by an intangible force, he molded her body to his. Her lips were soft and tasted of vanilla and cinnamon and her own special spice.

He lifted his head a fraction. Never had he needed anyone like he needed this woman. "What are we going to do about us, Lulabelle?" She stared at his neck for so long, he wondered if he needed to wipe something off.

"What I said to you in the hospital... I want to be sure." She glanced at him from the corners of her eyes then went back to studying his neck, avoiding eye contact.

"Look at me."

She shook her head.

Pressing his lips to her temple, he kissed the heart-shaped fleck and murmured, "What are you thinking?"

She looked up, misery pooled in the depths of her eyes. "Truth?"

His heart rolled slow and painful. "Always."

"I've made so many mistakes." She sniffed and ducked her head. "I don't want to make another one."

He splayed his hand through her hair and pulled her head to his chest. She was tearing his heart out. His throat hurt as his words rasped harsh. "With me?"

"Yes." She choked the word out.

His throat closed, leaving him unable to speak. Panic swirled through him. He believed with all his heart she'd been created for him. His biggest fear surfaced, forcing him to speak. "My arm?"

She straightened up, clipping his chin with the top of her

head. Her eyes were wide with shock. "You think this is about your arm?" She was shaking her head side to side before she finished the question. Both hands came up to frame his face, and he wanted to close his eyes and soak in the warmth of her gentle touch, but her eyes blazed earnest, and he couldn't stop himself from falling into their honeyed depths.

"It's not." She licked her lips and his stomach curled with desire. "It's about trusting the wrong people and thinking through why I did that." With a caress so soft it was barely there, she traced his eyebrows, the bridge of his nose, the curl of his ear, as though trying to memorize his face. "Truth?"

"Yes."

"I want to come to you whole."

His chest opened and he could breathe once again. "Your past is in the past, Lulabelle. It's not your future. Both men lied about who they were, in deed if not with words." He didn't know if what he said would help her, but he had to try. "I want you. But I want all of you, unchained to your past." And wouldn't he be wise to resolve some things in his own life? He pushed the thought aside. "How long do you need?"

Her fingers danced across his temple. "I think I need to pray about it."

A chuckle forced its way from his lungs, more air than sound. "My Lulabelle—praying."

She pulled his head down so they were brow to brow and almost cross-eyed with lips a mere fraction apart. "You taught me that."

He tipped his head and claimed her lips, determined to seal their bond, knowing he'd never again smell strawberries without thinking of her. Short of breath, he pulled back. "I love you." A hot ball settled in his stomach. She'd been honest with him. How could he be anything less? "What if there's nothing I can do about my arm?" *God, this hurts more than any beating I've endured.* "What if I can't come to you a whole man?" He shook his head, too selfish to walk away from her on his own accord. "In all your praying and thinking, just…don't forget that I love you."

She smiled and pressed a light kiss to his lips. "I won't forget." Slipping from his lap, she retrieved the thermos and bag. "Uncle Everett is waiting for his iced tea and cookies."

Feeling as though he'd lost part of himself, Jack stood and followed her into the barn.

The sweet scent of hay filled the dim interior. Dust motes danced on a stray sunbeam. A tall man dressed in bib overalls pitched a fork of hay into a box stall.

Lu made the introductions. Her great uncle extended his left hand without hesitation.

Gratitude washed through Jack as he shook the strong, calloused hand. "Nice to meet you, sir."

Sharp eyes peered from beneath bushy iron gray eyebrows. "Thank you for bringing our girl home." He accepted the treats Maudie sent along. "Sadie-cat disappeared into the loft a few days ago. Might have kittens up there."

Lu squealed and raced to the wooden ladder leading to the hayloft.

"Be careful," the men yelled in unison. They looked at each other and grinned.

"See you've figured out she's not the most graceful woman." Uncle Everett took a cookie and offered the open bag to Jack.

Lu's feet disappeared from view. They heard her above, calling and rustling through the loose hay.

"Needs someone strong to watch her back." Uncle

Everett looked up, munching his cookie. "Never figured that Ingersoll chump was up to the task."

The oatmeal cookie crumbled to dust in Jack's mouth. What did her uncle think of him? If Sam released him from SeaMount, he didn't know how he'd support himself, never mind a wife.

Wife. His heart floundered painfully in his chest.

Uncle Everett took another cookie. "I don't know about such things, but Maudie says the way Lu talks, you could be the man for her."

Cookie crumbs got sucked down the wrong pipe. Jack hacked till he was red in the face.

Uncle Everett banged him between the shoulder blades.

When Jack could take a breath and not cough, Lu's uncle tipped the thermos at him. "Well? Are you?"

Jack cleared his throat. He may as well go for broke at this point. "Yes, sir." His voice rasped over the words. "I believe I am." He glanced overhead. "She has a few things to work out. Wants to be sure she's not making another mistake."

Uncle Everett waved a cookie in Finny's direction. "Not much of a dog."

The puppy stepped delicately on bits of scattered straw and dirt, sniffing around the rusty disk of an ancient harrow. Beside it, the wheel and metallic purple fender of a motorcycle peeked from beneath a skewed canvas tarp.

"No sir, but Lu loves the little pup."

The old man harrumphed. "So what are your plans now that you have a bum arm?"

Truth was all he had to offer. "I'm hoping some of the damage can be repaired, but I won't qualify as an agent any longer."

"You wouldn't be happy being a desk jockey."

"Got that right, sir."

"You have a few of your own things to figure out."

"Yes, sir." Anticipation, exciting and terrible at the same time, rippled down his spine. Where was God calling him? How did Lu fit in?

From overhead Lu called, "I found them," followed by soft crooning and laughter.

"Well, don't take too long." Uncle Everett waved the half-empty bag of cookies toward the hayloft. "Maudie's already at work on a guest list for the wedding."

Chapter 32

Three weeks later

The wind off the ocean carried the tang of salt and the constant boom of the waves through the open windows of the gym. Controlling his breathing, Jack pushed through another set of leg presses before calling his workout done.

Slipping on a jacket, he grabbed a bottle of water and stepped outside to stand at the deck railing. Gray-green waves crashed ashore then foamed and churned in retreat, mirroring the emotions curling through him.

Behind him the door opened and closed.

"Go away, Aggie." He'd had it up to his eyeballs with the mollycoddling. "I don't want a drink, a cookie, or whatever it is you're bribing me with this time."

"Guess again."

The rough voice snapped Jack's attention to the man standing behind him. "Sam."

"You're moping."

"I'm not moping." He hoped his scowl put an end to that line of accusations, but in case it didn't, for good measure he added, "Men don't mope."

"Then you're acting like a love-sick calf."

Like he needed to hear this? He'd been poked and prodded and run through machines till he glowed in the dark. The prognosis turned out better than he'd expected, but less than he wanted to hear. He jerked his chin toward the bank of windows framing the gym and the new equipment Sam had installed. "Thanks for bringing them in for me."

Sam took a seat in a deck chair. "There's a 'but' in there."

"I can't do this job anymore." Jack threw back the rest of the water in the bottle, knowing what he had to say and not wanting to say it. But Sam deserved to know. "Truth is, God's calling me to something else."

"Figured as much."

Jack spun around and stared at the director.

Sam crossed his arms. "Could see you were fighting something."

Dropping onto a chaise lounge, Jack squeezed the plastic bottle till it crackled. "Taking my own advice and handing over the controls. Praying for an OPORD."

"If God sent out an operations order, you wouldn't have to live by faith."

Jack swung his aching leg up onto the lounge. "Got to know the mission before I can plan the execution."

"Pray it through." Sam paused. "Tell me about the boy, Simao."

"You know what I know." Jack adjusted the collar of his jacket. "He's a pickpocket and has a sister, Angelina."

Sam sat quiet, watching the gulls glide on the wind currents. Jack wished he knew what went on in the man's head. On second thought, maybe it was best he didn't know.

"Ethan is adamant about following up on those two." Sam rubbed a finger over his mustache. "Says the dreams keep coming."

Jack tapped the mutilated bottle against his thigh. Ethan and his dreams were nothing to scoff. The man seemed to have a direct line to heaven. "What are you planning to do?"

"Keep on it, though the turmoil in St. Beatrice is making it difficult to get information. Thankfully, Ava is happy staying at the villa with them while I unravel their story." Sam rubbed a hand down his face. "We keep collecting widows and orphans. Sophie and her girls, and now Ava, Simao, and his sister. Thinking I should have a halfway house."

Jack's heart skipped a beat then chugged heavy in his chest. *There are no coincidences.* He cleared the rasp from his throat, trying to remain calm. "For the past year, Isaiah 1:17 has needled me. I tried to live it out. At least, the first half of the verse."

Sam leaned forward. "What is it?"

"Learn to do good; seek justice, rescue the oppressed." When I stopped running I went back to that verse. Wanted to prove to God I was where He wanted me. The second half of that verse forced me to sit up and take notice.

"What's it say?"

"...defend the orphan and plead for the widow."

"Maybe you have your OPORD after all."

From the other side of the building, the laughter of children carried on the crisp breeze and a motorcycle rumbled past.

Jack shook his head, amazed and a little afraid this could be the answer to his daily harangue at the Throne of Grace. Needing time to ponder what transpired, he changed the subject. "Have you heard from Lucinda?" After two weeks of talking with her every day—sometimes several times a day—he hadn't been able to reach her for the last few days.

He wanted to call her grandmother but didn't want to worry the woman unnecessarily.

One side of Sam's mustache lifted. "You got it bad."

The zinger hit Jack hard in the gut. How many times had he gone round with Lu about the truth? Well, here it was and he couldn't deny it. Didn't want to deny it. "Yeah. I do."

"Thought you'd find yourself a quiet little church mouse." Sam's words drifted between them in the pure sunshine.

Jack's heart tripped. "Am I crazy to think it can work out between us?"

"It?"

"Yeah. The big 'it'. Love." He paused, uncomfortable with the direction of the conversation. "Not sure why I'm talking to you about this."

Sadness swept across Sam's scarred face before he looked away.

Way to go, Conroy. If anyone deserved someone to love, it was Sam. With his disfigurement it would take a special woman to look beyond the outside packaging. She'd have to be determined to break through the barriers protecting his heart. "So? *Am* I crazy? She doesn't know the final results of my tests."

"You prayed up about it?"

Jack looked out over the ocean. Foam laced the edge of the spillers rolling ashore. From the street side of the building the muted noise of the village blended with the constant roll and hiss of the water. "Yeah." *And I've interrogated Gray about marriage until he laughed in my face.* "Biggest worry—will Lu want me?" He fingered the cloth of his sling.

"Jack."

He rubbed a hand down his face. Just thinking about her, his brain conjured up her voice, so real and close. Sam was right. He had it bad.

"Jack."

He looked at Sam, questioning his sanity. The director's gaze was focused beyond his shoulder.

He twisted round in the chair. His heart dropped and pinged hot like spent brass.

Lucinda.

Red highlights twinkled like a fiery halo in her rich mahogany hair. An angel dressed in motorcycle leathers.

"Lulabelle?"

Lucinda wanted to sink to the chaise lounge and wrap her arms around him, and run away all at the same time. On the long cross-country ride, she'd thought of little else but this moment. Now that she was here she was unsure what to do. All the words she'd so carefully rehearsed had flown away on the cold wind.

"Lulabelle?" He started to rise.

Knees unable to support her weight, she sank to the edge of his lounge chair stopping him. "Hi." *Real bright, Lu.* He looked thinner and paler than she remembered.

Sam used the strength in his arms to leverage his body out of the chair. "Welcome back, Lucinda. I'm glad you're here. Please put the man out of his misery." He walked away whistling off key.

Jack's blue gaze traveled over her in a heated caress. "He knew you were coming?"

Flustered, she looked away on the pretense of placing her helmet on the deck next to the chair. "Yes."

Jack's eyes narrowed, his gaze nailed the door swinging closed.

Oh boy. That was the wrong thing to say. "Please don't be angry with him." This conversation wasn't going at all as she'd hoped. In her daydreams she would already be in his arms kissing him. All these stupid words were getting in the way. His hand claimed hers, and she jumped, her heart bouncing right up her throat.

"I'm glad you're here." His gaze held hers. "You changed your hair."

With her free hand she rubbed the ends. "It's the real me. Do you like it?"

"All I want is the real you, Lulabelle. And, yes, I like it."

She looked down at their interlaced fingers resting on her thigh. "I missed you." She'd missed him so badly she'd been heartsick from the wanting. "I have something to tell you."

His eyes shadowed dark. Stillness cloaked him. "What?"

How did one say this? She felt joyful and a little silly. Was she supposed to just blurt it out? His grip on her hand tightened painfully.

"Spit it out, Lulabelle." Deep lines bracketed his mouth.

She took a deep breath. "I went to church and talked to Deacon Beam." The words came out in a rush.

He exhaled, the guarded look in his eyes eased to a curious gleam.

She pushed a hand through her hair "It's seems so backwards that Jesus would die for me *before* I believed that He truly loved me."

"Do you believe it now?" His voice was whisper soft.

"Yes." She ducked her head. "I know my coming here might seem too soon, but I couldn't stay away. Does it sound corny that accepting Jesus' love made me feel whole?"

He collected her hair in his fist and tugged, making her

look at him. "Don't question it, Lulabelle. Accept it as the truth."

A sharp yip interrupted the moment.

Jack jerked with surprise.

Lu couldn't hold back the giggle tickling her throat.

"Where is she?" His eyes hunted over her tight fitting leathers, warming her to her toes. She slid off the chaise and on to her knees, twisting so he could see Finny, head and front legs exposed, riding safely in a pack on her back.

"Hey, pup." The softness in his voice melted away Lu's last bit of nervousness.

Finny's feet pushed at her back as he lifted the pup from the pack and set her on his chest, accepting slurpy puppy kisses on his chin. "You do realize these are not the kisses I've been dreaming of for the past three weeks."

He was going to give her a heart attack. She couldn't turn down the invitation in the heated depths of his eyes. Still on her knees, Lu placed her hands on the arm of the chaise separating them, and leaned toward him like a honeybee drawn to a flower. "Close your eyes."

His smile wavered. "Why?"

"I don't want to drown." His eyes were that blue and that deep.

"What?"

"Oh, forget it." She swooped in and planted her lips on his. He tasted of salt and musk and everything Jack. A man she didn't deserve, but would hold onto with every breath she took.

His hand cupped her cheek, fingers speared through her hair pulling her closer. All her thoughts dissolved in a mist of warm breath and contented sighs.

Jack's heart battered his ribs. She was here, safe and whole. He wanted this moment to go on forever. He didn't want to let her go. She'd made a momentous choice to believe in Christ. His brave Lulabelle. She was sure to keep him on his toes, asking the hard questions about scripture and her new faith. He had news of his own. Putting it off wasn't fair to her.

A cold nose slid up his throat. He released Lu in a huff of laughter. Pushing the puppy towards her, she started to move away.

"Stay." He wrapped his hand around her arm. "I have something to tell you, too."

A worried frown creased her forehead. She set Finny on the deck. "What?"

The knot in his throat was the size of a hand grenade. He swallowed a few times before he spoke, trying to keep his voice neutral. "The surgeon believes he can repair some of the nerves in my arm, but it will never come back fully."

She leaned closer. "We'll take what we can get and figure out the rest together." Her eyes drifted to the collar of his jacket. "I still don't understand the whole sovereign will of God thing." She peeked up at him out of the corners of her eyes.

His heart swelled with love for this feisty woman. The beauty mark on her temple begged to be touched. He was happy to oblige. Her skin was soft and smooth beneath his fingertips. "Truth?"

"Yes."

"Neither do I."

Her breath hitched. "You don't?"

"How can mortals understand all that God is and does?" He buried his fingers in her soft hair. "That's why we have to live by faith."

"I don't have a whole lot of that at the moment." Her voice carried a hint of a pout, and he couldn't help but smile.

"It will grow, Lulabelle." She'd be a force to reckon with once she fully understood what it meant to be a child of God. "So tell me, why are you certain Jesus loves you?"

"I jumped in front of the bullet."

His heart dropped then thundered on the rebound. She left him speechless.

"A wise woman once told me, I'd know love was real when I could willingly give up anything, including my life for that person."

He had no appreciation whatsoever for that bit of wisdom. "And what wise woman said this?"

"Ava."

Didn't that just figure. "There will be no more jumping in front of bullets, understood?" How had he missed that conversation? What other bits of questionable wisdom had the old woman shared?

Lu traced the curve of his jaw with her finger. "Don't look so fierce. I have no plans of doing it again. Unless you need me to."

He sat up straight. Never again did he want to see her stretched out on the ground, covered in blood. Before he could say a word, she placed a finger to his lips.

"You put your life on the line for me. I've never known that kind of commitment or love. What I did, there at the pawnshop, came from a place deep inside I didn't know existed. I didn't know I could love so deeply." She sighed. "All I'm trying to say is, Jesus' love has to be greater than anything I feel. Whether I understand it or not, I just have to believe." Her smile sizzled with radiance.

He snaked his hand around behind her back. Her crazy

conclusion was creating havoc with his breathing. The intensity of his love washed through him. He pulled her toward him.

She gasped. "The arm—"

His heart dropped. "Mine?"

"No." Breathless, she pulled back. "The chair's arm is digging into my ribs." She dodged around the wooden arm on the chaise lounge, leaned against him, and snuggled her cheek to his chest. "Where was I?"

He stroked her hair. With the warmth of the sun lighting up the red embers buried in the mahogany strands, it was like playing with soft fire. "You were telling me how much you love me."

"Hmmm." She draped her arm across his arm encased in its sling. "You're heart's pounding."

"Firebrands dressed in leather do that to me." Time to go for broke. "Do you remember the Bible verse about justice and oppression that I mentioned?"

She looked up. "Yes." Her breath fanned his lips with warmth making his blood sizzle.

"It ends "defend the orphan and plead for the widow". Sam wants a halfway house for widows and orphans."

"Ava, Simao and Angelina."

He nodded. "I don't have all the answers, but I believe that's the direction God's calling me." A big part of him was relieved he wouldn't have to sever ties with the agency and his teammates.

"I had Gran and Uncle Everett." Her eyes pooled liquid.

His nerves sang like the first time he'd hooked up to the static line in the belly of a C-130. "Lucinda." His heart thudded hard.

His use of her full name sharpened her gaze. "Yes."

"Marry me." He felt the shock ripple through her.

"Seriously?" She swallowed. Doubt muted the golden honey of her eyes. "Truth?" The word was a whisper.

"Yes."

"This seems so soon, and I'm a afraid…" She paused and cleared her throat.

His heart stopped and started again with a loud thud. "Afraid of what?"

"Well, look at me, Jack." Her voice trembled.

"I have. I'm not going to stop…ever. I love you."

"But am I the woman you want? Maybe you deserve someone better than me. Someone who's been a good girl all her life."

He cupped her warm cheek. "I'm willing to go slow and have a long engagement if that's important to you, but I deserve the woman God chose for me. That woman is you."

She blinked and tears spilled down her cheeks. A smile teased her lips. "So, what you're saying is, *I'm* God's gift to *you*?"

He would never hear the end of this. "Oh, yeah. The best gift ever."

"Truth?"

"Absolute truth, Lulabelle."

THE END

Also by Anita Greene

OUT OF THE WILDERNESS

Learn more about Anita
or sign up for her newsletter at her website:

anitakgreene.wordpress.com

About the Author

Anita lives in Rhode Island with her husband, son and spoiled Belgian Malinois. When she isn't writing, she enjoys reading, gardening, needlework, sewing and making cards. She hopes to one day get all her photos into scrapbooks.